Breaking

Babel

A Novel by

David Bard Kullberg

Andershire Books

Breaking Babel is an adaptation of David Kullberg's longer novel,
The War Against God, which is no longer in print.

Breaking Babel

Author website: www.davidkullberg.com

Requests for information: info@davidkullberg.com

Cover design by Carol Hunsberger, cah@imgrfx.com

Publishing services provided by Julie Klusty, jfklusty@gmail.com

ISBN 978-0-9884321-4-7

To Kelly

For your support, encouragement and advice, thank you. Most of all, thanks for all the hours of listening.

Love with all my heart.

Acknowledgements

For April, my middle daughter, thank you for all the late night phone calls from college, sharing the story's creation and its characters. To my other children, Keya, John, Joshua, and Michelle, I couldn't have done it without the motivation of your frequently asked question over a decade, "Aren't you finished with that book yet?"

For invaluable encouragement and support, I thank Finny Kuruvilla, D.J. Snell, Ken Beavers, and Mike Akers. Thank you Mike and Jan Loar, Martha Linder, Cheryl Cowen, and Connie Anderson for editorial help. For cover layout, thank you Carol Hunsberger.

Along the way, readers and friends who offered feedback and support. Thank you Bruce Kullberg, Krista and Tom Sisterhen, Bob Johnson, Doug Dicke, Marilyn Miller, Dick Crawford, Trace Thurlby, Larry Schirm, Linda Shafran, Hannah Armbrust, Jim Shumaker, Julie Klusty, Bob Trube, James Pyne, Greg Ganssle, Tom Slemmer, Howard Van Cleave, Bill Foster, and Stephanie Convey.

A special thanks to Kelly for her contribution to Katherine's letter.

Note to reader: A vision of the future

As a father I wondered how to best pass on a hopeful vision of the future to my five children. Many of us are drawn to great stories of conquest against the forces of darkness, advancing a kingdom of light, and love, and glory. We're hardwired to care, yearning to make a difference. We sense a call on our lives to build a better world. We have heroic notions because we believe life has meaning, and truth, beauty, and goodness are worth defending.

So, late at night between bedtimes and morning carpool, I began a journal. Soon a story emerged and abstract ideas became a novel, and the story's characters became my teachers and friends. Their conversations, faces, and choices filled my mind.

I also desired to explore and chronicle the confluence and clash of worldviews actively competing for the hearts and minds of a nation, and our world's future. All aspects of life have become contested ground. Nothing is exempt. Everyone participates. The contest is being waged every day, on every front.

What vision of the future have Christians embraced? What story to change the world has been advanced that captivates the hearts and imaginations of our young people, spurring them on to great acts of service and sacrifice?

Heaven has invaded earth, and Jesus rules with all authority from the Father's right hand; therefore, man's dream of Babel is ultimately futile. Through the Holy Spirit we are given the courage and conviction to play our part in our Lord's great historical narrative, and by shining His light we participate in loving God's creation back to life.

My journal became the novel, *Breaking Babel*. Thanks for considering the possibilities and exploring along with me.

David Kullberg

Breaking Babel

www.davidkullberg.com

Breaking Babel is an adaptation of David Kullberg's longer novel, *The War Against God*, which is no longer in print.

For that Hideous Strength confronts us,
and it is as in the days when Nimrod built the tower
[Babel] to reach heaven.

~ Spoken by Ransom in the C.S. Lewis novel,
That Hideous Strength.

When plunder becomes a way of life
for a group of men living together in society,
they create for themselves in the course of time
a legal system that authorizes it...
and a moral code that glorifies it."

~ Frederic Bastiat (1801-1850)

Chapter 1: The City of Man

Gordon Connelly quietly stared at the TV as a news story he was now familiar with continued: "Authorities are still looking into the tragic death of Lauren Connelly, wife of Texas Congressman Chad Connelly. Witnesses say her aircraft was shot down approaching a jungle airstrip in Guatemala. She was delivering medical supplies..."

Gordon turned off the TV and objected, "The transience of life requires we don't waste time attending funerals."

Berry Fields carefully observed the man, nearly twice her age, who had grown from romantic interest to kindred spirit. She asked, "But you're going anyway?"

"Yes, I leave for Austin in the morning," he replied, while helping Berry unfasten the top button of her black evening gown.

They had just returned from a political fund-raiser to his Manhattan flat. Gordon loosened his black bowtie and mixed two drinks, signaling a transition from his public to private world, into which few were invited.

Berry asked about his daughter-in-law, "Do you think Lauren was the target, or was it random?"

"It could have been either."

"Who'd want to stop Life Bridge from delivering medicine and food?"

Gordon glanced at Berry and shrugged. "I cautioned Chad about her involvement with PD Tech's agricultural project. And why was *she* flying a plane over the Guatemalan jungle?"

As Berry had come to expect, Gordon provided a possible answer without admitting what he knew. She wondered, "Speaking of PD Tech, what's going to happen to Philip Doyle?"

"Why do you ask?" Gordon responded casually. He handed Berry her drink and drifted towards the wall of glass overlooking the lamp-lit sidewalks of Central Park. "Is Doyle something to you?"

"Not really. Just college nostalgia – one of the gang. Nothing personal."

"That's good," suggested Gordon while looking out on the city. "I'm afraid Philip Doyle's on a collision course with reality."

With Gordon's attention drawn to the city below, Berry reacquainted herself with the flat's décor. She worked in Washington, D.C. and seldom visited his New York home.

As she appraised the spacious living area, slight frown lines appeared, creasing her otherwise smooth, sensual features. Rather than striving for comfort, the space felt more like a hotel lobby with stark, modernist furnishings set on an Italian marble floor, interrupted by an occasional Persian rug. She especially disapproved of the Greco-Roman art, framed by white marble columns, featuring paintings and sculptures of classical architecture and the gods of Olympus.

She chose to voice her displeasure with the artwork prominently featured above the fireplace. "Gordon, what's with this painting?"

Gordon glanced over and grinned, "*Julius Caesar Crossing the Rubicon.* The Roman Republic was weak and corrupt. Caesar did what was necessary to save it."

Berry decided to drop her complaint and opted for a leather couch where at least she could relax and enjoy her drink. Watching Gordon gaze into the city lights, she recalled his conversations at the evening's fundraiser. With the hint of a smile she asked, "Is it part of your job as chairman of the Eden Global Fund to worry about the world?"

He remained momentarily silent, as though seeking an answer from the world beyond the glass. Turning slightly towards her, he answered in a playful tone, "Why do you ask?"

Berry smiled, "Is it really worth the effort?"

Gordon could see her curious smile veiled in shadow. Her allure was more than beauty, now held in peaceful repose upon the couch. She personified the city he loved: the excitement of a million lights, the exaltation of the sensual and the energized quest for power. And like the city, she could be cynical, demanding and easily amused by those who refused to embrace the world's enlightened wisdom. He was confident he knew her, so he allowed her inquiry.

Looking down on the busy streets, he explained, "I see a world in chaos, spiraling out of control." He glanced back at her. "It's a question of survival."

"And you think *Tolerance for America* will help?"

"Wasn't it your idea?" he answered with an ironic grin as his vision drifted out across Central Park and the fervent activities of the New York night. A moment later he quietly added, "It's coming together. It's like looking through a window into the future."

Once again the room grew still. Shimmering candles cast shifting light and shadow. Berry spoke through an amused anticipation, "I wonder how long it'll be before they all figure out what's happening."

Chapter 2: Memories

'Where is Joshua?' Daniel Stone pondered his sister's question as he drove towards Austin for Lauren's funeral. But concentration proved difficult after twenty-eight hours on the road. It wasn't a need of sleep, an occasional roadside nap sufficed. Rather, he fought the mesmerizing monotony of reflected glare and the endless white lines leading him through the vast darkness of the Texas night.

He had hoped the long, quiet drive would give him time to reflect on his future mission work in Mexico. But by 4:00 a.m. all he had to show for a sleepless night was empty coffee cups and disjointed impressions pressing to be understood.

Leaning back against the headrest, not daring to close his eyes, he let out a long, deep breath. Now Lauren Connelly was dead, senselessly killed while delivering food and medicine. It was disheartening that the human mind could rationalize such action – that God would allow it.

As he approached Austin he was listening to a previously taped program on the college's radio station. The interview was being conducted by Rob Martinson, a former track teammate and now a teacher at their alma mater.

"Tonight we welcome a world-renowned authority on biblical prophecy, Dr. Allen Wilder," said Martinson. "He's authored nine books, published in twenty-eight languages, selling over thirty million copies. Dr. Wilder, welcome to our show and welcome to Austin."

"Thanks, Rob. We love visiting your beautiful city."

"It's obvious Austin loves having you. Tonight's conference has sold out, with two thousand attending. And I understand World Broadcast Corporation is televising the event."

"Our program will be seen nationwide," responded Wilder.

"And you're introducing your new book?"

"Yes, we're very excited. Pre-release copies of *Armageddon: The Battle for Jerusalem* will be available at the conference."

"I'm eager to read it. Your books explain much of what we see threatening our world today."

Daniel recalled his introduction to Wilder's writings in college. He'd started *The Returning King of Glory* at Rob's insistence, but soon lost interest. He felt the emphasis on the Rapture and the approaching apocalypse seemed counter-productive, even escapist.

Wilder continued, "Ancient prophecy is being fulfilled on the front page of our newspapers. The final battle for Jerusalem is fast approaching. The

3

Church is under assault. The global financial crisis has provided secular elitists with cover to disguise their agenda of a one world government, setting the stage for the rise of the Antichrist…"

Daniel broke away from the interview as he pulled into the parking lot of Glen's 24 Hour Diner. When he entered the restaurant, his first reaction was relief. Nothing had changed.

Glen was unmistakable, standing before his grill, dressed in whites, with his squat frame, balding head, and quick, continuous motion orchestrating the breakfasts of many with a maestro's skill. Shelly, Glen's wife and partner, sat in the back corner booth, engrossed in conversation with a young waitress.

Daniel surveyed the restaurant's décor – classic American diner with speckled laminate counters and tabletops, red vinyl seating and white ceramic floors with black accents. Also added to the mix were plants, student artwork and the traditional 'who ate here' memorabilia. Oddly, it came together with its own unique charm.

Glen's Diner hummed with activity, an inviting light in the lonely morning's darkness with its aromas of pancakes, bacon sizzling on the grill and fresh-roasted coffee. The diner created its own community, a busy place with purpose. This was Shelly's kitchen and her guests were her family. She felt that no one should leave the diner until they were ready to face the world. If someone seemed downcast, she'd share a hug and a word of encouragement, "God loves you. Now have a great day and don't forget to smile at a stranger."

"Daniel Stone!"

He responded to a greeting coming from the far back corner, as did everyone else in the diner. Shelly was on her feet, headed his way. She appeared the same, other than a bit of graying hair and a little more roundness. Her beaming face and personality overflowed as her presence filled the room.

"Daniel Stone, oh my stars!" she exclaimed, throwing her arms around him. She released the hug but kept her hands on his shoulders.

"Look, Glen, Daniel's here."

Glen peered over his shoulder and grinned. "I saw him walk in."

"Glen, did I actually see you smile?" Daniel prodded in fun.

"I think he did," answered Shelly, recognizing Daniel's accomplishment. She held his hands and stepped back to take a good look. His six-foot, muscular build was as she remembered, as was his casual attire of athletic shoes, jeans and a lightweight leather jacket. His thick and wavy black hair

4

was brushed peacefully back behind his ears, and his deep tan reflected a life outdoors. "Look at those red eyes. You've been drivin' all night. Let's get you something to eat."

Shelly led him to her booth. "Did you come for Lauren's funeral?"

"Yeah, unfortunately."

"Who could've done such a terrible thing?"

"I don't think they know."

"You've been gone too long. We haven't seen you since about the time your wife died. It broke my heart, hun."

"It's hard to believe Maria's been gone for six years."

Shelly commanded, "Now what would you like to eat?"

"I thought I'd take something over to the lake and watch the sunrise."

"Glen, one breakfast to go."

Glen glanced over his shoulder. "The usual?"

Daniel smiled. "Thanks for remembering."

Shelly asked, "How's your sister? Still in Mexico?"

"Katherine's well. She runs our education programs."

"She's an amazing young lady, and so beautiful."

Daniel waited, but he knew exactly where Shelly was leading.

"Shelly, she's not married and she hasn't seen Philip Doyle in years."

"Okay, you caught me. But I'm always the last to know anything."

Daniel resigned himself to Shelly's topic. "Katherine hasn't talked to Philip in ten years, since his graduation."

"Has she dated anyone else?"

"No."

"Does she still love him?"

"I guess so."

"You guess so? Spoken just like a man. She waits for ten years and you're not sure what to call it. Well, I know. I saw them together." Shelly pointed to a table by the window. "They'd sit over there and talk all night. I never saw two people with more to say to each other."

He nodded his agreement.

Shelly continued, "Philip never married either."

"I know."

"He was here this morning. You just missed him. Barney, our night chef, says Philip comes in about once a month, real early in the morning, and he sits by himself at the front window."

Daniel quietly listened as Shelly proceeded. "Barney said that Philip always looks through a scrapbook full of pictures and newspaper clippings

5

while he's eating. Then he leaves before the morning rush. Well, this morning I came in early and he was still here. He said he thought you might be in town for Lauren's service. But do you know what was a bit odd? He was wearing his old track warm ups. So I asked where he was goin'. Can you imagine what he said?"

"I have no idea."

"He was off to the track to close a door... figure that."

Daniel offered, "That's where they met."

Shelly paused in thought. "You know, Daniel, it's like one of those classical tragedies. Did you see the business magazine with Philip's picture on the cover? They talked about his company and how great he's doing. He said he didn't have time to get married. It's really sad."

Daniel nodded, "I don't bring it up anymore."

A young waitress brought Daniel's food, bagged to go. "Here you are, sir. Glen says there's no charge."

Daniel looked to Glen and waved. Glen acknowledged with a smile and a slight salute with his spatula.

"That's two smiles in one morning, Shelly. Is Glen getting soft?"

"We're happy you came in to see us." She reached across the table and touched his arm. "How are you doing?"

"I'm doing good, but... I feel like change is coming."

"Be patient," shared Shelly. "Walk in the light you're given."

Daniel left the restaurant and put closure to the troublesome conversation about Philip Doyle. Katherine's decision had been her only option.

Dawn's light was forcing the darkness to withdraw. Sunrise was only minutes away. He eagerly walked to the lake to revisit a time in his life that only the day before seemed inaccessible. Every building and landscape, every fountain and pathway revived a memory.

He headed for a wooden bench by the water's edge, framed in blooming azalea. He arrived moments before the sunrise reached out across the Sea of Glass, a secret name he and Maria had used to describe the lake. While in college, he'd come often to seek the Lord's direction. On this bench by the lake he shared the Gospel with his friend, Chad Connelly, and they prayed. At another time, seated with Philip Doyle, he tried to explain Katherine's decision, received his wrath and witnessed him cry.

On a previous morning, a lifetime ago, with the sun's first rays dancing across the water's mirrored surface, he had proposed to Maria. Here they had planned their life together, dreamed of their mission to Mexico and named the children they were never to have.

Chapter 3: Closing a Door

Philip Doyle sat motionless in the dark. He was seated in the first row of the Austin College track stadium. Compelled to act, he'd come to initiate a new beginning by closing a memory that had been left open far too long. Ten years before, as a student, he'd competed on this track with great success. And in this stadium, he'd met Katherine Stone.

He was ready, but unlike most obstacles in his life, time defied the sheer force of his will. So he waited for the light.

The other dimensions of the physical world had been formidable opponents as well. But they were succumbing to his work and to the efforts of like-minded scientists, delving deep within the atom and exploring the microcosm to the very "gates of creation." They'd found the keys and were unlocking the secrets of the universe at a furious pace. The mystery of matter was giving way to the ascendancy of mind.

In contrast, time remained a mystery – a fourth dimension taking the form of a ticking clock, forcing the present into the past, beyond his control. Philip was determined that strong, present action would reduce the past to useful experience and nothing more. Yet certain memories mastered him, and that was untenable.

He purposed to resolve his dilemma. He would act, not be acted upon. No longer would this stadium magnify his struggle. The door would be closed, once and for all, ruthlessly and efficiently.

As he waited, he recalled four years of victories. He loved the competition, and he loved to run. No balls or nets – just a race that went to those stubborn enough to win, willing to sacrifice and train, willing to overcome the pain when their bodies screamed to quit.

The 4 x 800 relay became his favorite event for the way it exemplified teamwork, with each member contributing their best – personal, yet interdependent. Daniel Stone ran first. Rob Martinson followed with Chad Connelly running the third leg. Philip ran the anchor leg because he refused to lose. The burning desire had not been learned, but existed indelibly within his nature. He drove the team by his will, leading them to four consecutive championships.

Throughout his youth he was dismayed how easily friends dismissed a loss. He concluded that he must be different and decided to set his own pace – to be the hero of his own life. Success would be achieved, and he'd never permit anyone to hold him back.

In the first light of dawn, Philip allowed his mind to drift, and once again *the* memory returned.

She first appeared at the beginning of his senior year, when he noticed her running the far straight away, his eyes fixed on her long, effortless stride. She seemed tall, the length of her limbs exaggerated by the continuous fluid motion. The lightness of her step transcended gravity, with each foot touching only a cushion of air. She held her head motionless, except for the long black ponytail swaying to the rhythm of her run.

Entering the far curve, she increased her speed and lengthened her long stride. By the straight away, grace gave way to power. He was captivated by the focused resolve in her eyes, the thrust of her chest, and the strength of cut muscle defining the arms and legs that drove her forward.

When she finished, she leaned slightly, resting her hands on her thighs, breathing deeply. He feared that if he looked away she might disappear. He asked his friend, "Chad, who is she?"

"Who?" Chad laughed when he noticed Philip's interest. "Oh, that's Daniel's sister, she's a freshman."

She walked towards them. "Chad, have you seen my brother?" She managed a smile through her deep breathing.

"He'll be here any minute," offered Chad.

Philip tried to look without staring. Just moving and talking became awkward. He felt flushed.

She turned and faced him. Her bright blue eyes were translucent, glowing as though lit from within. Her eyes promised a smile. He was driven to say something – anything.

"Hi, I'm Philip Doyle." He added, "Daniel's good friend."

She laughed, innocent and fun. "I know who you are."

"You do?" He wished to avoid sounding stupid.

"I've watched you run."

"How come I've never seen you before?"

"I didn't want to be seen."

"Hey, it's time to run," interrupted Daniel.

Both Philip and Katherine ignored the comment.

Daniel made the introduction. "Katherine, this is my friend, Philip Doyle. Philip, my sister, Katherine."

"Hi, Katherine," said Philip savoring her name.

"Come on, Philip, coach says to warm up," said Daniel. He ran onto the track with Chad. Philip didn't move.

"Why didn't you want to be seen?" asked Philip.

"I was just a gangly kid-sister," said Katherine.

"That would be impossible."

"Thanks, but it's true."

"Did you hide from everyone?"

She answered only with a laugh.

The longer she stood calmly before him, the more awkward he felt. "Hey, I'm…uh…after practice, are you walking towards campus? Can I join you?

"Ummm…" She paused. "Sure."

Over the next nine months they became best friends and lovers. They planned to marry someday, to experience life together. Loyalty and devotion marked their commitment. Nothing appeared incomplete.

But following his graduation, Philip noticed a change. Katherine avoided his apartment. He'd been preoccupied with finals and grad school, but as the distractions subsided, he grew aware of the tension between them.

"Katherine, what's wrong… and please don't repeat the same excuses?" He remembered her face, especially her eyes, sad and resigned.

"Philip, I can't come here anymore."

"Why not?" he asked, concerned she might be ill.

"Things have changed."

"What's changed? You no longer love me?" He remembered asking the question, but never believed it possible.

"I love you more than ever," she said anxiously.

"Then *what*?"

Visibly upset, she breathed deeply, gathering strength. "Philip, you won't like what I hold as true. You won't consider me your soul mate any longer."

"What are you saying?"

"I've become a Christian," she blurted out, as if to get it over with.

"You've done what?" he whispered in shock. He paused, observing her eyes fill with tears. "First Rob and Daniel, with your brother giving up architecture to be a missionary… and then Chad. Now you? This is crazy. Katherine, religion's an anathema to reason and science."

"But Philip, it *is* reasonable, and more. I thought of God when we slept under the stars in the white birch meadow. I wondered how and why the universe came to be, who was behind all the beauty. It's also about my heart." She stopped abruptly. Her appeal only revealed the gulf separating them. "I hope you'll understand," she offered, clinging to a fragile resolve.

"Of course I do. You love another man."

"Jesus is not 'another man.'"

"Then who is he?"

"He's the Creator who became one of us." She fought back the swelling tears. "He's God in flesh and blood, showing us the depth of his love."

"That's irrational nonsense." He fought to control his reaction. He couldn't imagine life without her, and yet she stood before him a stranger. She quietly waited.

Philip persisted, "Let's talk about this, like we always have. That's been our strength. Right?" When she remained silent, he continued, "Jesus was a man, not God. If he were God, then he wouldn't be a man because a man can't be God. I don't know why you all have so much trouble seeing that. Now, you're asking me to share your affections with another man. Even if he is dead, it's impossible. I've given you all my heart. I only ask as much from you. It must be all or nothing."

Katherine spoke deliberately, trying to steady her trembling voice. "Philip, this is the saddest day of my life. I love you, but things are different. A marriage between us, as we are now, can never work. I know you don't understand. A few weeks ago I wouldn't have understood either."

Confused and angry, he struck back with words he'd never forget. "I don't know who you are. I'd like you to leave."

She did, ten years ago, and he'd not seen her since.

Philip's thoughts returned to the present. The stadium was a door through which the past haunted him. Although only a symbol, sometimes a break from the past required the destruction of symbols.

Taking off his warm-ups, he stretched his tall, lanky frame, performing a ritual for the last time. He began running the four hundred meter oval, oblivious to the demolition crew's arrival in the morning's light.

How many laps he ran, he didn't care – just another one faster than the last. Construction workers waited and watched, no one sure what Philip Doyle was trying to accomplish, no one aware of the past from which he was running.

He ran until his legs were numb and his lungs burned. His dry throat ached with each breath. His stomach churned and he threw up.

He was finished. The sensory experiences of running gave way to jack hammers resounding and the smell of diesel fuel. Retrieving what he'd brought, he walked to a trash dumpster and tossed in his warm-ups and scrapbook. Then he climbed into his Mercedes and drove away.

Chapter 4: The Call

Daniel Stone basked in the warmth of memory as he meandered through the Austin campus. He eventually found his destination.

The morning's sun illuminated two giant red oaks, guarding the gated entrance to the East Garden outside Edwards Hall Auditorium. The great oaks stood as an imposing discouragement to those who did not belong. But to those who were welcome, their massive canopies, like angels' wings, shaded and protected the weary from the searing midday sun. It felt good to see these two old friends. They must have agreed, bidding him welcome with a cool breeze and the gentle rustling of their leaves as he passed.

Entering Edwards Hall, Daniel's thoughts turned to architecture. As a young boy living with his mother and sister on the Sierra Mesa plateau leading to the Grand Canyon, he pondered design and construction, whether by the forces of nature or by human hands. He grew up believing that someday he'd build homes for people, but not until he first experienced the Craftsman style in the elegant, artful workmanship of Edwards Hall did he imagine that architecture could be his life's work.

Treasuring the Craftsman tradition and its reverence for the integrity of natural materials, he regarded the architect's design as a goodwill treaty with nature, an effort to cease the endless war between man and his environment. But he soon received a much greater vision for his life.

The old Daniel Stone had known enough to stay away from the One who calls. As a young boy, he sensed God knew him and loved him. The crucifixion and the Easter story tugged at his heart, and he believed that someday he'd answer the call. But with the age of accountability came an opposing desire. He feared the God of his youth might challenge his right to run 'his own life.' So he hid, hoping to be forgotten.

But his love of the artistry and genius visible in creation drew him back. He desired to *know* what was real, to somehow *enter* into goodness and truth, to truly *see* beauty. And he realized that to be reconciled to others, to the earth, and to this Creator he was beginning to know, he'd have to turn away from his pride and surrender his heart. Humility was the door to a larger life.

Now he wanted to live heroically in the Great Story of creation, the fall and redemption. He envisioned communities where families and friendships thrived: neighborhoods, places to worship and to heal, markets and schools. This desire grew into his calling, and he became a missionary pastor and builder with his wife, Maria, and his sister, Katherine, among the poor in Mexico City.

Daniel entered Edwards Hall auditorium. The morning sun pouring through the leaded glass windows filled the room with a golden haze. The atmosphere inspired reverence for the sacred enterprise of passing on wisdom and truth to eager hearts and minds, beyond the commonplace and profane.

Daniel observed Rob Martinson, sitting alone at a front desk, facing two hundred empty chairs. "Good morning," spoke Daniel. A faint echo answered as his voice reached out into the empty auditorium.

"Daniel Stone, all the way from Mexico. I was hoping you'd come."

Rob rose to greet his old friend while conducting the evaluation that accompanies reunions. He'd first met Daniel at track orientation their freshman year. Now, fourteen years later, Daniel still looked like a runner though his handsome features had matured, and he showed the evidence of hard work.

As Daniel approached, Rob recalled his friend's dominant feature – his eyes. At rest, although Daniel was seldom at rest, his dark blue eyes were pools of thought. When animated, his eyes revealed a probing intensity that could make someone uncomfortable if it weren't for his inviting smile and gentle presence. Katherine had described her brother as having a warrior's eyes – not angry but shining, revealing inner strength and determination.

Daniel waved his left arm towards the empty seats. "What happened? Word get out I'd be recruiting?"

Rob laughed. "My first class isn't until 1:00. What are you up to?"

"Thought you might like to show me what's new on campus."

"Love to, but can't. I have a meeting with Allen Wilder, the prophecy writer."

"I heard your interview with him while driving into Austin."

"Then you know about tonight's conference?" said Rob.

"Yeah, sounds interesting."

"Can you come? His knowledge of prophecy is amazing."

"I'm seeing Chad later this afternoon. But I should be free tonight."

"Great. I'll leave a ticket at the door," said Rob. "What direction are you headed?"

"I thought I'd go over to the track. You know, relive the glory days."

"You don't know about the track?"

"Know what?"

Rob started for the door. "Come on, I have time to show you."

When they reached the stadium, the demolition was underway. They watched as the asphalt was ripped up and loaded onto waiting trucks.

Daniel spoke first, "Hard to imagine all the blood, sweat and tears that asphalt has absorbed over the years? I don't know. It just doesn't seem... respectful."

"Know who's responsible?" asked Rob.

"What do you mean?"

"The major donor to the new stadium?"

"Who?"

"Philip Doyle."

Daniel was silent. He recalled the day he first introduced Philip to his sister. He remembered their passion for one another. But today, both he and Philip were saying goodbye to the women they loved, one by cherishing the memories, the other by trying to forget.

Daniel concluded, "Philip's not destroying the old track to build a new one. He's building a new track to destroy the old one."

Chapter 5: What Are They After?

The constellation of PD Technologies was set like a jewel in the wooded hills outside Austin. Philip Doyle had chosen the four hundred acre property for its small lake, trout stream and diverse terrain. Sixteen PD Tech offices and research labs grew in harmony with the site. Thanks to design suggestions by Daniel Stone while they were students, the office environment celebrated its natural surroundings with wide-open vistas and access to fountains and pools flowing through indoor gardens and courtyards.

Philip's original inspiration for PD Tech was born at the dinner table during his teenage years. Although his father was a successful businessman, it was his visiting uncle, a brilliant biochemist, whose hyperactive mind guided many conversations to the limitless discoveries and innovations made possible in a quantum world.

Philip would listen late into the evening, fascinated as his uncle described a world of abundance, cloaked in mystery yet waiting to be discovered by creative imagination. The microchip, biotechnology and genomics were hammers to shatter paradigms. Shortages identified opportunities and provided the motivation to transcend the status quo. When his father joined in, bringing practical application to theory, the world exploded with possibilities, guaranteeing Philip many sleepless nights.

Science became Philip's window to the world. While lying awake, he dreamed of innovations that would provide the resources necessary for human flourishing.

With financial backing from his father and uncle, Philip embraced the challenge to apply theory to practice. He established a research incubator to develop technologies used by manufacturers to create products and services.

Philip realized that PD Tech's success would depend on his ability to attract and retain talented scientists and engineers, or partners as he preferred to call them. He built incentives into the company culture with stock options, generous research budgets and flexible work schedules.

He succeeded in creating a feeling of purposeful community, occasionally having to remind partners to go home, although he was known to sleep in his office suite many nights. Even his uncle joined the new enterprise, bringing with him a personal portfolio of valuable patents.

For the past ten years, PD Tech's main success had come from developing and licensing advances in the discovery of specific plant genes and sequencing entire genomes. They had created tools to dissect plant genes in order to identify desirable traits such as increased yields without increasing water or fertilizers. Also, using genetic markers they developed new hybrids cheaper, cutting the time to advance new varieties from five years to several months.

PD Tech was publicly traded on the Nasdaq with a market capitalization of over a billion dollars. Investors had been rewarded and nine hundred employees owned more than two hundred million dollars of PD Tech stock. The business model worked, and Philip's dream had become a reality.

****

Chad Connelly noticed his reflection in the glass of PD Tech's front entrance. He was momentarily distracted by a random thought. He didn't look old enough to be a U.S. Congressman. His slight 5'10" frame contributed to his boyish looks, while his light brown hair, worn parted and combed over, would fall across his forehead in response to the slightest breeze. The conclusion was unavoidable; he looked like a college kid. His charcoal gray suit and red tie, which he wore even on hot Texas days, helped a bit, but he still could be mistaken for a grad student on a job interview. His father's stature and expectations rose up as if on queue, but left the moment his reflected image disappeared. Upon entering the lobby, the ever-present aching shock of Lauren's death once again tightened its grip.

Chad knew he needed to talk with Philip, his former college roommate, best man and now an influential constituent, whose project may have contributed to his wife's death. He'd met with Philip many times over the past six years of his congressional tenure to discuss business and government, but none like this. He was still wrestling with the reality of his loss. He didn't want to think of the why or who, but Philip had requested the meeting.

From the lobby a young woman called a 'scout' led him along pathways and water gardens to an enclosed patio adjoining Philip's office.

Philip rose to greet him. "Chad, thanks for coming." He motioned for Chad to have a seat at the table occupying the center of the courtyard. "Again, I want to tell you how sorry I am about Lauren," he spoke from a place of shared grief. "I don't know what to say or where to begin."

Chad had come to expect such awkward moments. When Philip's eyes swelled, Chad broke in, "There really isn't anything to say. But thanks. You're a good friend."

"How are Adam and Ruthie?"

"They're trying to be strong for their dad. I don't think it's become real to any of us yet."

In an effort to move past the difficult moment, Chad turned his attention to Philip's latest painting-in-progress, resting on an easel several feet away. He walked over to the canvas and studied the profile of a young cowboy, slouched on his horse, watching over a cattle drive. The cowboy, weathered beyond his years, stared across the rugged landscape towards a vast, open sky, exploding with color: pale bluish purples and soft pinks bleeding into orange and red. But what struck Chad was the intense longing etched in the young man's face.

"It's hauntingly beautiful," said Chad. "What are you trying to say?"

Philip shrugged, "If I had the words to explain it, I wouldn't have to paint. It's the third of a set. Next time you're at the house I'll show you the others."

Chad returned to the table. "Our Guatemalan embassy says there's a rumor someone wants to stop your agricultural project."

"But we haven't started."

"It's you, your reputation. People expect stunning results."

"But who… I never imagined Lauren was in danger. She was just using her contacts to help us."

"Lauren believed your algae program would bless the people she was committed to help."

Philip spoke softly, "She was a remarkable woman."

After a momentary pause, Chad changed the subject. "What can I do for you?"

"I know this is a terrible time to ask. But I'm leaving for New York immediately following Lauren's service, and then I'm flying to Israel."

"It's okay. It helps for me to stay busy."

"Someone's attacking our stock. Fabricated stories about PD Tech suddenly appear, hyped by the same media people every time. When the stock price drops, Eden Global and your father's partners buy more."

Chad waited silently, not sure he wanted to hear about his father's possible activities.

"We believe someone's orchestrating the media. Our research team has analyzed over a hundred media people, breaking down several thousand articles and news reports about PD Tech by content and form. We've identified five media people as the common links for most negative articles and news reports leading to the stock price declines. We can only speculate who's behind them. Here's the list."

Chad glanced at the names. "I know Chuck Bellows from Business Daily News and Maurine Niven of World Broadcast Financial Network. They're friends of my father." He expressed his annoyance, "Do all roads lead to Gordon Connelly?"

"They may attempt to use the stock as leverage to break up PD Tech in order to acquire our algae genetics."

"A takeover?"

"That's what it looks like, but it doesn't make sense. Our ownership structure makes a takeover virtually impossible.'""

"Are you ready to launch the Farm Initiative?"

"We're making good progress. I'm meeting soon with some of our licensees for Mexico and Central America. Lauren selected them. They're honest, hardworking, family people looking for an opportunity."

When Chad didn't respond, Philip continued, "I know you have limited influence with your father."

"I have no influence."

"Well anyway, could you look into it?"

"I'll see what I can do. Gordon once advised me against Lauren's involvement with your project."

"Maybe he can provide some answers."

"I'll talk to him, but it's not something I look forward to."

Chapter 6: Ideas Have Consequences

Chad and Daniel spent the afternoon by the pool at Chad's red brick, Georgian-style home.

Daniel asked "Have you seen Philip lately?"

"I saw him earlier today. After the memorial service tomorrow he's headed to New York for a stock analysts' meeting, and then to Israel to meet with a subsidiary partner."

"Do you know about the track?"

"I'm speaking at the dedication next year."

"How's Philip doing?"

"He has a problem." Chad recounted his conversation with Philip about the stock manipulation.

"What's your father's story?"

"He married my mom after college. She was a beautiful girl with a sweet spirit who grew up in west Texas, the daughter of a devout Christian doctor who probably gave away more services than he charged for. Her marriage to my father was difficult from the beginning. They moved to New York and she hated the lifestyle. She disliked his friends and their cutthroat business practices. She once called them a brood of vipers.

"After I was born, they split, and my mom moved back to Texas. Gordon's always been indifferent towards me, complaining I'm too much like her. But recently he's tried to bring me into his circle of influence. I think he assumes that because I'm a politician, I must be more like him than he thought.

"As chairman of Eden Global he controls the flow of billions of dollars around the world. Although he's extremely wealthy, his ultimate goal is power. To Gordon, it's about walking into a room of presidents and world leaders, with everyone knowing who really holds the levers of power. It's not about visibility, but about the rich and famous paying homage, like swimmers knowing they survive only by the grace of the shark below."

"Will you talk to him about Philip?"

"I'll try," said Chad. "And there's something else concerning my father."

"What's that?"

"Do you remember Berry Fields?"

"Sure, and I was glad when your college romance with Berry broke up."

"You don't need to remember that well. Anyway, after she transferred to Berkeley her senior year, she went on to graduate school there. We'd talk occasionally. She somehow met Gordon and he hired her. She works out of his D.C. office, managing his personal affairs.

"A few weeks ago I ran into a friend who works for a Christian TV station in Dallas. He'd heard a rumor that Gordon was a large anonymous donor to Wilder Ministries? I figured it had to be a mistake, so I called Berry. At first she laughed at the possibility, but she's looking into it."

Daniel asked through a perplexed grin, "Is your father a closet believer?"

"Not a chance, he hates Christianity, especially in light of my mother's faith. I guarantee you, if he's contributing to Wilder's ministry, it's because Wilder benefits his interests."

"Why would he do it?" asked Daniel.

"I don't know."

"What about Wilder?"

Chad shrugged, "Allen Wilder's reputation has always been solid." After a momentary pause Chad continued, "Did you know Rob joined Wilder's staff?"

"I knew he was meeting with Wilder this morning."

"Rob agreed to head up their teaching seminars. I'm hoping he'll shed light on Gordon's purpose. But I have to be careful. My father only acknowledges my existence because of my political career. And unfortunately, he knows that without his help, my chances are slim of ever becoming a senator."

Chad remembered, "Right before my mother passed away, she asked me to respect my father and pray for him. But she warned, 'Never allow him to entice or deceive you into losing your soul.'"

"I hope you follow her advice."

Chad grinned, "It's time for me to pick up the kids. How long are you staying in Texas?"

"For a couple of weeks."

"Good," said Chad as they stood to leave. "Before you go back I'd like to discuss Life Resources."

"Whenever you're ready."

****

Daniel sat beside an excited Rob Martinson as they waited for the featured speaker, a rising celebrity, Dr. Allen Wilder. The festivities were hard for Daniel to fathom. The worship music set the stage for the main event. A doctor of theology was presenting his views of end-times. For Daniel, after years in Mexico using his hands, mind and heart, this American phenomenon was both troubling and amazing.

With a warm welcome, Wilder walked out onto the stage. He was about fifty, smaller than Daniel had imagined, with a slight build, short cropped gray hair combed back, and wearing a dark blue suit. Spontaneous applause greeted his trademarked intro, "We live in exciting times...

"Israel is God's clock. The gathering of the Jews proves we're in the last hour. Although we don't know the exact time, I'm convinced we are the blessed generation that will experience the Church's rapture out of this world..."

Daniel's thoughts drifted as he listened for several minutes. He'd never focused on end-times prophecy, but the longer he listened, the more questions he had. Didn't Jesus and the New Testament writers insist the kingdom was at hand, two thousand years ago? Did Matthew 24 really refer to the generation of people living today? And what did Christ's claims of authority mean to us now?

He refocused on Wilder, "The Tower of Babel still casts its shadow over the hearts of men. Global unity is the world's most enticing religion with its promise of peace and prosperity.

"But be on your guard, for all utopian dreams will appear as the seductive slavery of Egypt, once again calling God's people to leave behind the harsh freedom of the desert.

"Man's attempts to achieve peace are doomed to futility. The longing for a united world order will not tame the divisive nature of a rebel's heart. Yet the fool's paradise is an enduring dream until idealism is crushed by brute force.

"We don't know when the Tribulation will begin or when the Antichrist will come to power, but we can feel the darkness surrounding us. Governments will fail. Israel's enemies will be emboldened and her allies weakened. Fear will cause people to abandon their freedom to those who promise security. The world is being prepared."

Wilder paused before shifting direction. He discussed several prophetic interpretations in detail, then launched into his close. "How should we live in the expectation of Christ's imminent return? Will he find us evangelizing the lost... or wasting our time on a thousand irrelevant distractions like trying to reform this world, as if the rising tide of evil can be prevented?

"Are we not required to separate ourselves from the world? Are we not expecting many who have called themselves believers to deny the faith during a time of testing?

"I say to students, your degrees won't be needed. The mission fields are where you belong.

"To business people, invest in the Gospel. It's the only future you have.

"To those troubled by elections, forget politics. The Antichrist will soon rule this lost world, and all who govern will serve him. Don't be deceived trying to save a condemned world.

"To you who fret over the environment, don't spend time worrying about what will be destroyed in the coming Tribulation.

"Don't waste precious time polishing brass on this sinking Titanic. Instead, be committed to saving as many passengers as possible.

"God bless you and good night." Wilder lifted his hands and waved, acknowledging a standing ovation more enthusiastic than before.

Daniel took a deep breath and tried to process the experiences of the past sixteen hours. The lack of sleep had finally caught up with him. His first day in Austin after six years had been long, but meaningful. He was enjoying his time with friends, although the emotional reunion only added to his growing premonition that change was coming to his life.

Chapter 7: The Attack Begins

Philip Doyle was flying first class from New York to Tel Aviv. After four hours in the air he finally fell asleep, and he was dreaming.

In his dream Katherine suddenly appeared. She stood before him, just beyond his reach. She moved gracefully, dressed in a flowing robe, the purest white, her long black hair resting softly on her shoulders, her expression radiant.

"Philip," she spoke with a lover's smile. "What are you doing?" she asked with the innocence of a child.

He fought to get up, to go to Katherine. But he was powerless to move.

Katherine stopped. "Philip, why don't you answer?"

His desperation could generate no sound.

Katherine's eyes turned sad. Her voice conveyed a deep sorrow. "I don't know who you are." She disappeared.

"No!" He awoke with a jolt. When he realized he'd been dreaming, he leaned back and closed his eyes. His heart was pounding.

"I failed her," he said, his eyes still closed.

"Failed who?" asked Brenda, his personal assistant who often traveled with him.

"Katherine, and I failed myself."

"How did you fail her?" Although no one at PD Tech talked about her, everyone knew that someone named Katherine Stone was the reason Philip never dated.

"I couldn't go to her because…" He paused, opened his eyes and looked at Brenda. "Something I'm holding onto prevents me from going to her."

Gazing off into the space before him, he continued, "I don't have Katherine because of what I am, not because of what I'm not."

"And what's that?"

The dream left him a sick, empty feeling. "I'm not sure."

Uncomfortable with personal revelations, Philip made a half-hearted attempt to redirect the conversation. "Maybe I should start thinking about someone else."

Brenda shared a good-natured disbelief. "Remember when you were on that magazine's list of the country's most eligible bachelors? They asked me what it was like traveling the world with Philip Doyle. I said it resembled traveling with your older brother. I told them you acted like the most married man I'd ever known."

"Is it that obvious? Am I that sad? To be waiting my entire life for someone who's never going to be with me?"

"May I ask how long it's been since you've seen her?"

Philip spoke through a long sigh. "About ten years."

A door cracked open, and for the first time Brenda glimpsed into Philip's vulnerable sadness. "Why don't you go see her?"

He stiffened and slammed the door. "She broke it off. It was her choice. I wasn't what she wanted."

"Do you really believe that?"

"It doesn't matter what I believe." He turned away.

Philip stared out the window as the aircraft approached Israel's coastline. He realized the Holy Lands were significant to many, though not to him. The attraction of religion to seemingly intelligent people was beyond his comprehension. Yet he wanted to believe that he harbored no bitterness towards Katherine, or God, if there was one. That was her decision to make. It was her right to walk away. She wasn't obligated to him for what she believed or how she acted on those beliefs. But when he thought about it, he sensed his resentment just under the surface. Wasn't everyone, including Katherine, obligated to live in a reality based on reason?

The subject frustrated him so he returned to thoughts of his Friday afternoon in New York. Although business was good, the meeting was a bust.

He disliked the stock market, though he knew it was necessary. PD Tech's continued growth required access to capital markets. The stockbrokers who'd recommended his company in the past had profited from PD Tech's success. But the previous day's analysts' meeting had been rough. The mood in the room, from greetings to questions, was stiff and foreboding.

He wanted to say that his audience's apprehension was unwarranted, based on fear and not the facts. But he did understand. Although the stock analysts were involved in the cold, calculated business of capital, their success came from insight and intuition, and their ability to anticipate the future. What was known was reflected in the current price of any stock, PD Tech included. Therefore everyone in the room knew that careers and fortunes were at the mercy of the next bit of information. They all feared being left out, to be the last to know.

Enter the rumor, or more specifically, 'the rumor on the street,' that source-less, vague, shadow of truth.

The market movers had listened as he laid out present realities. Profits, growth and margins would exceed Wall Street expectations. No hidden problems, the business plan was proceeding on schedule. PD Tech was in great shape.

'But…?' They didn't challenge him directly, yet he sensed their skepticism.

His father had cautioned, "You're a hero now, but if there's a premonition you're sailing into rough seas, Wall Street will turn against you. Remember, those who call you friend will abandon ship before being swallowed by the seas where you sail."

When they landed in Tel Aviv, Philip mentioned to Brenda, "We'll be met in the airport by Lydia Shafran, a bioengineer who is ARD's Coordinator of Project Development. It's her job to keep me informed of ARD's progress towards meeting our goals."

As they entered the terminal, a woman in her early forties, with short black hair and dark features came forward and introduced herself to Brenda after greeting Philip. Brenda found Lydia's manner confident and serious, yet friendly.

On the drive to Jerusalem Lydia shared her story, "…After graduating from MIT, I continued to do algae research for several years in America. I returned to Israel when Ezra Levi offered me a position."

Brenda asked, "What's it like working for Ezra?"

Lydia smiled, "Challenging. He's an off-the-chart genius, but demanding and eccentric."

Philip added, "Ezra came to me five years ago because he needed financing to continue developing his algae production systems. He agreed to give PD Tech control because he saw I was also committed to algae's potential to provide the world with renewable energy, nutrient-rich foods, and a cleaner environment. It's worked out beautifully. Without the partnership, neither our genetically modified algae strains nor his ARD production units would be cost competitive."

Lydia looked at Philip, her face animated by the possibilities, "You know, with your algae genetics and ARD's production technology, there's a new agricultural revolution in the making. From Israel to Texas, the dry and desolate lands will bloom with fields of blue-green algae: consuming carbon dioxide and saline water, producing protein, animal feed and renewable chemicals, and enough green crude to keep the wheels turning. It's going to happen some day, just as we envisioned."

Their conversation drifted from Israel's history to Middle East politics.

24

Philip gazed at the rocky and barren hills that dominated the landscape. From one perspective, the land possessed a rugged beauty, yet from another, he could hardly understand what all the fuss was about. They finally reached Jerusalem and the historic King David Hotel.

Strolling like tourists through the Old City, Lydia's colorful commentary helped Philip and Brenda begin to grasp Jerusalem's significance. Intrigued by the ancient city's history, Philip ran his fingers along the stone walls defining the 'Via Dolorsa' where Jesus had carried his cross. He felt oddly uncomfortable touching something physical that had witnessed the historical event as reality.

Philip absorbed the sounds and energy of busy streets, bustling bazaars and small shops filled with people managing to ignore the ever-present danger. He tried to understand the sightseers of many religions and nationalities touring holy sites.

Lydia explained, "They're pilgrims. They've come to a city where they believe God once resided and where many think he'll return. They're each searching for a deeper faith."

Philip let the conversation drop. Her comments roused questions, but it wasn't a path he was comfortable with.

Lydia stopped. Her attention was fixed on a Muslim mosque with a huge gold dome. They stood beside her, waiting.

"It's called the Dome of the Rock, and it's actually an Islamic shrine. The Muslims built it more than thirteen hundred years ago on the approximate location of the first and second Jewish Temples. You can imagine how that might be a sore point," she said with an ironic grin.

"The thought crossed my mind," he smiled back.

"The mosque nearby, south of the Dome, is Al-Aksa. Both buildings are located within the thirty-five acre site called the Temple Mount."

They resumed their walk to a terrace with steps leading down to the Western Wall. Lydia continued, "Now for some history. The original Jewish Temple, built by King David's son, Solomon, was demolished by the Babylonians in 586 BC. Then the second Temple, the one Jesus taught in, was the site of terrible bloodshed and fiery destruction as Roman soldiers stormed the Temple Mount in 70 AD.

"Several different Muslim nations controlled Jerusalem from 638 until 1917, with a few exceptions during the crusades in the Twelfth and Thirteenth Centuries. In 1917, the British occupied Jerusalem after defeating the Ottoman Empire during World War I. When Israel was created as an independent Jewish state in 1948, war broke out with the Arabs. Jerusalem was divided, and the Old City, including the Temple Mount, was controlled by the Jordanians.

"During the Six Day War in 1967, Israel captured the Old City and reunited Jerusalem. The Israeli Defense Minister, General Moshe Dayan, allowed the Temple Mount to remain under the control of the Supreme Muslim Religious Council. He'd hoped to establish good will, but instead the Jews' lack of resolve to hold on to their holy site was viewed as weakness."

Turning to Brenda, Lydia reminded her, "Remember what I said about Ezra Levi being eccentric."

"I do."

Lydia continued, "To fully understand Ezra, you must appreciate his determination to build a new Jewish Temple on the Temple Mount. A large model is displayed in their lobby, as well as exact replicas of sacred instruments and apparel for temple worship."

Philip responded, "That's a side of Ezra I don't know."

Philip noticed Lydia staring past him as she answered, "Most people don't."

Lydia's expression grew intense and focused. The strain revealed a fear that concentrated in her eyes and spread to her tightening mouth. Philip turned towards her alarm. A young man, perhaps Palestinian, was walking directly towards them, his movement intentional, with his hands concealed in the pockets of a long coat.

Philip glanced quickly back at Lydia. She was locked in a dreadful apprehension. She grabbed his arm, "Come with me."

Philip resisted her tug and turned again towards the object of Lydia's fear. He studied the man's approach: a hundred feet, ninety feet, continuing towards them.

Lydia began to panic, trying to force Philip and Brenda down a narrow side street. But Philip again refused to yield and pulled away. The commotion caught the attention of two Israeli policemen. They noticed Philip watching the Palestinian who had quickened his step as he made the final approach. When he started to lift his hands out of his coat, two Israelis jumped in-between with guns drawn, yelling for the man to lie on the ground. Their quick search uncovered a handgun in each pocket.

With no desire to become further involved, they slipped through the gathering crowd and hurried back to the hotel. Philip spoke first, "Who was he after?"

Lydia asked, "I'm not sure… and besides, what were you going to do, ask him?"

Philip's slight shrug revealed he wasn't sure why he'd not followed her lead.

She slowly shook her head. "Do you believe in angels?"

"No."

Lydia smiled, "Well, maybe you should." Her expression turned serious, "Was that man coming after you?"

"I don't know."

"Maybe you should think about returning to America."

"Not until I've visited ARD."

"Okay, but be careful. I'll have security sent to the hotel. Stay inside tonight and I'll pick you up in the morning."

Philip paced in his hotel room, trying to evaluate a course of action. He paused when he heard "PD Technologies" coming from the television. *Weekend Update* was on World Broadcast's Financial Network.

The interviewer asked, "Today's guest is Clifton Roberts, the chief investment strategist for the Eden Global Fund. Clifton, you attended an analysts' meeting yesterday with Philip Doyle, the CEO of PD Tech. What's your assessment of the company's future?"

Roberts answered, "In the past we've recommended PD Tech and their imaginative business model. However we're no longer confident Mr. Doyle is capable of maintaining their present growth rate and profit margins, so we're downgrading the stock."

"Damn," muttered Philip. The tightness in his chest warned he was indeed sailing into rough seas. Another attack was coming. But who was his enemy? And who would resort to violence? He had no idea what to think.

Chapter 8: Quest for Power

Gordon had attended Lauren's memorial service and insisted Chad bring Adam, who was eight, and Ruthie, who'd just turned six, to the lodge for a few days. He'd said to Chad, "I'll have some visitors on Sunday, then the lodge will be yours for the rest of the week. It'll be a chance for you to be alone with the kids for a while."

Though in a fog of grief, he accepted Gordon's offer to have his Gulfstream pick them up Sunday morning in Austin.

Gordon's Land Rover and driver were waiting at the airport in Jackson Hole, Wyoming and carried Chad with Adam and Ruthie north towards the ranch. The two thousand acre estate Gordon called "East of Eden" was located on the eastern edge of the Teton Mountains. Chad once asked if the name held any significance. Gordon only grinned, claiming the Tetons surely rivaled the original Garden of Eden, and considering his ranch's location, East of Eden was appropriate. Chad doubted the explanation was the complete truth.

The driver pulled up to the front entrance. The kids were greeted by a young lady who was to take them riding. Chad paused as he gazed up at the lodge's rustic beauty. Surrounded by cottonwoods and towering pines, with hewn log walls and a green copper roof, Gordon had built East of Eden to replicate, on a more intimate scale, the lodge houses of Yellowstone and Yosemite.

Chad's vision was awash in memories. He and Lauren had been married on the back patio with the mountains in full view. The day after the wedding they'd sent the guests home so they could enjoy their honeymoon alone in one of the most beautiful places on earth. Summer vacations and weekend retreats marked the kids growth as stepping-stones along the way.

Gordon had suggested Chad might need to get away. But he'd come for the opposite reason, to be immersed in memories of times with Lauren, times of love, and adventure and beauty.

He fought back the tears. Now was not the time. But later, when he was alone, he would allow himself to cry.

Chad entered the lodge and ambled down several steps into an open sitting area. The décor was Mission style with Rocky Mountain art and Native American artifacts. He admired the massive stone fireplace that rose

28

from the center to reach the ceiling forty feet above. Coming out from behind the stone tower, he paused to take in the grandeur of the Grand Tetons, visible through the transparent back wall.

Chad hesitated by an open glass door as he observed his father seated with two men and a woman at a wrought iron table on the stone patio. He was reminded how someone would always notice Gordon first. His striking physical profile ignored his fifty-eight years. He possessed thick silver-gray hair, which he brushed comfortably back. His charming smile contrasted his dark eyes that were sharp and severe.

Over six-feet tall, tan and fit, Gordon was as comfortable on horseback as in a New York boardroom. Although he didn't frequent the gym, many a younger man or woman regretted accepting his challenge to climb the stairs to his twelfth floor New York office. Gordon always pursued the advantage. Dissipation wasn't permitted.

Chad's next thought seemed as strange as it was interesting. The only person he knew who possessed similar traits of strength and focus was Philip Doyle. His father and Philip were similar in their disciplines, yet they sought divergent ends. Gordon purposed to dominate and possess, whereas Philip succeeded by empowering those around him.

The conversation at the table ended and Gordon's visitors exited the far side of the patio to take a golf cart to a boat on the river. Chad waited for them to leave and then walked out to greet his father.

Gordon smiled, but expressed concern as Chad approached. "Are you alright?"

"I'm okay."

"Lauren's service was beautiful. Her mission outreach was impressive."

Chad couldn't resist, "Before mom died she donated the remainder of your divorce settlement to Life Bridge."

Gordon appeared indifferent, "I'm not surprised. Lauren was a lot like her. They both influenced you."

With a slight grin Chad asked, "And that's a bad thing?"

"It's noble they both desired to be helpful. But the world will be engulfed in flames and anarchy before our problems are solved by love, forgiveness and charity."

Gordon motioned for them to sit at the patio table. "You wanted to talk to me?"

Gordon noticed Chad watching the three guests riding the golf cart to the boat dock. Gordon asked, "Do you know Blake Merrill, president of Amber Grains?"

"I thought that was Merrill. Amber Grains is often the subject of our Ag Committee hearings. How long have you known him?"

"Several years. He's a brilliant scientist whose company feeds more people than anyone in history."

Chad wondered, "Does Amber have the answer to future food production?"

Gordon responded through an ironic grin, "What are the options... the family farm?"

Chad pushed back, "Industrial farming has it own drawbacks."

"It beats starvation."

When Chad once again looked at the visitors on the boat Gordon continued, "Merrill believes in the science but not in the intelligence of people to adopt it. Social action and government have a part to play."

"That's where you come in?"

Gordon laughed. "We all want the same good end."

"That depends on the means."

"Chad, you're becoming too cynical."

"And my cynicism's not justified?"

Gordon stood up smiling. "I need to join my guests on the boat."

Chad noted, "I understand, but let's continue our conversation at dinner."

"We can do that. I'm not leaving for D.C. until late tonight."

As evening approached, Chad was once again alone with his father, enjoying dinner on the patio against the backdrop of the sun descending on the Grand Tetons.

Gordon asked, "Now what is it you wanted to talk about?"

"Why did you downgrade PD Tech?"

"It's no longer a good investment. Why do you care?"

"Philip's a friend."

"Friendship and business seldom mix."

Chad responded with a slight grin, "Don't you have friends?"

"I surround myself with those who possess mutual interests."

"Like what?"

"Feeding the world, for example, like my guests on the boat today. We accept the challenges of this world instead of waiting for the next one."

"And to do this you seek power?"

"Power is simply the ability to accomplish what must be done." Gordon smiled at Chad's disapproving expression. "Don't look so shocked. Necessity has thrust this role upon us."

30

"Sometimes I think you create the necessity."

"Chad, with my help this world can be yours. You're so close to real power, to the ability to move the world. Yet you don't see what it takes to acquire and hold it."

Gordon stood and walked to the edge of the patio. He lit a cigar as he gazed into the disappearing sun setting the Grand Tetons ablaze. Chad joined him.

Gordon pointed toward the mountains, "This is why I come here." He glanced at Chad, "Anything else?"

"What's your problem with Philip? I understand business as usual, but isn't PD Tech a rather small fish in your world?"

"Doyle has become a romanticized symbol of a creative entrepreneur building a better tomorrow. What he does is not important. It's the idea that's dangerous, the impulse to diffuse power, believing that change and progress come from individual actions."

Chad didn't hide his surprise, "Why's that a bad idea?"

"Individual actions no longer matter. We don't need a bunch of little guys acting on their own, meddling in the future. The future must be planned, with our problems solved by those who know how. Not the chasing of impossible dreams."

Chad almost objected, but stopped. He wanted to end the conversation. The ache had returned. To hell with the world – the world would have to take care of itself. Better yet, God made it, let him do it.

Chad just wanted to be alone. He wanted to hold the kids. He wanted to go upstairs to the same balcony where he and Lauren had often sat, and lose himself in his memories.

Chad offered token resistance as he started to leave, "America was founded on the idea of everyone pursuing their impossible dream."

"But the world has changed."

"I hope it hasn't changed that much."

Chapter 9: A Foreboding Struggle

At home in Austin, Philip studied his image in the bathroom mirror. He appeared the same: six foot three, the slender frame of a distance runner, short brown hair, deeply set light brown eyes, and cut facial features drawn taut. Yet this observation brought no comfort because he didn't recognize what he saw.

He expected the mirror to reflect creative confidence. Instead, he saw uncertainty, even confusion. Ever since his visit to Jerusalem, he sensed a foreboding struggle, unlike any before.

It was 6:00 a.m. and he was preparing for battle. He'd fought many over the years and usually won, although winning wasn't always necessary. He'd built his success on both the victories and the setbacks.

Yet when he looked into the mirror, he didn't see a warrior to defend his PD Tech against Eden Global, Wall Street rumors or even a Palestinian assassin. Instead, he saw the streets of Jerusalem, the stones and their testimony, and the intensity of people waiting for God.

He felt swept up in a struggle bigger than his own story, something swirling around him, carrying him towards an uncertain end. Regardless, his course was clear. It was time to go to work.

After an early morning meeting with his managers, Philip retreated to his office. He sat at his computer at 8:30 a.m. Central Time to watch the opening of the stock market. PD Tech's descent was continuing as the stock gapped down at the opening another point to 103.53.

He stared at the screen as if searching for understanding, but there was nothing except the slow, steady downward ticks. He finally looked up to see Brenda standing in the doorway, quietly waiting.

"Good morning," she offered.

"I'm not so sure," he countered. "Could you do something for me?"

"I'm ready."

"Contact the business shows and arrange some interviews for later this week. It could get ugly and I don't want our stockholders and partners to think I'm not defending their interests."

"I'll get right on it."

After Brenda left, Philip glanced back at his computer screen and grimaced. He took a deep breath, let it out slowly and then walked from his office to the adjoining courtyard where his father, Art Doyle, was waiting.

"Thanks for coming in."

Art expressed concern, "Brenda told me the details of your close call in Jerusalem."

"I'm not sure what to call it."

"I'm glad the guy couldn't get his hands out of his pockets."

"Lydia said it was angels."

Art smiled, "Well, it makes sense they'd be hanging out in Jerusalem. Did you see what's going on over there now?"

"No, I didn't."

"Palestinians are demonstrating in Jerusalem against the so-called Israeli occupation."

"How bad is it?"

"Going from bad to worse."

Philip shook his head.

Art continued, "You've had quite a weekend. What's your sense of things?"

"Someone's launching another attack."

"Why?"

"I don't know. We're not vulnerable to a hostile takeover. Even the slim possibility of someone inflicting enough damage in order to pick up some of the pieces would be impossible as long as..."

Philip paused until his father asked, "As long as what?"

When Philip didn't answer, Art offered a suggestion, "As long as you're running things... right?"

Philip nodded. A realization was coming to light.

Art proposed a thought, "Who wants break up PD Tech?"

Philip responded, "Eden Global and Gordon Connelly's friends seem to be the main players."

Art offered, "Are there others."

"There must be. Gordon couldn't be responsible for his daughter-in-law's death, or the incident in Jerusalem."

Art concluded, "Your uncle and I agree that it's not just Gordon. Someone else wants a piece of PD Tech."

Philip flashed an ironic grin, "Now I definitely feel better." There was a slight pause, then Philip moved the conversation forward, "What would you do?"

Art smiled, "I'd take the next step."

"That's what I told everyone this morning. We're rolling out the program in six months."

"Good for you," encouraged his father. "Push it as hard as you can. It'll move slowly enough on its own. What's your plan for dealing with corrupt governments and local gangs?"

"We don't pay bribes. Our program is designed to keep the money dispersed locally. We're focusing on strong, local families with entrepreneurial or farming experience, and historical roots in their communities.

"With Lauren gone, the selection process will be more difficult. She worked in many of these communities for years. Her people know who's dependable, and the locals trusted her. I can't ask anyone else because of the danger, so I'll have to somehow do it myself."

Art offered support, "What can your uncle and I do to help?"

"There actually is something. I'd like for both of you to come back to work."

Art laughed, "You can't afford us."

Philip smiled back, "Let's just say you're protecting your investment. Tell Uncle Bret we need someone in the lab who can make decisions intuitively. We don't have time for lengthy studies.

"And Dad, someone has to keep the financing together. This attack may unnerve some of our investors in the new algae rollout. If things get much worse, our partners are going to see their hard-earned wealth start to evaporate. That's why I need two Texas legends to come on board to instill confidence that we can win this battle."

"I'm game, and I know you can count on Bret. So it looks like we're in."

****

Working late on Wednesday evening, Brenda received a call for Philip. He'd returned to his office after finishing the Chuck Bellows' interview for Business Daily News from PD Tech's studio. Everyone in the office believed Philip had done a terrific job. However, when he signed off, Bellows and two stock analysts undermined everything he'd said. Brenda was certain Bellows intended to make Philip appear deceptive.

Brenda informed Philip, "Chad Connelly's on the phone."

Philip answered, "Chad, how are you?"

"I'm all right."

"How about Adam and Ruthie?"

"They're struggling. The lodge brings back lots of memories. Life's hard enough to understand without having to explain it to kids. How are you holding up? I saw the stock's down over ten percent this week."

"I'm treading water. We don't believe we've seen the real damage yet."

Chad asked, "Aren't Gordon and his friend's also losing money?"

"I'm sure they hedge by selling short."

"Doesn't seem right."

Philip explained, "It's within the rules of the game, but it's symptomatic of Wall Street becoming a parlor game for speculators."

"Did you get my message?"

"Yeah, Brenda told me."

"It seems you and my father disagree."

"About what?"

"As close as I can tell, Gordon and his friends believe they're qualified to rule the world, and he's convinced you're not cooperating."

Philip laughed and then asked, "When are you coming back to Austin?"

"Sunday... By the way, did you talk to Daniel at the service?"

"No. I saw him but I arrived late and had to rush out to catch my plane."

"That's too bad," said Chad. "He's visiting friends in Dallas for a couple of weeks. I'll be spending next week in Austin before I go back to D.C. Hopefully, we can get together to discuss how Lauren was helping you."

"Sounds great."

"Philip, Lauren was very excited about what you're doing."

"Thanks, that means a lot."

When Philip hung up and returned to work, he realized that was just what he needed to hear.

****

Early Friday evening Brenda stuck her head into Philip's office. He was leaning back from his desk with his hands behind his head and elbows extended to the sides. Before looking up at her, he glanced one last time at the market close of 91.98 for the week. The stock had lost twelve percent of its value during the week. Unless something changed or he figured out *who* and *why,* his plans would be derailed before he ever got started.

He looked up at Brenda, "Why don't you go home."

"Thanks, I think I will as soon as you finish taping your interview for *Investors Week*. We'll need you in the studio in about an hour."

"Okay, remind me at the fifteen minute mark."

"Also, your flight for New York leaves at 7:00 in the morning. I emailed your itinerary. First you do the *Wall Street Recap* and then the Business Network's *Week in Review*. Would you like for me to go with you?"

"No thanks, I need you rested for next week."

"By the way, take a look at the news out of Jerusalem."

Philip brought up WBC News on the wall monitor. He quietly watched mass demonstrations in Jerusalem between rock-throwing Palestinians and Israeli soldiers. The world was getting crazier by the day. He wondered if those who still possessed some level of sanity had enough time to save it.

Chapter 10: The Wrong Direction

The light from Glen's offered a safe haven from a stormy sea. Philip entered the diner late Saturday evening. He took a seat at the counter and greeted the night chef. "Hi, Barney, how's business?"

"Real good, Mr. Doyle. What brings you in on a Saturday night?"

"I was in New York today. They asked me to stay and have dinner at a five star restaurant. I said definitely not. After a hard week, my mind's set on a Deluxe #1 at Glen's 24 Hour Diner. And here I am."

Barney agreed, "A fancy New York restaurant versus Glen's, hardly a contest."

Philip moved to his favorite table by the window. He chose Glen's because he needed a hiding place, somewhere to escape the battle, even if only for a short while.

Still, only one activity ensured a moment's relief. He pulled from his pocket the only diversion capable of holding back the storm – ten letters, each with a picture, sent to him over the past ten years to wish him happy birthday. They were the treasures of an impossible love, ten letters from Katherine Stone.

He received a letter each year, on or near his birthday. The first one shocked him and ignited his expectations. But even though she'd reached across the divide, she never eliminated it.

He rejoiced when the second one arrived. After the third, he expected them. More than that, he lived for them. No matter how he felt – lonely, angry, forsaken – he only had to make it to the next birthday. She seemed to intuitively know what he needed. Anything less, he'd have starved to death. Anything more, short of being in her arms, would never be enough.

When a new letter arrived, he read it with both joy and sadness. He cherished each revelation, savoring every conveyance of affection, from the 'Dear Philip' to the 'Love with all my heart.' Her words were the evidence of his hope, and with each letter, he loved her more.

He immediately went to an excerpt from the last letter that captured his feelings about the past week. He was uncomfortable with the religious emphasis, yet he appreciated her ability to beautifully express "building in the ruins."

...We live in a time of intriguing irony – characterized by people rejecting the 'big story,' and yet millions gravitate toward grand epics and myths to help make sense of their lives. The most popular of these epics offers the power of simple virtue and the eternal worth

of human beings, the conquest of evil, and the value of adventurous friendship.

Perhaps there really is a great story, a hero and a band of brothers and sisters, and perhaps we have heroic notions because there are battles to be won. Truth changes us as it changed the cowardly friends of Jesus who deserted him at the cross but were transformed by the resurrection. They were no longer afraid of death, nor life, nor the world and its idols.

Truth is not abstract and unembodied, but alive. Wanting relationship with us, in us, the Author risked entering his own play and became the sublime hero. He revealed that our lives are subplots in the epic that began before, and will continue after, our short time on earth – and that our lives are unending.

His kingdom is both now and not yet. And for now, the work of the kingdom is always with us. It begins right where we are planted, best in fellowship with others. Bringing water to the thirsty and good news to the poor. Binding up the broken-hearted. Announcing freedom to captives. Dancing where there was mourning. Revealing dignity where there was shame, and praise where there was despair.

This is our great adventure, even though lived an hour at a time. Culture-making, world-changing, kingdom-advancing is about the faithful commitment to build in the ruins. Not to coerce but to shine forth a light so lovely that all will be drawn to His presence...

He reread the passage. Her words lingered in his mind as a haunting melody, a revelation from someone who'd seen beyond the visible. Someone who had seen what he at times felt was possible. For this special moment he was not alone, and he could rest.

He finished reading through the letters. He rebuked himself for trying to eliminate Katherine's memory by building a new track stadium. How foolish, but he'd felt compelled to act. Something had to be resolved. Some unsettled conflict was directed at his heart, outside his control. He assumed this struggle originated with Katherine, but he wasn't certain anymore. The harder he pushed away, the more he felt he was heading in the wrong direction.

Philip prepared to leave the restaurant. He needed to avoid emotional distractions. His life's work was at risk. With a battle to win and a business to save, he had to stay focused.

There it was again – the feeling that he was going the wrong way. He considered the thought, and then reacted as he always did. He suppressed it.

Getting up from the table, he paid his bill and walked out into the darkness.

Chapter 11: New Direction

After returning from East of Eden, Chad spent the next week at his home in Austin. Daniel dropped by the house after returning from Dallas.

Chad fixed a cup of coffee and joined Daniel at the kitchen table. "I've done a lot of thinking about Life Bridge. The decision to continue the ministry is easy. They do excellent work with a dedicated staff, and it's well funded from Lauren's family and my mother's estate. I don't know if I've told you about my maternal grandfather."

"Not much, other than he was a Christian doctor with a generous heart."

Chad told the story. "As a young doctor, after World War II, he lived in west Texas and provided medical services for many of the oil wildcatters and their employees. They often couldn't pay him so they'd give him stock certificates instead. Most of them were worthless and for years he just filed them away.

"When Lauren shared with my mother her dream of the ministry, mom contributed the money she'd received from Gordon. She also located a box of these old oil certificates and gave them to Lauren to see if they had any value.

"It took quite an effort to track down their current status. Some had gone under, but many of those original drillers had found oil and over the next forty years had sold to oil companies who'd sold or merged with bigger companies and so on. Anyway, Lauren ended up with millions of dollars in oil company stocks.

"So Life Bridge was born and now provides food and medical assistance in fifteen Central and South American countries. They have seventeen employees and help support the work of over fifty missionaries and hundreds of volunteers. The structure's in place. It just needs leadership."

Daniel observed, "That shouldn't be difficult, unless you intend to continue helping Philip."

"Are you familiar with what he wants to do?"

"Only vaguely. I'd see Lauren whenever she came to Mexico City, and for the past couple of years she was very excited about Philip's algae farms. But I don't know many details."

Chad proceeded to explain Philip's algae concept from production to distribution to the variety of products including protein, animal feed, chemicals and green crude oil. "His strategy is to provide, at minimal cost, algae production units to small, local communities that fit a specific criterion. They will select qualified families to create a board, provide management and labor, and run the operation as a for-profit enterprise.

40

"To stock the farms, PD Tech has made phenomenal progress through their genomics research, developing super-hybrid algae strains adapted to specific environments and desired product mix.

"It's quite a remarkable vision. Philip looks at the program as a long-term investment in the people of Central and South America. He believes it's extremely difficult for people to overcome poverty unless they're able to liberate *themselves* from the daily needs of food and energy.

Daniel sat quietly, considering Chad's request. For several months he had sensed new challenges lay ahead. He explained his thinking, "When I was driving to Austin I kept focusing on Lauren's description of Philip. She was convinced that God was using Philip's deeply ingrained understanding that freedom and prosperity are tied to productive work at the individual family level. I agreed with her then, and it's something I'd like to be a part of."

"I know Philip will be thrilled you're involved," said Chad, smiling. "There's a good chance that what happened to Lauren was isolated to a particular location and we can avoid that area."

Chad stood up and headed for the den. "I've invited Rob to join us tonight. Before he gets here, there's an interview on WBC of someone who recently visited the ranch. The Reverend Buzz Nelson... ever heard of him?"

"Isn't he the liberation theology guy from years ago?"

"Yeah, that's him, except he now calls it social justice."

By the time Daniel got to the den, Chad was watching the program in progress. Nelson was being interviewed by WBC reporter, Clarence Daily, the host of *Faith in America*.

B. Nelson: "...we're spending too much for corporate welfare, too much for the military, and too much to support Israel's oppression of the Palestinians."

C. Daily: "What role can people of faith play in the debt debate?"

B. Nelson: "It's unfortunate how many Americans have been misled to believe government is the problem, when, in fact, our government is the one institution with the legitimate role to protect all the people, especially the disadvantaged. Who better than our elected representatives to make certain the wealth of America is used for the common good of all the people?"

C. Daily: "Congressman Chad Connelly of Texas has accused the administration of strangling the economy with new regulations on everything from healthcare, to energy, to farming and food production."

B. Nelson: "And just who does Mr. Connelly represent? The President has led the way to protect consumers from greedy insurance companies, big oil interests, and the monolithic, agricultural industry that controls patented seeds and chemicals, charging whatever the market will bear for the sustenance of life."

Chad turned down the sound. "That was odd."

"That he quoted you?" said Daniel.

"No, I'm used to that. It was odd that Buzz Nelson took a direct shot at Amber Grains." He explained to Daniel, "Nelson was at Gordon's ranch with Blake Merrill, the president of Amber. It's not a nice way to treat your friends."

Rob Martinson arrived to share the evening with his former college track teammates. The conversation soon turned to a discussion of his first week working with Allen Wilder. Daniel mentioned he'd finished reading Wilder's new book.

"What did you think?" asked Rob.

"I thought it was interesting, but I question how he manages to interpret every current event as further evidence that the Rapture and Tribulation are just around the corner."

Rob laughed, "That's because they are. Look at Jerusalem."

Daniel asserted, "But conflicts in the Middle East are not new."

Rob insisted, "Our present government in Washington will abandon Israel. Everyone knows it. The battle for Jerusalem is coming, and only God can defend his city. Just like scripture says."

Chad wasted no time redirecting the topic to finding out if his father was contributing to their ministry. He asked Rob, "I've heard a rumor my father's funding Wilder, but it's hard to believe because Gordon has always been hostile to Christianity."

Rob responded, "I have no idea. No one has mentioned it, but I'll see what I can find out."

Chad wondered out loud, "What could Gordon want from Wilder?"

Rob stated, "I can assure you of one thing, Wilder doesn't take orders from anybody, especially for money. He's as honest and committed as they come. If Wilder accepts money from him, it's because Gordon doesn't ask for anything in return."

Chad was perplexed, "It shows I still don't understand my father."

Chapter 12: Strawberry Fields Forever

Chad arrived at his Washington, D.C. office on an uneventful Tuesday morning. It was now four weeks since Lauren's death and he was on autopilot, just going through the motions. He wasn't motivated to work, but there were important matters needing at least his presence. He even hoped the busyness of the nation's capital might help relieve the painful emptiness. So far it hadn't helped.

He stopped by his office manager's desk. She mentioned a possible noon appointment, "Berry Fields called, inquiring if you were free for lunch. She offered to update you on your father's activities."

"Please call her and ask if the Capital Brewery on Maryland Avenue at 12:30 will be okay."

An arms-length friendship with Berry Fields was a harmless indulgence Chad had allowed for the past four years, ever since Berry had started managing his father's personal affairs from Gordon's D.C. office. Chad admitted this weakness while checking the restroom mirror. But Berry was an indulgence with limits, like a rich dessert, beautiful to the eye but impossible to eat. He'd learned from personal experience that if he took even one bite, he'd pay the price.

He had paid the price in college. Berry had captivated his heart for eight months and then she moved on. He'd crashed to earth with a thud, left gasping for breath, fearing he'd never recover.

After meeting Lauren, he refocused his life, grateful for a love established on a firm foundation. Once Berry started working for Gordon, he'd talk to her occasionally, but now saw her in a different light. The spirit that once held his fascination disallowed her loyalty or commitment to anything other than a whim and the wind that moved her.

Chad noticed two men seated at the table next to him abandon their conversation and stare towards the restaurant's entrance. He grinned, guessing what might have caused the interruption. He was right. Berry stood inside the door. She spotted him, returned his smile, and started towards the table.

Her entrance was an event. Who did she know? Who was acknowledged? She took in everything with casual disinterest, especially those who watched her, from glances held a moment too long to outright stares.

Those experiencing Berry's presence first noticed her hair, a classic strawberry blonde, lightly brushing her shoulders, lifted by the continuous motion of energized curl. Although her present style was sophisticated, Chad recalled that in college her curls were never under control, only varying degrees of suppression.

Fourteen years before, the blonde curls with their reddish hue belonged to a college freshman named Sarah Fields. A nickname originated quite naturally from her devotion to the Beatles' music of the 60s and her retro-enchantment with their psychedelic period. With a little help from her friends, she invented a new description of herself. From then on, the former Sarah Fields was known as Strawberry Fields Forever, or simply, Berry.

She loved her new name precisely because it wasn't a name. The moniker more aptly described what she aspired to be: imagination without boundaries, undefined, yet knowable as an attitude, an image, an awareness. She dreaded the limitation of being known as a 'something,' unless that something involved mystery – a mystery revealed when the revelation amused her.

Chad stood to greet her. As he accepted the hand she offered, he was drawn to her eyes – exotic, alluring, with an ever-present hint of whimsy. He was always struck by how light blue they were, almost a bluish gray, vividly set in high cheekbones, showcased against her light, gentle complexion. The soft, inviting lines of her facial features were beautiful, yet approachable.

During their college romance, he'd also been intrigued by her originality and whimsical nature. Every conversation could be a journey to a destination unknown. She spoke often of meaning hidden in mystery, and he found it enchanting. But he never escaped the feeling that beneath all the enigmatic behavior one would find a world that revolved for the amusement of Berry Fields, alias Strawberry Fields Forever.

"How have you been?" asked Chad, helping Berry with her chair.

"I'm fine," she responded through a warm smile. "I wanted to personally tell you how sorry I am about your loss."

They discussed Lauren's death, the memorial service and his week at the ranch with the kids. Berry asked, "Is it uncomfortable when people ask about her?"

"Actually not," said Chad with a warm smile. "She's in my thoughts all the time anyway. In fact, talking about her is the best way to bring temporary relief."

He decided to mention, "Daniel Stone has agreed to become the new executive director of Life Bridge. We worked out the details yesterday."

Berry was delighted, "I haven't seen Daniel since college. Did he ever remarry after his wife died?"

"No, he hasn't. It's hard to believe it was six years ago."

"Has he been in Mexico all this time?"

"Yeah, with his sister, Katherine. But he was ready to consider something new. He's even going to continue the ministry's work with Philip."

Berry was surprised, "Was that why Lauren's plane was shot down?"

"No one knows. We'll avoid any dangerous areas."

Berry's doubts were evident, but he didn't want to get bogged down in a discussion of security. "How are you doing? Is there a significant person in your life?"

"No, Gordon keeps me busy and I travel a lot."

"What about Gordon? I often wonder what kind of woman would interest my father."

Berry reviewed the menu and then answered, "First, let me tell you what your father said when he hired me. He agreed to my salary request and then increased it. He explained that the first amount was for my work, the second for my discretion."

She laughed while changing the subject, "How was your time with him at the ranch?"

"It was a nice visit. We both have low expectations. He's such an enigma to me that I don't worry about it."

Berry smiled. "I'm sure at times he feels the same."

Chad continued, "How he views the world confuses me. Yet on the other hand, if he started making sense I'd really be worried. I don't know how he sleeps at night.

"For example, I asked him why Eden Global recommended selling PD Tech's stock. He alluded to investments, and then criticized Philip for believing that individual actions make a difference. He called it a dangerous idea. It's like he rejects something quite reasonable because it doesn't fit his view of things. Anyway, when one considers the size of Eden Global, is PD Tech really worth all the effort?"

"What effort's that?" asked Berry.

Chad wondered whether to confide in her. What would it hurt? Philip was being slaughtered daily and PD Tech's stock was in a tailspin. He remained undecided and instead redirected the conversation, "Have you been able to find if Gordon gives money to Allen Wilder?"

"Gordon donates to a lot of things."

"But a Christian ministry?"

Chad let Berry order lunch while he considered his options. He again considered whether to tell Berry what he knew about the stock manipulation. He looked towards the bar television. Maurine Niven was hosting the noon report. Reading the closed caption, Chad followed the interview with a journalist who'd written an article for *Equity Journal* entitled, "Can Philip Doyle Still Lead?"

Chad concluded there was little to lose by asking Berry for help. For some unexplainable reason he did trust their friendship, and if he were going to help Philip, he had few options.

"Berry, I'd like your help, but this needs to stay between us."

"Sure."

"I recently talked to Philip. He's convinced that PD Tech's stock price has been manipulated for the past year and a half, and Eden Global may be involved."

"What does Philip mean by manipulated, and is this the same 'effort' I asked you about a moment ago? You know, when you ignored my question." Her voice possessed a good-natured tease.

His boyish grin acknowledged her jab. "I guess so."

"Is Gordon's aggressive move against a company uncommon?"

"No," agreed Chad, "but the extent of the effort compared to the relative small size of the victim seems unusual."

"To accuse them of stock manipulation seems a little farfetched."

"Philip's people have done a lot a research that shows…"

Berry casually interrupted, "Isn't all this rather… circumstantial? What if it's no more complicated than Wilder's doing something beneficial and PD Tech's a bad investment?"

Chad learned back and answered with a grin, "I don't think so."

Berry returned his smile. "Okay, what would you like from me?"

"It's simple. Without compromising any sacred trust between you and Gordon, if you hear of a reasonable explanation for either, please quench my curiosity. It may only be another stock deal to Gordon, but Philip's a close friend, and I'd like to help him save his company."

Chad looked away, returning his focus to the television above the bar. The stock quotes scrolled along the bottom of the screen until the letters PDT flashed across in red. PD Tech was already down more than two dollars for the day. He wondered how Philip was handling the pressure with everyone expecting that the worst was yet to come.

Chapter 13: Defending the Alamo

Philip stared blankly at the screen. It was late Thursday afternoon and PD Tech closed at 86.57, down twenty-three percent from a high of 107.25 in just one month. The onslaught had continued with a rumor circulating that the company was insolvent. Another rumor claimed improper accounting procedures.

In a matter of weeks, PD Tech had lost over two hundred million dollars in market value. No reason justified the loss. The objective was clear. Someone intended to drive him out. The inconceivable was their goal, and a specific strategy had come to light. Through the media, a story was being constructed that pinned the stock losses on his "ill-advised" venture into algae production.

Philip let go of his thoughts and resumed listening to his father, who was talking with his Uncle Bret and Charles Lee, who headed up PD Tech's research team.

Bret asked, "At what point do things break down?"

Art responded, "We're in great shape financially, but that ignores a pressing problem. The employee stock losses have created an explosive situation. At some point we can expect the board to be approached by indignant stockholders and shell-shocked partners who'll argue that Philip's head-long leap into the blue-green algae abyss has irresponsibly squandered investor equity."

Philip asked, "Would anyone advise we abandon the algae initiative?"

Charles clarified a point, "That would upset Ezra Levi, and we don't believe dropping the algae project at this time will stop the attacks, only change their approach."

Silence greeted Charles's final observation. Their present strategy appeared to be the best course of action.

Art asked Philip, "I hear you're going to Mexico this weekend."

Philip nodded, "I'm visiting our training center in Mexico City. We're bringing together about twenty highly qualified families for a pilot presentation. In light of the importance of this first group and the opportunity to show Daniel Stone what we're doing, I decided I should be there."

"You leave in the morning?"

"Yeah, I'll be back on Monday."

Art continued with another question, this time with a slight grin, "Is

47

Katherine still in Mexico City?"

Philip's answer was barely audible, "Yes she is." After a brief pause, he turned to Charles, "What do you think they'll do next?"

Charles answered, "We're expecting something dramatic to occur soon in order to shock the partners and investors into a fear-driven demand for change. At that point it might be difficult for the board not to cave."

Philip asked, "How do we counter what we don't know?"

"Remain diligent," said Art, "and keep moving forward."

Bret added, "…and hope they make a mistake."

Sitting alone in his office courtyard, Philip closed his eyes and let go of the intense concentration that always held him upright. He surrendered to gravity, sinking back into the chair's contour. He blocked out everything except the steady, deep gurgling of water surging through the rock garden. His thoughts turned to Katherine. He'd soon be entering her world, and his hopeless desire to see her floated to the surface.

****

Katherine woke in the middle of the night to her racing heartbeat and the chill of cold sweat. She sought discernment and prayed. She pictured Philip, and fear swept over her. Her eyes swelled. Something seemed wrong.

Through the open window, the night sky lit her bedroom. The light revealed the paintings on the wall, artistic expressions of faith, created by Mexican believers she knew and loved, that pointed to the source of her comfort and trust.

She wondered if Philip's expected presence in Mexico City the next day was the reason for her anxiety, even though she had no reason to believe she'd see him. As she lay quietly and listened, she felt there was something more. She prayed for his safety.

When she finished, a recurring theme filled her consciousness, this time stronger than ever before. The season of deliberation had passed and a pressing thought required action. She'd tell her brother in the morning. She, too, would soon be leaving their mission, but this time not to follow her brother. This time she was going home.

****

At 6:30 a.m., Philip was preparing to leave Austin for Mexico City. Brenda Hanover received the call she was expecting. Only one person had the audacity to call before sunrise.

"Hello, Mr. Doyle."

"Good morning, I hope I didn't wake you."

"Of course not. You can't wake me because I dare not go to sleep. How are you holding up?"

"I'm fine. Like any good Texan in a tough fight, I woke this morning thinking of the Alamo."

"The Alamo?"

"You know, Davy Crockett. Early in his life he was revered as a courageous fighter, then he died at the Alamo."

"And?"

"I wondered what he thought, standing in their little fort outnumbered more than thirty to one, watching a vast army preparing to overrun their meager defenses."

"And what was Davy Crockett thinking?"

"How he'd so obviously gotten himself in the wrong place at the wrong time."

Brenda laughed as Philip continued, "I'm counting on you to hold the fort."

"Like Davy?"

"Sure. Think how famous you'll be," teased Philip.

"What are you doing now?"

"I'm on the plane, reviewing the profiles of the people coming to the training center. I feel like I know them."

"In what way?"

"Just like all of us at PD Tech, they're looking for an opportunity to be productive and provide for themselves and their families. I think it's a good match."

The plane landed in Mexico City and Philip made his way through the terminal to the valet pick up area. A driver was standing alone, holding a sign for 'Philip Doyle.' He opened the back door of a black Mercedes limousine. Philip climbed into the car and slid across the seat to the center. He leaned back, blocking out the sites and sounds.

His thoughts turned to Katherine. He remembered the times she'd visited the family ranch. His memories were filed away like faded home movies: her laughing with his mom and dad on the front porch, riding horses along the shallow creek beds, dreaming of a life together under the vast canopy of starry nights.

These events had occurred. The pictures in his mind were proof, but he yearned to again experience the unique passion that had once possessed the center of his life.

His stream of memories was disturbed when the car turned into a narrow alley and stopped.

Not recognizing the surroundings, he leaned forward to question the driver. Before he could speak, two men entered the car, one from the front passenger door and the other from the left side. The men wore knit caps and clothes, covering the lower halves of their faces. Philip's immediate instinct was to escape. He dove to his right, trying to open the door. He heard a click just as he grasped the handle. It was locked.

He shot a glance over his left shoulder to the man now seated across from him. The resentment he was about to unleash on the invaders was abruptly stifled by a large black handgun pointed directly at his face.

He stared into the dark hole at the end of the gun's barrel. The implied threat imposed a sufficient restraint. He did nothing.

The weapon, held calmly in his assailant's hand, did not elicit fear. It was simply a tool. Only when he looked into the man's eyes did the weapon's threat become real. The gunman's eyes were without life, as cold and black as the steel in his hand. Philip was suddenly gripped by the very real possibility that his life could be ended by a hunk of metal, exploding out from the black hole, crashing into his face. He realized he was confronting death's agent, and from that moment he understood his life was in someone else's hands.

Philip heard the door lock click open. Another man entered the limo through the right side, and then the door closed sharply. He motioned for Philip to place his hands behind his back, and his wrists were taped together. His briefcase was forced open to look for anything of value, and then, along with his cell phone, tossed into a dumpster. A cloth bag was placed over his head, and his face was forced down against his knees. The car lunged forward.

Philip listened, but no sound was distinguishable from the drone of busy streets. The car pulled into a space that echoed like a large garage and came to a stop. The doors opened and two men pulled him from the back seat. After being searched, he was led down concrete stairs. He listened for clues of where or why. He wanted to speak, but remained reactive, waiting.

Strangely, nothing happened. They stopped and he heard a door open. The tape binding his hands was cut, and he was shoved several feet forward. The creaking metal door slammed shut behind him. The lock was bolted from the outside. Muffled voices, light and laughing, started outside the room. The congratulatory sounds faded with distance, ending when a second door was closed at the end of a hallway.

Philip slowly removed the hood. He was standing in a dingy, one room apartment with a grime-covered cast iron sink and an adjoining bathroom with no door and filthy, orange-brown rusted fixtures. The kitchen sink was framed by trash-covered wood shelves with flaking paint, so faded he didn't recognize a color. The adjacent corner contained a thin, stained mattress lying on a metal bed frame. The center of the room held an old circular wood table with two metal chairs and a badly frayed upholstered chair with side table and lamp. Along the ceiling, on the wall opposite the door, was a row of glass blocks, protected by a heavy wire mesh allowing daylight into the room. The last thing he noticed was a camera mounted on the ceiling in the far corner, focused on the door.

After a quick survey, Philip ignored the room. He couldn't think of anything but the gunman's eyes. They haunted him. He'd just faced evil as a living reality, as though a spirit of evil was using the gunman for its own purpose. Philip wasn't able to discern its source, but he believed it was more than some misguided soul with bad life experiences or poor education.

Adding to his confusion was the constant feeling that some undefined influence loomed over his struggle, something he did not understand, something beyond his resources to fight.

Chapter 14: *Reading the Script*

Leo Marone was sitting in a leather chair in the living room of Gordon Connelly's Washington, D.C. condominium. Gordon had met with the CEO of Uni Energy several times in Italy to advance his strategy for developing PD Tech's algae genetics after the takeover. But this was the first time the Italian had asked to meet in America. He figured it was related to Philip Doyle's disappearance.

Gordon had known Marone for three years and was impressed with his connections. In his late thirties, Marone had studied and worked in Rome, New York, Dubai and Singapore. Fluent in four languages, he was savvy and persuasive with an innate intelligence. Always dressed in stylish, tailored suits, his strong, angular features highlighted restless, dark eyes. Gordon found him to be engaging with a gracious manner, accented by a touch of aristocratic arrogance.

Gordon asked, "Why would Doyle's disappearance bring you to Washington?"

Marone replied, "I believe I know why he was taken."

"Why?"

"Our future partners are getting restless."

"Our plan was working. His own board of directors would have eventually ousted him. And besides, I didn't know I had competition."

Marone continued in his indirect style. "There are those who questioned how long it would take."

"Let me clarify the ground rules, Leo. You're not to say anything that would make me an accessory to a crime."

"That's not my intent. But it is my opinion that Doyle's disappearance provides an opportunity to close the deal."

"That depends…"

Marone calmly asked, "On what?"

"Whether my son's friend is alive, and stays alive."

"That's important to you?"

"With my help, Chad could someday be President. But if Doyle dies, and Chad believes I'm involved, he'll never join me. That would be unacceptable."

Marone proceeded, "Your son and the people at PD Tech need to understand there are powerful interests involved."

"And you know who?"

Marone's silence was answer enough. Gordon proceeded, "What are you proposing?"

52

"It's possible those holding Doyle might let him go if, let's say, PD Tech agrees to sell their algae business."

Gordon's suspicion grew as he studied Marone before answering, "You're suggesting I pass this on to my son?"

Marone shrugged as he answered, "Of course, I have no way of knowing, but it might be the only way to save Doyle."

Gordon's tone carried a warning, "Someone is treading on dangerous ground. I don't care when or how the algae business is separated from PD Tech, but Doyle must live. That's non-negotiable."

The hint of a smile crept into Marone's expression. "I'll use whatever influence I have to ensure his release. In the meantime, PD Tech must understand the necessity of acting immediately."

Gordon rose to his feet. The severity of his features and his movement towards the door signaled their meeting was over. "My son's due here in an hour. I'll mention your suggestion."

****

Chad showed up at Gordon's condominium visibly shaken by Philip's disappearance. He planned a direct confrontation with his father.

Gordon opened the door. "Hello, Chad. Come in."

Chad walked by him into the living area, "Are we alone?"

"Yes." Gordon walked to the bar and poured a drink. "Would you like something?"

"No, thanks. I came over because Philip Doyle's missing."

"I saw the news."

"Do you know what happened?"

"Why ask me?"

"Because you're involved," stated Chad, pressing the point.

"How's that?"

"I believe Eden Global and your business partners executed the media attacks on PD Tech."

"So?"

"This thing with Philip smells like a set-up. What are they after? What are you after?"

"Are you accusing me of something?"

"Don't play coy games with me. I want to know who did it or I'll bring the full force of my congressional office against you, and we *will* find out what you know."

Gordon appeared to excuse the threat, "You'd find I know nothing about it."

"Nothing's beyond your influence. I want to know the truth."

Chad could see instant fire in Gordon's eyes and a tense contraction of his jaw. He'd succeeded in pushing his father to the edge and braced for an angry rebuke. Instead, he witnessed an absolute mastery of emotion as Gordon's features relaxed with a slight smile as he calmly explained, "Chad, I certainly didn't kidnap your friend. That's not my style. But instead of accusing me, perhaps you should consider that I might be trying to keep him alive."

"Why would you do what?"

"Why wouldn't I?"

Chad was astonished. He'd anticipated an irate frontal assault and instead received a request for gratitude. Without admitting anything, Gordon had turned the conversation upside down by countering with an impossible proposition. Chad was amazed at how Gordon always seemed to be one step ahead.

"Do you know what happened, or who did it?" asked Chad.

"No."

"Do you know someone who does?"

"I'm looking into it."

"How do you know Philip's alive?"

"I *believe* he's alive," answered Gordon, "and I haven't heard otherwise. What do you think?"

"I don't know…"

Gordon said nothing, only stared back at Chad with a grin that seemed to say the conversation was proceeding just as Gordon had anticipated.

Chad's utter frustration pushed him towards the door, "We'll talk about this again, soon."

"I'm available any time."

Chad started to leave, but stopped. His anger subsided enough to start thinking. He turned back to his father, "What would you recommend PD Tech do?"

Gordon was pleased with his son's recovery. "I'd start by unloading everything connected with algae."

Chad realized he was being schooled in how the game was played. He couldn't tell if his father was helping him save Philip or furthering his own interests, or both. He asked, "Is there anyone PD Tech should talk to?"

"The other algae companies couldn't afford it and someone like Amber Grains would ignite the conspiracy peddlers."

"Then who?" asked Chad with the sense he was reading from a script.

"I'd wait to see who contacts me, maybe a company not presently involved in algae."

Chad walked out and hurried to a cab waiting for him at the curb. He didn't want to go back to an empty apartment so he instructed the driver, "The Capital Brewery on Maryland Avenue."

He'd gone to Gordon's as a U.S. Congressman demanding answers and left with a message for PD Tech, possibly from Philip's enemies. As he rode through the nation's capital in the back of a cab, Chad once again found himself comparing Gordon and Philip, two men remarkably alike, apparently locked in a battle. Gordon and Philip were both confidently committed to visions of the future made possible by their audacious imaginations and iron wills. Each had developed the talents and resources to attempt to make their vision a reality.

The problem from Gordon's perspective was that he and Philip had incompatible visions, and Gordon understood that Philip's vision of individual empowerment was an *idea* that couldn't be tolerated.

Chad only hoped that his father's desire to win his son was strong enough to cause Gordon to use his influence to save Philip's life.

Chapter 15: Octaviano

At 9:00 p.m., as instructed, Daniel walked along a road next to the Mexico City park, Bosque de Chapultepec. Before long a dark Toyota SUV pulled up behind him. The vehicle stopped and the back door opened. A big man, over six feet, dressed in black, stepped out and waited. Daniel turned and walked towards him, stopping about ten feet away.

"I'm Daniel Stone."

"You want to see Octaviano?"

Daniel nodded and climbed into the back seat. They drove for twenty minutes before parking in the alley behind a small restaurant called The Smiling Texan. He entered through the back door with the two men who'd picked him up. At a corner table he found a distinguished yet casually dressed Hispanic man, about sixty, with thick, black hair, mustache, and huge grin.

"Daniel, mi amigo bueno. I picked this place for you."

"Octaviano, it's great to see you." Daniel looked about the room. "But isn't this all a bit melodramatic?"

"I'm not paranoid, my friend, only cautious. Have a seat."

They ordered dinner and caught up. Daniel explained what had been going on in Austin with Philip and the Algae Farm Initiative. "U.S. security in Guatemala believes that Lauren Connelly's death is somehow connected to Doyle's project"

"Powerful interests control the food business."

"But enough to shoot down a plane?"

Octaviano grinned at his friend's reaction. "Money and control, Daniel. The powerful take their cut and the rest of us struggle to survive."

Daniel responded with a reluctant grin, "That seems a little cynical."

"Do you mind if I explain the world Mr. Doyle's entering?"

"Please do," said Daniel sincerely.

"Do you know my background?"

"Not much, other than you grew up on a farm in northwest Mexico."

Octaviano nodded slowly as he reached back for a distant memory. "I come from a long line of farmers. Back in the late 60s, after several lean years, some Mexican scientists trained at one of your universities persuaded my father and other local farmers to adopt modern agriculture."

"The 'Green Revolution," offered Daniel.

Octaviano nodded. "My father was a proud, smart man who wanted the best for us. He was skeptical of all their promises, but he had no choice.

"Soon he was planting hybrid wheat on his sixty acres. At first, yields improved but within a few years he was in way over his head. He had to buy expensive hybrid seeds every year, chemicals, and new equipment. All of the farmers depended on global grain pricing, and worst of all, credit. Soon growing debt forced him and many of his friends to sell their farms for practically nothing and move into the city looking for work. He found a job as a truck driver, delivering chemicals to the industrial farm that had gobbled up his land."

Daniel responded, "I've heard stories like that in Mexico City."

"Look what happened," shared Octaviano sadly. "From Mexico to Argentina, and even within the U.S., thousands of self-sufficient family farmers were forced off the land. Instead of finding the promised prosperity, they became indentured through debt, bankrupted by cheap imports, or otherwise intimidated into abandoning their land to those big enough to survive.

"The unemployed flooded into the cities. Families were destroyed. Rural communities scattered, leaving behind ghost towns. People lost their dignity as they depended on food aid just to live, aid that further undermined the remaining local farms.

"You see, Daniel, food isn't a commodity as the American agribusinesses claim. It's the sustenance of life. And a farm is not an efficient factory. It's a multigenerational community and culture. It's a hard life, to live off the land, to humanely raise livestock, but it's a fulfilling life – self-sufficient and liberating.

"But that's not where we are now. The giant agribusinesses, in league with bureaucrats, bankers and absentee landowners, are creating a new feudal system, and we're the serfs.

"There are many powerful people with their fingers in the pie. Any one of them could either feel threatened by Doyle's project or could want to control it."

Octaviano flashed an ironic grin. "From what you've told me about Doyle, I'd say he's a revolutionary, like me. Doyle and I understand that people must liberate themselves and their communities from the corruption that would enslave them."

Daniel responded with a slight laugh, "Philip's not a communist."

Octaviano frowned. "That's a tired word I no longer embrace. My struggle isn't for power. I have no desire to enthrone another dictator. I work for freedom and democracy in local communities, the only place where it can truly exist."

Daniel regretfully changed the subject, "I want to know more, but I need to ask a favor."

Octaviano eagerly obliged, "Anything, my friend. I owe you much."

"You don't owe me."

"Oh yes I do." He looked at the man standing by the back door. "Orlando, when I was in prison for 'political crimes,' Daniel got my kids medical help, made sure they could read, and helped their mother find work. He even visited me in prison." He looked back at Daniel, "That's why."

"You don't understand. I'm only passing on what's been given to me."

Octaviano smiled, "Okay. So how can I help you?"

"Could you find out what happened to Philip Doyle?"

"Possibly. It appears to be a local group. There's talk they're squabbling over what to do with him. I'll check it out and get back with you. Is there anything else?"

"There is something," Daniel continued smiling. "The world you and I, and even Philip, long for can only be found in a person, not in revolutionary systems or good deeds."

"And I suppose that's Jesus?"

"Who else? That's because the only way to change the world is to change you and me."

"Always the missionary," said Octaviano with a wide grin. "I have to go, my favorite American, but I'll talk with you again. Soon."

"Take care, mi amigo bueno."

Chapter 16: Smile of Assurance

Daniel entered the home he shared with his sister. "I'm back."

"In the kitchen," answered Katherine as she glanced at the clock. It was 11:45 p.m. Taking one more look at the pictures of Philip, she pushed away from the table and walked into the living room. Daniel lay sprawled across the couch. She dropped into a cushioned chair.

"I'm exhausted," he said.

"What have you been up to?"

"I met with Octaviano tonight. Other than that I've been following a lot of dead ends."

"Do we know anything yet?"

"Octaviano heard Philip's still alive. He's looking into who did it and what they're after."

Daniel had scheduled for them to say goodbye to their Mexico City mission in the morning. He also felt it was best for Katherine to return to Arizona. "I'd like for you to go home tomorrow afternoon."

"Not until Philip's found."

Daniel spoke patiently, "I need you to go. I can't do what I must if I'm worried about you wandering the streets looking for him."

Katherine raised her voice, "Until I know Philip's safe, I'm not leaving."

He didn't respond to his little sister's stubbornness.

She spoke again, "Why aren't you saying anything?"

He smiled, "Mom said you're to do whatever I say."

That comment prompted the launch of a chair pillow that ricocheted off his forehead. Jumping to her feet, she pelted him with one pillow after another. He threw his arms over his head for cover and didn't see her bound across the room. She wrestled him to the rug and resorted to a favorite tactic from childhood, grabbing the skin under his arm.

"Stop!" he called out laughing. "I give up."

"I'm going to make you pay this time," she said, squeezing even harder.

"I have something to tell you."

"Oh, yeah?"

"A real something…" said Daniel.

She tightened her hold, "You're not getting out of this one."

"I'm serious. I promise – it's good."

Katherine relaxed her grip and let him up. "Okay, I'll hear you out. But it better be good." She sat cross-legged on the rug while Daniel propped himself up against the couch. Her thoughts turned to how much she loved the smile animating his face. It was her favorite smile. She first remembered seeing it when they were kids in Arizona, on a Sunday afternoon after a stirring church service about the life of a Christian soldier. At least the sermon stirred Daniel, he was twelve and she was only nine.

That afternoon they hiked the pine-covered hills bordering their property, exploring paths through the woods, open meadows and creek beds. Their favorite resting place was a rock outcropping located on a steep hilltop. Within these rocks stood one much larger than the rest, one they called Stone Mountain.

Filled with adventurous awe, they climbed through the rocks to the top of Stone Mountain. Pausing to rest in the shade, they looked out from their high vantage point towards the Grand Canyon. Daniel was lost in a daydream. When he awoke, he hopped to his feet and announced, "Like our pastor said, someday I'll be a great warrior for God."

Katherine marveled at her big brother as he confidently approached the front edge of the huge rock. He held his walking stick at his left side and with his right hand slowly drew it upwards as if unsheathing a sword. With both hands he held his sword directly in front of him and solemnly proclaimed, *"Behold the word of God. Sharper than any two-edged sword."*

Then he spun around, boldly facing the vast expanse. He raised the sword, his arm extended, pointing it upwards, out towards the canyon and the distant horizon. He spoke again, repeating what he'd heard that Sunday morning, his voice strong and clear.

"Now have come the salvation and the power and the kingdom of our God, and the authority of his Christ... They overcame the evil one by the blood of the Lamb and by the word of their testimony. They did not love their lives so much as to shrink from death."

Katherine never forgot the expression on Daniel's face when he glanced back at her. It was the same that lit his face tonight, as they confronted the unimaginable. But more than a smile, it was like the expression of one who has seen the future, and has returned, knowing the joy at the end of the journey, the joy of a promise, the joy of assurance.

"Last night," shared Daniel, "I came to this conclusion. The enemy of our souls wants to destroy Philip. But he has taken a calculated risk by cutting Philip loose from what has bound him. I believe the Holy Spirit will use this opening. I must be prepared."

Katherine leaned towards him, her eyes shining. "Thanks for being who you are. If you insist I go to Arizona, I will go. But I'm asking, Daniel, as one who has shared many struggles with you and stood by your side all these years, please don't ask me leave. This is where I belong."

"Katherine, if you stay, you must agree not to argue with me, even if you don't understand."

"Okay."

"And if I go to Philip, you can't follow me."

She paused, longing to qualify his requests in a hundred ways, but she knew there was only one answer. "I agree."

****

Katherine and Daniel stood before their mission family and shared their decision to turn over any remaining responsibilities of the mission to the local leadership, a process they'd begun long before.

They celebrated the passing of the torch by recounting the many stories of conversion and faith. The passing of Daniel's wife, Maria, was remembered. They affirmed their love for the people. Friends shared and future visits were discussed. They prayed for Philip. The new leaders gave thanks for their sacrifices and prayed to send their friends into the future with God's peace and protection.

Daniel reflected on the blessings they'd witnessed, but he couldn't deny the frustration he sometimes felt. It seemed that people knew *what* they believed – their hearts told them they belonged to Jesus and they wanted to someday be with him in heaven. And they also knew the importance of trying to live a *good* life. But what they didn't seem to understand was *why* they should live a *different* life – why they should take up their cross and follow him.

The church's new Mexican pastor preached a message from Matthew 13 and the parable of the wheat and tares. The pastor said, "When our enemy is causing the greatest trouble, he works hard to conceal himself, for his plans are most easily defeated when his presence is discovered. Therefore, when he comes to plant his tares, he hides in the dark. Unfortunately, darkness may be present because we neglect to shine the light."

Daniel knew he was leaving the church in good hands.

Chapter 17: Philip, Gordon and the RAJ

Gordon was enjoying a Sunday afternoon on the patio at East of Eden. Berry, sitting beside him, spoke playfully, "I have to admit your objectives are sometimes a mystery to me. I can make sense of the financial and political goals, and I share your dislike of religion, but at times it seems like you're fighting a war against God."

Gordon grinned. "Call it our glorious fight for freedom."

"Are you sure there's nothing personal?" Berry's pale blue eyes were aglow, having captured the retreating sun's fiery light. The upward curl of her lips revealed her amusement.

"Why do you think that?" he asked.

"Chad told me."

"What?"

"His mother was a Christian." She paused, enjoying that she'd chinked his armor. "My college friendship with your son has helped me understand the mysterious and powerful chairman of Eden Global."

When Gordon offered no response, she proceeded, "Then your animosity towards God is as much personal as philosophical?"

Gordon answered, "There are greater issues at stake than personal vendetta. As you and I have often discussed, I find religion insulting and a dangerous roadblock to solving the world's problems."

Berry laughed at his rare, animated expression. "And I thought you aspired to spend eternity with the born again crowd."

Gordon scoffed, "Could there be anything worse? Do you know my deepest desire right now?"

"No. What?"

"You."

"Me?" she answered with a pretense of innocence.

"Yes, but tomorrow may be different. And no holy man is telling me what to do, one way or the other."

"One more example like that and your *tonight* will be different," she advised smiling. "But come on, Gordon, if there's a God, do you really think you can win?"

"I do," he spoke with casual certainty. "The odds are against him."

Gordon glanced towards the peak of Grand Teton. "Many people believe God will show up one day to crush the rebellion with a bunch of angels and impose his kingdom by force. But that would be his admission of failure."

"And you know about such things?" asked Berry with a disbelieving grin.

"One must know his adversary," said Gordon. "There *is* a war between man and God. There always has been. And if there's a God who allows such a struggle, it's because he intends for his people to win it *his way*. Then he might send some angels to mop up and secure the victory."

Berry asked, "And what is *his way?*"

"A self-governing conscience… but for all practical purposes, it's an absurd and dangerous concept. Jesus was asking indulgent children to be responsible adults." Gordon continued with mocking distain, "After two thousand years, it's safe to say it's not going to happen. People won't be happy until they're freed from the consequences of making their own decisions."

"You seem sure of yourself," she teased. "What about Chad? He embraced Christianity."

"He'll change."

"Why?"

"For one thing he married someone too much like his mother. Now that Lauren's influence is gone, his ambitions will bring him to me."

Gordon's phone vibrated. He glanced to see who it was. "Hello, Leo."

Berry watched Gordon's demeanor change from casual to exasperated. "Who the hell is RAJ…? How…? What do you mean, you have no influence?" Berry was reminded of how rare it was to hear surprise in Gordon's voice, especially mixed with aggravation.

When he set down the phone, she asked as casually as possible, "Was that Leo Marone?" She waited patiently.

Gordon nodded and resumed staring towards the mountains before offering, "Looks like Doyle's in more trouble than we figured, and Leo's not going to be any help." He reached for his phone and stood to leave, "I need to make a call."

As Gordon walked away Berry heard, "Darius, I need you to…"

****

Brenda Hanover hurried through the restaurant to the bar section of the Austin Bistro. She noticed that the wall-mounted television was tuned to WBC's Sunday night edition of Maurine Niven's Financial News. Charles Lee and PD Tech's attorney, Hank Miles, stood to greet her.

As they expected, Niven introduced her program with PD Tech. "Today, Philip Doyle and his future leadership of PD Tech were the subject of an emergency meeting of their board of directors. Sandy Willis has a report from Austin…"

"Maurine, I'm standing outside PD Tech offices in Austin, Texas where the fate of local tech hero, Philip Doyle, was the topic on the board's agenda. A black cloud has hung over this campus all weekend, anxiously awaiting any word. The board chairman, Philip's father, Art Doyle, has joined us. Thank you for your time, Mr. Doyle."

"Thank you, Sandy. Everyone's extremely concerned for Philip's safety. We've offered our assistance to the U.S. and Mexican governments and we're satisfied they're doing everything possible to find him."

"Did the board take any action?"

"We've assigned an interim management team to follow through on the board's directives which include updating our employee partners and evaluating the future of the Algae Farm Initiative…"

WBC's next story showed a large demonstration outside the headquarters of Amber Grains in Omaha, Nebraska. The camera closed in on the Reverend Buzz Nelson speaking to the crowd, "My new book, *Starving for Profits*, rips away the curtain, exposing the worldwide tentacles of corporate greed. We are grateful that Amber's seeds can feed the world's growing population, but does that give Blake Merrill a license to steal – to drive up food prices and extort windfall profits from a starving world?

"Our nation cannot allow such power to be controlled by giant corporations such as Amber Grains? The wealth, resources, and productive farmland of the world belong to the people of the world…"

WBC broke away in the middle of Buzz Nelson's speech. Maurine Niven's voice carried an increased intensity. "WBC has just learned that the U.S. Embassy in Mexico City has received a demand from a terrorist group called RAJ. In exchange for Philip Doyle, they're demanding the release of three men held in a Mexican prison. These men were convicted of an Aztec Airways bombing that killed ninety-eight passengers. RAJ is threatening to execute Mr. Doyle within thirty days if their demand isn't met. Authorities believe RAJ was responsible for the murder last year of German industrialist, Markus Breslin."

Brenda gasped, "Philip's still alive. Will they make the exchange?"

"They don't usually negotiate with terrorists," offered Hank.

Charles Lee added, "This contradicts what Gordon told Chad. Either Gordon was lying, or he doesn't have as much influence as he thought."

Chapter 18: Turning on the Light

Philip reclined on the bare mattress with his back against the wall. It was Sunday evening, ending the third day of his captivity. He hadn't moved for a long time. The lamp was off in his makeshift cell, and he lacked the motivation to turn it on. He was preoccupied with what was outside the room, so he sat in darkness.

He didn't know who abducted him, and he could only guess why. Gordon Connelly was the prime suspect, obviously involved in the stock manipulation. He had the wherewithal to orchestrate the attacks, but Philip couldn't believe Gordon would risk kidnapping in order to make money on a stock deal.

Whoever was responsible, he was surprised they hadn't killed him already. If their purpose was to break-up PD Tech, then his life didn't matter. He was just the guy who had to be eliminated.

He thoughts drifted to his tour of Jerusalem and Lydia's description of the religious and political issues surrounding Israel, including Ezra Levi's determination to build a new Jewish temple. The Middle East religious conflicts confused him. Katherine's faith confused him. In fact, everything about God and a spiritual world intersecting the material world eluded his ability to seriously embrace.

His total frustration, on top of emotional anguish, caused him to do something he'd never done before. He muttered, "God, if you're there and know what's going on, and if you actually care…" He paused, not believing either and questioning whether to continue. But he decided he had nothing to lose. "I'd really like to know who you are, if you are. If I'm going to die, I'd at least like to know if Katherine's right."

Was he losing his grip? "Philip, you're talking out loud to God." He needed a distraction or he would go crazy. He turned on the light and looked about the room. He'd already checked the drawers and cupboards, and they contained nothing of interest except enough canned beans to keep him alive.

He once again considered the boxes piled in the corner. Amongst the junk and worn out clothes he came upon a small stack of books. He didn't like reading in Spanish, but saw no choice. Boredom drove him to review each book. One looked particularly interesting with a brown leather binding that was extremely old. The name on the outside was illegible, and the spine was broken. He carefully opened the cover. The title was *Ben-Hur: A Tale of the Christ* written by Lew Wallace in 1880. The edition was printed in English.

Philip vaguely remembered the movie. The chariot race and the sea battle were exciting, but the emphasis on Ben-Hur's mother and sister and their illness had lost his interest. When opening the book, his eyes were drawn to a hand written note on the inside cover: *Ben-Hur was the best selling American novel of the nineteenth century.*

The table of contents showed a Chapter VIII entitled, *The Promised Kingdom.* He wondered if *Ben-Hur* could shed light on some of his questions. As he skimmed the chapter, he remembered how he felt when touching the stone wall along the Via del a Rosa.

He was impressed by the prose, *Henceforth our lives will run on together like rivers which have met and joined their waters.* The perception of human action, *May we without trial tell what a man is? There are people to whom fortune is a curse in disguise.* And the writer's comment about purpose and destiny. *Intelligence is never wasted; intelligence like God's never stirs except with design.*

However, it was the coming kingdom that especially sparked his interest. Chapter VIII involved a conversation between Simonides, who had served for many years as a family servant to the Ben-Hurs in charge of the family treasury, and Judah Ben-Hur after he returned from his long absence as a slave on a galley ship and in Rome. Judah was now incredibly wealthy and Simonides explained to Judah how he should use his fortune to aid the coming 'King of the Jews.'

Simonides began: *Poor will the King be when he comes—poor and friendless; without following, without armies, without cities or castles; a kingdom to be set up, and Rome reduced and blotted out.*

In Simonides, Philip hoped he'd found a way to understand the Jewish hope of Ezra Levi. And from that beginning maybe he could discover where Katherine fit in. The thought that *Ben-Hur* might be an answer to his prayer also crossed his mind, but that would mean the book had been sitting in the room in anticipation of his request. He had no idea what to do with that possibility. He turned to page one and started to read.

Chapter 19: Ben-Hur

The story of *Ben-Hur* took place at the time of Christ. Judah Ben-Hur, a young Jewish man from a prominent Jerusalem family, was wrongly accused of attempting to murder the Roman Consul. He received a life sentence as a galley slave aboard a Roman ship of war. During a battle he saved the commander's life, accompanied him to Rome, and became his adopted son. While in Rome, he learned the art of warfare. He later returned to Jerusalem to search for his missing family and to seek revenge.

Due to Ben-Hur's military training, great wealth, and passionate hatred of the Romans, the Jewish anti-Roman political faction saw him as the ideal candidate to organize, equip, and lead a small clandestine army. This military force was to aid the coming 'King of the Jews,' who Simonides believed to be Jesus of Nazareth.

Philip didn't recall the military and political emphasis in the film. The book's major theme was centered on Judah Ben-Hur's efforts to determine Jesus' purpose. Specifically, was Jesus the promised Messiah and what was the true nature of his kingdom?

Reading through the first several chapters, Philip savored every word without distraction. He was captivated by the rhythm and substance of the literary prose as an escape from his lack of an alternative.

The author recounted the search for truth through the eyes of the three wise men. The Greek wise man especially struck a chord with Philip:

> *There was a relation between God and the soul as yet unknown. On this theme the mind can reason to a point, a dead, impassable wall; arrived there, all that remains is to stand and cry aloud for help... I believed it possible so to yearn for Him with all my soul that He would take compassion and give me answer.*

As he read on, Philip allowed himself to understand the Christmas story's significance. He was reminded of Lydia Shafran asking in Jerusalem if he believed in angels:

> *[The shepherd] moved towards the fire, but paused; a light was breaking around him, soft and white, like the moon's. He waited breathlessly. The light, deepened; things before invisible came to view; he saw the whole field, and all it sheltered. A chill sharper than that of the frosty air – a chill of fear – smote him. He looked up; the stars were gone; the light was dropping as from a window in the sky; as he looked, it became a splendor; then, in terror he cried,*

"Awake, awake!"

Philip wanted to understand, so he purposed to read with an open mind. But he'd moved a step beyond. When the words touched his heart, he didn't object. In his present quandary, the peace and comfort were welcomed.

As for changing his thinking, he foresaw no threat. No matter how competently the words pressed their message, they were *not* going to influence his personally constructed philosophy of life. So within his compromise between control and peace, he allowed the story to be told.

A conversation between Ben-Hur and his mother helped Philip understand the competing forces at the time of Jesus. Ben-Hur's mother explained:

> *The prayer of the barbarian [Roman] is a wail of fear addressed to Strength, the only divine quality he can clearly conceive.*

As she continued, Philip saw himself:

> *The Greeks have their great glory because they were the first to set Mind above Strength... The sway of the Greek was a flowering time for genius...*

Finally, in the mother's impassioned eloquence, Philip saw the powerful sense of destiny that drove Ezra Levi, and the deep ties of Judaism to their traditions and the land of Israel:

> *But was the Hellene [Greek] the first to deny the old barbaric faith? No. My son, that glory is ours;...the wail of fear gave place to the Hosanna and the Psalm.*
>
> *So the Hebrew and the Greek would have carried all humanity forward... but... over Mind and above God, the Roman has enthroned his Caesar; the absorbent of all attainable power; the prohibition of any other greatness.*
>
> *Yet the glory of the men of Israel will remain a light in the heavens... for their history is the history of God.*

Philip knew little about monotheistic religions, but he figured that any proper relationship between a man and a sovereign God should be grounded in humility. Katherine illustrated this in her letters.

On the other hand, in *Ben-Hur*, Israel's leaders had found a way to define their relationship to God in a way that justified the transfer of authority from God to man.

In college Philip had rejected religion. He believed that supernatural belief systems were constructed to serve human ambitions. He wasn't interested in fabricating a 'god' to serve him, anymore than he'd waste his life pursuing the alchemist's delusion or the sorcerer's fantasy. That was irrational. He deemed the search for the supernatural to originate from the same quest as the Roman conqueror – *the absorption of all attainable power.*

He'd reasoned that it was only rational to submit to what he loved and valued. So if there were such a God deserving to be loved, then this God would have to reveal himself. Philip knew he could no more choose God than a wild horse would, on its own, submit to a master. God would have to initiate, get his attention, and enable him to overcome his natural unbelief.

Ben-Hur now framed Philip's perspective. The stage was set. Rome, history's most powerful empire, ruled the world. The Greek culture had advanced learning and the power of ideas. Thrown into the mix was the surging sense of destiny inciting the Jews, with their proud heritage and growing belief that the Messiah was coming to blot out Rome and usher in the earthly kingdom of their father, David.

Philip was fascinated by the prospect of Jesus stepping into this arena.

Chapter 20: *Under the Cover of Chaos*

Art answered his phone, "Art Doyle."

"Mr. Doyle, this is Leo Marone. I'm president of the Italian company, Uni Energy. We provide energy development services to the petroleum industry throughout Europe and the Middle East. Although we've had no previous experience with algae, we're interested in its potential. I've heard PD Tech's seeking a buyer for its algae technology."

Art asked, "Mr. Marone, do you know Gordon Connelly?" He wanted the Italian to know he understood the game.

"Do you mean Gordon Connelly of Eden Global?"

"That's the one."

"Yes, I know him."

"Just wondered." From that point on Art answered Marone's questions. "PD Tech was not ready to sell... They'd not yet determined a price... He didn't know when..."

"Mr. Doyle, when do you think you'll have the answers?"

Art moved to end the exchange, "Let's talk next week? We'll prepare the answers to your questions as soon as possible."

Leo Marone replied, "That'll be fine. But I have one more question. We're assuming your Israeli subsidiary, ARD, will be included in the deal."

Art was surprised by the stipulation, and he wasn't sure what to say. He decided to probe Marone's resolve. "Your request may not be possible."

"Mr. Doyle, I hope you understand how serious I am. The inclusion of the ARD technology is a requirement."

"I'm not certain we can deliver ARD."

Marone asked, "Since there's no possibility of a deal without it, why can't you deliver ARD?"

"Our agreement with Ezra Levi allows him to buy back ARD's stock if we no longer pursue the algae business or if Philip leaves PD Tech."

Marone was silent on the other end of the phone for so long that Art wondered if they were still connected. Finally Marone spoke, "Please call me next week with the answers to my questions."

"I certainly will."

Art got up slowly and walked to the window. He looked out upon the PD Tech research labs and thought of sixteen-year-old Philip, his bright face lit by the opportunities explored during their dinner table discussions. And now Art was observing the realization of that dream as the many creative partners went about their work of improving the lives of people they'd never meet. It was a marvelous process, and it touched his heart in a way that seemed almost spiritual.

****

The demonstrations in Jerusalem had intensified with larger crowds and escalating violence between protesters, counter-protesters, and Israeli soldiers becoming a nightly occurrence.

Ezra Levi had been pulled into the drama on the streets of Jerusalem, often leading counter-demonstrations, demanding the forced evacuation of the Palestinian rioters from his beloved city. His dim hopes of ever worshiping in a Jewish temple on the Temple Mount frequently threw him into fits of despair. His public tirades and flamboyant style made him a lightning rod for the Jewish opposition to the Palestinian demands.

At night, under the cover of chaos, with opposing groups marching towards each other – chanting, throwing rocks and bottles – separated by soldiers with weapons drawn, a lone gunman hid, waiting for an opportunity. At just the right moment, his patience was rewarded, and he was able to fire three rounds, point blank, into Ezra Levi's chest. He then dropped the gun and disappeared into the panicked crowd, stampeding in every direction as soldiers closed in.

Chapter 21: A Dead Man's Wish

Early Sunday evening the PD Tech team led by Art and Bret Doyle were focused on determining how to sell the algae. The ARD requirement from Marone weighed upon Art's mind, and he hadn't yet envisioned a solution. Art received a phone call from Israel.

"Mr. Doyle, this is Lydia Shafran. Do you know who I am?"

"Yes, you're Philip's contact person with ARD. You were with him in Jerusalem."

"Yes sir, and did he tell you I'm also a close childhood friend of Ezra Levi's wife?"

"Yes, he mentioned it."

"I'm with Deborah Levi right now. Ezra died this evening."

"Oh no!" exclaimed Art. "What happened?"

Lydia offered what they knew about Ezra's death. Bret, Charles Lee and Brenda were also sitting in the room, listening on the speaker. When Lydia finished describing what details were available, she shared a message from Ezra's wife. "According to Deborah, just a couple of days ago, Ezra told her he'd been contacted by an Italian company called Uni Energy."

"I know who they are."

"Ezra told Deborah that Uni Energy's president, Leo Marone, had promised him a position in a new company they were creating if he'd agree to a buyout of PD Tech. Ezra had not given up on working with Philip and he was also aware of the Marone family's ties to the Arabs, so he declined the offer. In fact, he stated emphatically that he'd not work with Uni Energy."

Art asked, "How's Deborah doing?"

"She's very upset. Ezra had advised her that if anything ever happened to him, she should try to keep ARD with Philip."

"Does Deborah have effective control of ARD?"

"She doesn't control a majority of the stock. But hopefully the board of directors will support her, though it could be quite a battle if someone makes a strong offer."

Art and Lydia wrapped up their conversation and agreed to talk later in the week. After hanging up, Art voiced his frustration, "Now what do we do? A dying man's last wish is for ARD not to be sold to Uni Energy. So how can we sell it to Marone to save Philip?"

The room remained silent.

****

Art Doyle received an expected call from Lydia Shafran. Eight days had past since Ezra Levi's death. It was Monday morning. He had talked with Lydia several times over the past week. Charles Lee and Bret were listening with him.

"Hello, Lydia. Did they have the board meeting today?"

"Yes, and we're at a stalemate. Deborah's slim majority held, but the other half is pushing for acceptance of a very serious offer from Uni Energy. Quite frankly, it's far more than we'd ever get anywhere else."

"Can she gain a solid majority to prevent the sale?"

"It's possible, but you guys aren't helping. We learned Friday that you've lost your funding commitment for the algae farms."

"I'm afraid so."

Lydia continued, "That, combined with uncertainty surrounding Philip, the continuing media attacks, and the declining stock price are undermining our case that PD Tech is the best long-term option."

"I understand," responded Art as he ended the call and agreed to keep in touch.

Art hopped up from his chair and paced the floor. "How do we tell them that we need for Deborah to sell to that scoundrel?"

Art's intercom buzzed with an incoming call from Leo Marone. Art answered, "Hello, Mr. Marone."

Marone got straight to the point. "Are you aware we made a generous offer for ARD?"

"I am."

"This is all unnecessary and counter-productive to our mutual interests. If PD Tech were to announce we've finalized a deal contingent upon ARD accepting Uni Energy's offer, then I'm confident we'd come to a successful conclusion quite soon."

Art answered back, allowing his frustration to show through, "Pressuring a grieving widow who's following her late husband's wishes is not my style."

"It's not about style, Mr. Doyle. It's about the bigger picture. But the choice is yours. The outcome is in your hands. I'll be waiting to hear from you. Good bye."

Art looked from Bret to Charles and gave his assessment of their situation, "Dammit."

Chapter 22: Mystery

Philip listened past the unceasing stillness to the faint muffled sounds of a distant outside world. He'd been sitting in what felt like a slowly shrinking room, enduring the stale odor with little sunlight, eating canned beans with foul-tasting water, not seeing or talking to anyone, and not knowing what was going to happen. But worse yet, having no control over his fate.

He exercised and for hours paced back and forth across the room. This had become his response to frustration, but he reminded himself that it could be much worse. He was still alive, which meant there was hope. He had water to drink, a flushing toilet and electricity, although his light bulb had just burnt out. The canned beans were a gourmet meal compared to the alternative of starvation, and seven 4 inch square glass blocks lined up along the top edge of an outside wall allowed enough daylight to not only read his book, but also inform him he'd been detained for twenty-three days.

There was a camera in the corner along the ceiling, and he assumed it worked, but had no way of knowing. He'd run every possible escape scenario through his mind dozens of times. Nothing struck him as even remotely possible, but he still reviewed the possibilities every day.

The food and water kept him alive but did not prevent insanity. That job was accomplished by his ever-present, new best friend, Ben-Hur.

For as long as he could remember, he'd purposely moved towards specific goals by taking action. He wasn't drawn to pondering the great intellectual questions of life. Only in a locked cell with the total absence of choice and freedom of movement, under the threat of death, would he ever allow himself to be absorbed with the issues confronting Ben-Hur. Having read through the book twice, and some chapters several times, he would intently discuss God's kingdom, Roman and Jewish politics, history and quantum physics with Ben-Hur as he paced the floor.

He discovered the source of the Jewish hope he'd seen in Ezra Levi, as from a passage that described the Jewish perspective at the time of Jesus. He read out loud as he walked, *Upon such a people... so proud, so brave, so devoted, so imaginative – a tale like that of the coming of the King was all-powerful... They were assured he was to rule the world, more mighty than Caesar; more magnificent than Solomon, and that the rule was to last forever...*

He had come to comprehend why Levi wanted to build a new temple on the Temple Mount. Levi apparently believed that from this temple, from an actual throne in Jerusalem, the Jewish Messiah would come to rule the world.

During his first week of captivity he was convinced Levi was a religious nut. Then for the next few days he wondered if maybe Levi was right. Many Christians talked about Jesus' coming back to Jerusalem to rule the world. But finally he came to the conclusion that the question didn't have an answer that was knowable, which created a problem for anyone who thought it did. For how does one live a long-term, multi-generational life in a short-term world?

Yet he couldn't stop thinking of his visit to Jerusalem. He couldn't shake the feeling that the ancient city was different. That beyond the stones and the busyness of tourists and daily life, there was something timeless and spiritual, which explained why his father had suggested that's where angels would be hanging out.

What was it, that feeling Jerusalem evoked? Philip's pace quickened the more he stretched for an answer. The idea of mystery came to mind. Yes, that was it, "mystery." Not as something difficult to understand that would soon be discovered, but more like an eternal unknown, a mystery that reminds us that there are things beyond our ability to ever know.

Philip thought much about such things for the first time in his life. The one conclusion he'd come to about this mystery was that not even Philip Doyle could afford to ignore the question.

****

As had become their standard practice since Philip's abduction, the circle of friends dealing with the Uni Energy – ARD stalemate gathered to determine their options. Chad Connelly was also in town for the meeting. They were running out of time with only seven days left before the thirty-day ultimatum by RAJ expired.

To make matters more stressful, the PD Tech board, pressured by partners and investors, was asking that a more rigorous effort be made to find a buyer for the algae genetics in hopes the stock would recover. The board and partners weren't informed of the choices or consequences facing them. Art didn't believe it was in anyone's interest for their dilemma to become public.

For two hours they rehashed every option. Since Deborah Levi's group hadn't caved in to Marone's offer, PD Tech would have to pressure Deborah and Lydia Shafran to sell out to Uni Energy. After much deliberation, they agreed that no matter how it was defined, the Uni Energy deal was disguised extortion. And besides, as pointed out by Bret Doyle, the option was predicated on a vague inference from Gordon Connelly that Marone had the wherewithal to ensure Philip's safe release.

Art stood before the group. "So we agree not to succumb to extortion by threat of violence?"

Art took one final look around the room until he was satisfied. "Then it's unanimous. If we try to do good by giving in to evil, then what kind of world are we left with? I believe we're doing what Philip would want us to do. We'll have to wait and pray for a miracle…"

Chapter 23: The Unexpected

A timid knock interrupted Daniel and Katherine's evening debriefing of what had become a daily frustration. After twenty-six days they'd made no progress towards locating Philip. Daniel opened the front door to find a mother and her two daughters who attended their mission church standing on the front porch,

"Teresa Diego," said Katherine with her typical delight as she stepped forward and offered her hand. "What a wonderful surprise. Please come in." She placed her arm around Teresa's shoulder and led her in with the two girls following.

Katherine turned to the girls. "Daniel, you know Paulina and Ana?"

"I certainly do." He retrieved an extra chair from the kitchen.

Katherine invited them to sit down. "Now, girls, refresh my memory. How old are you?"

"I'm twelve," offered Paulina. "And Ana is ten." Ana smiled her agreement.

They briefly discussed school and church, but it was obvious that something was bothering the girls' mother.

Katherine asked, "How is Marcos? I haven't seen him in a couple of years."

"That's why we came. I'm worried for my son," said Teresa.

"Can we help?"

Teresa, confused and upset, looked at her older daughter when she spoke, "Paulina heard Marcos on his phone, and she thinks he knows about the American you're looking for."

Katherine shot a glance at her brother, who moved to the edge of his chair. Daniel spoke calmly to the girl, "What did Marcos say?"

"He talked about leaving Mexico City when the American was dead."

"Do you know who he talked to?"

"No," said Paulina.

"Where can I find Marcos?" said Daniel.

"He won't tell us where he stays," answered Teresa, "but he used to go to a bar in La Condesa." She pleaded for help, "I don't believe Marcos wants to do these things. Can you find him?" Looking from Katherine to Daniel she added, "He always liked you both, and I don't know who else to talk to."

After discussing all the information that might be helpful, Katherine thanked the Diegos for coming and assured them that she and Daniel would do everything they could to find him.

Daniel spoke to Katherine, "After twenty-six days of nothing, we hear of someone who might be involved, and Octaviano wants to talk to me tonight. Maybe we're about to break through."

"What about the police or the embassy?"

"Later, I have to meet with Octaviano now."

Early that day, Daniel had received the much-awaited follow up call from his best source. Octaviano had instructed him to come alone to Poco's Tequilla at 9:00 p.m. Walking through the sparsely filled bar towards a dark corner in the back, he once more prayed that Octaviano would provide a way to Philip.

"Daniel, it's good to see you again."

"And you, too."

"Have you discovered anything useful?"

Daniel answered, "I have the name of someone who might be involved."

"Who?"

"Marcos Diego, a boy about eighteen. He sometimes hangs out in a bar in La Condesa."

"The bar is probably Raul's."

"How about you?"

"Much better, but first you must promise me, as an oath, because both of our lives will be at stake, you won't tell anyone what I share with you tonight."

"What about the security people at the U.S. Embassy?"

"No one, or I don't talk."

Daniel nodded, "I agree."

"A local gang was hired to abduct your friend. The gang splintered into two groups. The radical faction, called RAJ, took over the operation and announced their ultimatum for the release of the three terrorists.

"But someone doesn't want Doyle killed, and whoever that is hired an elite team of mercenaries that operates out of Columbia. These men are from several countries, mostly trained years ago by your Special Forces. They're the best, and expensive. I'm fortunate to know one of them, a former comrade. They've been hired to take out RAJ."

Daniel asked, "What do you mean by 'take out?'"

"They've been hired to kill the RAJ people before they execute Doyle."

"Do you think they can do it?"

"Of course. These RAJ are a nasty bunch, but they're just a gang. The Columbian team, they're elite soldiers. The hard part is to keep Doyle alive."

"When is it supposed to happen?"

"Soon. My old friend has been here for a week mapping out the operation."

"What about Philip?"

"They'll get a huge bonus if he survives. And they're paid extra to take him back to Columbia and hold him for a while." Octaviano leaned forward and in a hushed tone shared, "They don't want to take him back to Columbia. They earn most of their money wiping out RAJ and keeping your friend alive. Abducting people is messy and drags out the operation."

Daniel interrupted, "So what will they do?"

"They're sure Doyle is in a separate location. So, I told them we'd get him out during the fight. Then your friend will be alive and the mercenaries will have an excuse for not taking him to Columbia."

Daniel was skeptical, but with a glimmer of hope. "Do you have a plan?"

Octaviano sensed Daniel's confusion and offered, "You think about it. When they find out where RAJ is holding Doyle, I'll survey the area and draw up a plan. Then we can decide."

"Any idea when?"

"Probably Friday or Saturday, but be ready any time… And remember, you can't tell anyone, even the police or American intelligence. If the wrong people show up, some will die, and their blood will be on your hands. Equally important, my dear friend, I'll be a dead man. There will be no place for me to hide. Do we understand each other?"

"Yeah."

"Will you look for the Diego boy?"

Daniel nodded, "I'll try Raul's."

Octaviano offered one last suggestion with a wide grin, "If you find him, ask for a key. We'll need it unless you intend to blast your way in."

To enter Raul's was to penetrate shadows and a wall of sound: music, laughter, the clanking of glass, voices straining to be heard above the din. Daniel moved about unnoticed. His dark features, casual dress, and natural comfort with the culture made him as inconspicuous as an American could be. His confidence in his objective countered the oppressive atmosphere he felt.

He worked his way towards the rear of the bar where he spotted Marcos Diego engrossed in conversation with a woman and two older men in their thirties at a table along the back wall.

Daniel moved over to the bar, ordered a drink and waited until Marcos left his table for the restroom. Daniel met him there. They were alone.

"Marcos."

The young man turned and their eyes met. Marcos recognized him and instinctively sought a path of escape. Daniel casually blocked his exit.

"Marcos, it's okay. You know I'm your friend."

"What do you want?" he asked with restless hostility.

"Your mother's worried about you. And we need…"

The restroom door opened and one of the men who'd been sitting with Marcos stumbled in half-drunk. A scowl crossed his face when he saw his young companion talking to a stranger. Marcos lowered his eyes, betraying fear of the man. He challenged Marcos, "Do you know this American?"

"Yes," Marcos nervously replied.

"What's he want?" the man demanded through a slight slur.

Marcos hesitated long enough for Daniel to answer the interrogator. "It's no problem. I recognized Marcos from our mission… when he was young… that's all."

The interrogator swore in a mocking tone when the third man from the table came through the door. He was as short as Marcos and wore a ball cap pulled down, covering his eyes from Daniel's view. He and the other man whispered back and forth until Marcos' interrogator left, motioning for Marcos to follow him.

Daniel sized up the man standing between him and the door, attempting to guess his intentions. Daniel still couldn't see the eyes hidden below the cap's bill. A thin moustache grew above a grim, closed mouth. The tattoo of a black snake rose out of the top of the man's colorless t-shirt. The snake watched Daniel from the man's neck.

The awkward silence felt threatening. When Daniel moved towards the door, the man pulled out a knife with a 4 inch steel blade.

Daniel froze and then slowly took a step backwards. A thin grin appeared on the man's face as he ordered, "Wait."

The interrogator reappeared. He smiled seeing his friend's knife and addressed Daniel through a drink-induced slur, "Someone wants to talk to you." Then he laughed, "Maybe you can tell him about your mission."

Daniel was led down a dimly lit hallway and out the back door into a dark alley. Several hands pinned him against a block wall. The beam of a large flashlight was directed at his face, obscuring his vision while he was searched. Shadowy outlines moved about. A voice behind the lights demanded, "What are you doing here?"

"I just asked Marcos…" A fist flashed out of the darkness, striking his side. The blow collapsed his lungs, instantly eliminating any strength in his legs. He fell to his knees, gasping for air. He spied peripheral movement and anticipated another blow. Four hands grabbed his jacket and pulled him to his feet as he struggled to breathe. He stood still, hoping his legs would hold.

"Why did you talk to Marcos?"

"Because his family…" The next blow struck his chest, driving him back. His head slammed against the wall and he fought to keep consciousness.

An older man spoke with authority from behind the light, "I know who you are. I know of your mission church. What's Marcos to you?"

Daniel's chest ached. He strained to take in enough air to answer. "His family comes…"

"You're worried for his soul?" the man asked with amused malice.

"I am," answered Daniel. He felt a chilling oppression sweep over him each time the man spoke.

"You're a fool for coming here." The voice carried light laughter, apparently finding humor in Daniel's pathetic quest. "Listen, missionary, I never want to see you around here again. Let him go."

Someone shoved him from the back just as he was struck from behind. He fell face down onto the gravel, unconscious.

Daniel awoke to the sound of people talking while walking around him. He struggled to his feet. His leather jacket had been stolen and his pockets were empty. He felt a little better recalling he'd not carried his wallet. Bending over, he lifted his pant leg and removed a spare car key from inside his sock.

On his way back to the car, his heart was heavy as he prayed for the souls of the men in the alley, men who had no way of knowing that within a few short days they'd be dead.

Chapter 24: Hopeless Dread

Chad stood at his office window, watching the afternoon rain strike pools of water collecting on the Washington street. He thought of Berry. He'd had lunch with her several times since returning to work in D.C. Despite any misgivings, he wanted to be updated on his father's activities. As for any interest in Berry, he excused himself. His heart had been ripped out of his chest, and he figured it was only natural to be drawn to someone that distracted him from the pain, even if only for a moment.

When his thoughts turned to Philip, feelings of dread washed over him. Only three days remained before the thirty-day deadline. Daniel had called, saying he had a potential lead, but there was nothing new to report on either end.

No one knew if Philip was still alive. Efforts to find him had stalled. RAJ wasn't well known, and no connection could be found to the three men in prison. The abductors hadn't communicated since their original demand, and their silence frustrated efforts to determine their identity or location.

Mexico City's size and the absence of leads made the search for one kidnapped American among eighteen million people quite impossible. Total surprise and the lack of an urgent agenda by Philip's abductors contributed to the ineffectiveness of prevailing U.S. and Mexican strategies. Their plan appeared to be nothing better than waiting for a break.

Art Doyle and the group at PD Tech had given up on selling the algae business to Uni Energy before the deadline because of the impasse with ARD.

Chad had explored the possibility of a prisoner exchange, but each of his requests to the President had been re-routed to the State Department where they garnered the expected procedural response of "we don't negotiate with terrorists." Gordon had explained that with the election so close, not even he could get the White House to do something that would make the President appear weak on terrorism.

He reviewed his calls. One name prompted him to put on his headset and walk back to the window. The rain was letting up, but the dark gray ceiling pressed even lower.

He placed his call to the young congresswoman from North Carolina, Macy Southerland, who'd been in his freshman congressional class six years before. Since that time they'd developed a friendship and trust based on a shared vision for the country. He regularly sought her insight.

Macy's father had been a congressman from their conservative district for sixteen years. She and her father had shared a dream. One day he'd step down, and she'd run for his office, but a heart attack forced his early retirement.

By the next election, the unexpected vacancy resulted in a splintered party and a bitterly contested primary. As a consequence, the opposition captured the district for the first time in over two decades.

Over the next two years Macy worked to repair the damage. Then she took a bold step to reach her dream. She ran for Congress, relying on the same values, intellectual capacities, and personal charm that had served her father. She united her party's base, adeptly framed the campaign issues, and won the next election by a landslide.

After briefly discussing family matters and Philip, Macy brought up the reason for her call. "I heard your name today in unusual circumstances."

"Where was that?"

"I was having lunch in Georgetown with some girlfriends and while waiting to be seated, a woman standing next to us mentioned 'Connelly' to a couple of men. When I glanced at them, they stopped talking.

Chad wondered if it involved his father. "Did you see anyone interesting?"

"I did," said Macy, "they were there to meet with Darius Cain."

Chad asked, "I know Darius Cain works for the President. What exactly does he do?"

"Darius is the President's Special Projects Facilitator. He apparently has authority over all White House policy administrators in order to set project priorities."

"Is he effective?"

"Unfortunately, I think he is. Our subcommittee on the Middle East has worked with him. Darius is an effective power broker, both personally and professionally."

"You know him personally?"

"We've had lunch."

"Lunch?"

"The people's business only, Chad."

"Is he single?"

Macy acknowledged Chad's tease. "Okay, so he asked me out. But I kindly refused. He's not my type. Whatever his interest in me, I guarantee it has nothing to do with my convictions. So enough of that. When I saw that the people at the door had joined him I had to go over and say hi – right?"

"Sure. Did Darius ask you to join them?"

"No, hardly, but he was gracious. He even introduced me to his friends."

"And who was there?"

"The first was Buzz Nelson. I remembered his name from my father's occasional criticisms of the religious left. Do you know who he is?"

"Yeah, he's been to my father's ranch."

"And the other man was someone named Clifton Roberts."

Chad interjected, "That explains why you heard 'Connelly.' Roberts is the chief investment strategist for Eden Global. Who was the woman?"

"Someone with the White House, Andrea Clark."

"She's the head of a new program called Worldwide Food Security."

Macy quipped, "Quite a group. Maybe Roberts was selling some mutual funds."

Chad smiled, "You should have joined them."

"I'm sure their conversation was interesting, but probably not as much fun as lunch with the girls."

"I'm certain it wasn't."

"Well, that's all I have."

"Thanks for watching out for me."

"You're welcome. Next time we'll invite you."

"Wouldn't miss it."

Chapter 25: Peak Food

Chad arrived at D.C. Books and Café with a clear head after a brisk two-mile walk from his office. The rain had subsided and the rising city lights replaced the dull gray of a dreary afternoon.

Having completed the afternoon's uneventful phone work, Chad wanted to revisit his conversation with Macy. The bookstore offered a suitable environment for research. He purchased a sandwich, picked up Buzz Nelson's bestseller, and plugged his laptop into an outlet by the window.

The mention of 'Connelly' by Andrea Clark at a luncheon with the unlikely trio of Darius Cain, Clifton Roberts and Buzz Nelson was a fascinating puzzle begging to be solved.

Chad quickly surveyed the material on his table. The sandwich won. After a quick bite, he picked up Nelson's book, *Starving for Profits: Genetic Engineering and the Corporate Takeover of the Sustenance of Life.*

Clever title, he thought, as he stared blankly at rows of headlights moving along the street outside the bookstore. As dusk slipped into night, he tried to imagine a connection or motive for the Georgetown meeting, but nothing jumped out at him. Nothing shed light on what his father might be up to.

Reading Nelson's biography on the jacket cover, he noticed "Chairman of Solutions for Humanities." He wondered what that might be about, so he visited their website. Twenty minutes later he'd determined three main policy interests for the progressive think tank located in Boston.

The first section promoted a collective social movement they called "unity consciousness." Another section presented public policy initiatives to enforce separation of church and state in every area of public life. But it was the last section that shed light on the luncheon's purpose. Solutions for Humanity was advocating a dramatic increase in government control of genetic food production.

The meeting was beginning to make sense. Buzz Nelson and Andrea Clark were both advocates of the centralized oversight of food production. The presence of Darius Cain showed the program to be a White House priority.

Chad sat back and once again watched the cars, this time through pouring rain. Why would Clifton Roberts of Eden Global show up at a lunch in D.C. to discuss agriculture?

He also wondered who was behind Solutions for Humanity? An initial search of board members and advisors provided the typical list of liberal activists and academics. He considered reviewing the donor lists on the 990 tax forms, but instead took the easy way out and opted for his favorite internet conspiracy theorist with the handle, 'Light in a Dark Corner.'

Chad went to the site, entered his password and typed 'Solutions for Humanity' into the search. When the information appeared on the screen, he skipped ahead to the contributors. Again, just like the board, the list was comprised of rich liberals and progressive foundations. Chad grinned at the use of euphemisms for names: Share the Harvest, Tax Policy for Civic Responsibility, and the Consciousness Unity Movement.

Since the C.U. Movement was the largest donor he searched their name and skimmed the bio, but found nothing of interest. He had perused rabbit holes many times in the past, and he feared this one could be endless, so he closed the computer and went back to Buzz Nelson's book.

An hour later he was ready to move on. Nothing particularly struck him other than the book's radical recommendations. Nelson's basic message was that world population was increasing faster than normal advances in food production technology. The peak food concept combined with Nelson's claims of water shortages, soil erosion, and climate change made the need for genetic seed development vital to prevent mass starvation.

Nelson was thoroughly convinced, almost to the point of panic, that the capitalist business model, as practiced by companies like Amber Grains, was not capable of meeting the challenge. Nelson advocated that only drastic government action could head off a global catastrophe.

Chad shared some of the same concerns, but Nelson's extreme proposals would only create additional problems. Chad sensed that some people when faced with a crisis, out of fear, grasp the problem so tightly they often stifle the very means to a solution. Or worse yet, there are others who will leave no potential crisis unexploited.

He was ready to go back to his D.C. apartment. He headed for the door with umbrella in hand. As he passed the magazine rack he noticed Allen Wilder's picture on the cover of *New Evangelical Thought*. The caption read, "Allen Wilder: The Rise of a Prophetic Voice."

Chad purchased a copy and exited the store.

Chapter 26: *From the Shadows*

Katherine approached the front door of her home. A sound coming from the side of the house startled her. Peering into the darkness, she stepped back from the door and moved slowly towards the corner of the house. Searching the shadows, she heard her name in the hushed whisper of a woman's voice.

"Is someone there?" She spoke in the direction of the sound.

"It's Teresa Diego."

Katherine turned the corner and discovered Marcos' mother. She reached out and held her arm. "What is it Teresa? Why are you hiding?"

"No one can know I'm here."

"How can I help you?"

"I talked to Marcos. He told me he saw Daniel. Is he all right?"

"Daniel's fine."

"Marcos wants out of the gang, but no one can leave. What can Marcos do? He's afraid and begged me to ask Daniel for help."

"Are they going to kill Philip?"

Katherine waited, fighting back her own tears as Teresa cried. "I think so. Marcos said something is happening soon. He said he's sorry."

"Is there any way Daniel can talk to Marcos or meet with him?"

"I don't think so."

Katherine called Daniel and explained Teresa's visit.

Daniel was emphatic, "Tell Teresa she must talk to Marcos. She can't give up. I have to know where they're keeping Philip, and I need a key."

"Where are you now?"

"I'm trying to find Octaviano."

Katherine insisted, "We'll do whatever we can."

A brave little girl stood by herself in the dark. It was late, and she'd been waiting for more than two hours. Another group came through the door, out into the alley behind Raul's. She wouldn't have to wait any longer. Her brother was among them.

"Marcos," she called out, determined to be heard above the drunken laughter and chatter.

Five men with two female companions turned at once. A woman spoke first, "Look, the little girl's calling for Marcos. Who is she?"

With an anxious irritation Marcos' responded, "Paulina, what are you doing?" He assured the others, "That's my sister. I don't know why she's here."

"Don't be mad, Marcos. I just wanted to say goodbye."

Marcos didn't move but waited for instructions. The same woman spoke up again, this time with a drunk's authority, "Go on, Marcos, give your little sister a goodbye hug. It's cute."

Her suggestion went uncontested and was encouraged by the drunken laughter of others. Marcos walked briskly to Paulina as the group started to drift down the alley.

She hugged her brother's neck and whispered, "Where is the American? Daniel needs a key."

Marcos looked at his sister and laughed. Then he spoke loud enough for the others to hear, "Goodbye, Paulina, and yes, I promise to come back for your wedding."

He picked her up off her feet with a big hug and spoke into her ear, "I'll put the key under the oil drum at the bottom of the stairs. He's in a warehouse. I don't know…"

One of the men commanded, "Come on, Marcos."

Paulina kissed her brother's cheeks and whispered, "Run away as soon as you can."

Marcos set her down and hurried towards the others. He turned and demanded, "Go home and don't worry your mother." Paulina gave a quick wave and darted down the alley in the opposite direction.

Only one person remained as anxious eyes followed Marcos and the group passing under a light on the side of the building. When they disappeared around the corner, she took a deep breath and relaxed her grip on the revolver in her coat pocket. She'd doubted she could ever shoot someone, but if anyone had threatened the precious little girl trying to help her brother, she wondered for a moment what she would have done.

Katherine left the shadows to catch up with Paulina and find out what Marcos had said.

Daniel received a phone call from Octaviano. "I have news, Daniel. It'll be tomorrow."

"I'll be ready."

"Will you have a key?"

"I think so."

"Good. I'll call when it's time to go."

Chapter 27: Villa Marone

Gordon Connelly stood in the grand ballroom on top of the world. The elegance of the late Renaissance villa, a proud architectural treasure nestled in the Italian Alps, affirmed the wealth, power and privilege of aristocracy.

Leo Marone was the heir, having been trained by his forebears to manage the family business and their extensive holdings. Leo accepted the responsibility as an honor. He also relished the opportunity to distinguish himself, for of all the portraits gracing the halls of Villa Marone, no countenance held more ambition than his own.

Merchants and brokers for more than four centuries, the Marone family zealously cultivated their relationship with the Arab world. This evening's party was yet another celebration of their long and lucrative friendship.

Gordon surveyed the ballroom, soon discovering his host surrounded by presidents of multinationals and princes of Arabia. Although Europe's business and governing elite were well represented, the Arab presence at Villa Marone demonstrated the Italian family's extensive influence in the Middle East.

Making his way through the guests, Gordon reflected on how he'd rather not be the center of attention. He found the spotlight limiting, even irritating. When he entered a room, he didn't want people rushing to his side, seeking his attention the way they did the young Italian's.

Gordon preferred controlling the levers of power from behind the scenes. Yet the guests at Villa Marone were aware of Gordon Connelly's presence. Conversations momentarily halted and people stared when he crossed the room. His physical stature enhanced his image, communicating a demeanor of distance, unapproachable to anyone without specific purpose.

People relished the most recent Connelly rumor – power and influence that mysteriously appeared, and then quietly vanished – leaving the observer wondering if an event happened naturally or was orchestrated from the shadows. This was Gordon Connelly's world and he did nothing to discourage their speculation. Every moment they wondered only added to his mystique. And the mythology surrounding a story could be a more sophisticated and subtle expression of power than the truth. Their whispers were a prayerful homage they paid in awe of such power.

Gordon approached the circle of people competing for the host's attention. Marone looked past them to acknowledge his friend. "Good evening, Gordon. Are you enjoying our party?"

"I'm impressed." He allowed Marone to introduce him to several guests.

Marone started their conversation on a positive, "I'm sure you noticed how Allen Wilder has reacted to the riots in Jerusalem."

"That's why you haven't heard from me."

Marone proceeded, unsure of what Gordon meant, "Wilder's total emphasis is now on the final battle for Jerusalem. This should accomplish what you've asked for. Saber rattling, the nightly outbreaks of violence, and the constant threat of war will continue to feed Wilder's end-time predictions. My Arab friends have assured me they'll keep it going through the election."

Gordon responded, "Wilder's interpretation of the present violence in Jerusalem is just as I anticipated. But remind your friends that an actual war will create too many volatile unknowns, and we can't afford to lose control of how the public perceives the conflict. The Arabs must keep the militants on a short leash until after the election. Then Israel can be forced to surrender Jerusalem."

"That is understood," said Marone.

"Good. Have you heard any more about Philip Doyle?"

"No I haven't. The people I thought could help lost their influence."

"If you find out who ordered the abduction, let me know?" The severity of Gordon's gaze made Marone momentarily uncomfortable.

Marone smiled and nodded, "Certainly."

Noticing they were about to be interrupted and hoping to change the subject Marone asked, "Where's your creative inspiration? I haven't seen her tonight. I trust you're not keeping her only to yourself?"

"She's here," assured Gordon as he was pulled aside by an approaching guest.

Marone continued to mingle, although his interest was diverted by an occasional glance towards the grand ballroom door. His patient watch was rewarded by her arrival. Aloof, centered in her own presence, she made her way into the room. Noticing everything, gracious in her acknowledgement of the attention she received – unaffected, beyond flattery – enjoying the natural phenomenon of eyes following her as she walked by.

It was a game. She was a game, with her own rules. A game she allowed few others to play. And Marone enjoyed playing.

Her path towards him was indirect but guaranteed. She exuded an air of the nonchalant. She was her own time, and it would wait. She'd acknowledge him, and he in turn, by his smile and interest, would make a statement to those present that this young lady, unknown to many yet so beautiful, was greatly esteemed. As a result, an aura of mystery would follow her throughout the evening.

Marone smiled and took a step in the direction of his anticipation. His gaze followed the line of her neck through the blonde curls of reddish hue, to her shoulders and the black evening gown that framed them.

The fabric of her gown flowed as a melody to the whimsy of her nature – soft, light, and delicate – a covering to the eyes, though transparent to the desire of a man's soul – of the purest sheer – finding shape and form when clinging to contours and symmetry that stirred the imagination.

Their eyes met and she stopped just short of his reach. With a light laugh, he took the final step to close the gap. He reached out and she placed her hand in his.

"Berry Fields, what a pleasure to see you."

"And nowhere would I rather be than Villa Marone. It's an enchanted castle where dreams must come true."

Marone teased, "I've seen your friend here this evening, so I doubt my dream will come true. But that's all right. Seeing you move across the floor is as much of the sensual as a mere mortal can absorb."

Berry smiled into his eyes and moved closer. She slipped her hand underneath his dinner jacket with her palm resting on his heart. Her eyes, sultry and playful, held him. Softly she whispered, "That's because, Leo, my dear friend, seduction is my weapon of choice."

Marone again laughed lightly, thoroughly enjoying the exchange. "Does my heart reveal my thoughts?"

"Yes it does, Leo," she said with an amused, sensual smile that caused his heartbeat to quicken. "And it's a shame my affections belong to another." Her active eyes shifted to Gordon Connelly as he came up beside her.

"Who am I rescuing from whom?" asked Gordon.

Berry moved to Gordon's side, slipped her arm through his and rested against him. Her mischievous eyes played with their host. "Leo was about to tell me something wonderful about Italian men, but you interrupted him." She turned to her host, "You were saying, Leo?"

Marone laughed. He wasn't about to be drawn in. "I'll only say my friend is a most fortunate man to possess the essence of a spring breeze."

"And brilliant besides beautiful," added Gordon.

"Then let's share her with our guests," stated their host with exaggerated enthusiasm. "Come, we have important people to meet."

Chapter 28: The Next Step

Katherine knelt at her bed. When she finished praying, she leaned back against the wall. There was nothing left to say: no more verses to quote, no way to obligate God, to press him or lead him. She breathed deeply, attempting to expel the nervous pressure that gripped her. She believed that prayers made a difference, and she was determined to remain at her post. All that was left for her to do was trust Jesus and rest in his arms.

The ringing of Daniel's phone caused a shock of nervous energy. She heard his voice coming from the living room. The excruciating wait for Octaviano's call was over. She hopped to her feet and hurried to hear the news.

When she entered the room, Daniel was standing at the front door. He'd finished the call and was staring into the night.

"Daniel."

He turned towards her. She noticed his distant gaze.

"Are you sure?" she asked.

Slowly his eyes focused and he smiled. He walked back into the room and hugged his best friend. "I'm sure I'm going... but after that I don't know."

Her eyes swelled. "I can't lose you, too."

He gently assured her. "Recently a wise sage told me, 'Walk in the light you're given.'"

"Shelly at Glen's Diner?"

"Who else," he answered, smiling. He kissed her cheek and hurried out the door.

Daniel jogged a half-mile to the designated intersection and waited. He hardly noticed the busy Saturday night traffic as he wrestled with his decision. He was totally out of his element, with each step taking him down an unfamiliar path. Yet he stood on the corner, committed to whatever awaited him, because he'd set his will to take the next step. Not so much as a conscious act of faith and trust, but more like the determination to follow through on what he required of himself, to act on what he believed to be the right thing to do.

The expected black SUV pulled up. Orlando stepped out and opened the door. Daniel slipped into the back seat and the car pulled into the traffic. Neither Orlando nor the driver spoke for the fifteen minutes it took to reach Poco's Tequilla. Octaviano exited the bar and joined Daniel in the back.

Daniel greeted his friend, "You do have a flare for the dramatic."

"From watching your American movies."

"So it's tonight?"

Octaviano smiled, "Are you anxious, my friend? This is different from missionary work."

"I think so," Daniel acknowledged with an uncomfortable grin.

"You have good reason to be concerned. We have a problem. The Columbians located RAJ's base and have discovered a warehouse where they're keeping Doyle. The building is in an industrial area on the south side that's a maze of manufacturing and warehousing, with many abandoned buildings scattered about."

"You mentioned a problem," said Daniel.

"Yeah, my friend thinks they've wired the warehouse with explosives. Last year RAJ kidnapped and executed a German businessman. When the police found him, he was dead from a gunshot to the head, but his room had been wired with explosives to detonate if the door was forced open."

Daniel asked, "Is that why you told me to get a key?"

"I thought it was possible. You see, Daniel, there are many moving parts… Now for the plan."

"Will the key bypass the explosives?" asked Daniel.

"Probably."

"Did the Columbians go into the warehouse?"

"No, they're certain RAJ set up cameras."

Daniel didn't know if he could handle any more "information."

Octaviano asked, "Do you still want to go in?"

"I'm listening."

"RAJ usually hangs out at Raul's until midnight. At 2:00 a.m. the Columbians will penetrate RAJ's base and take them by surprise. Hopefully before anyone can trigger the explosives with a remote."

Octaviano unrolled a drawing of several buildings and streets. He explained as his fingers glided across the drawing. "Here's the warehouse. We'll be parked here. You'll approach through this building."

"How do I get in there?" asked Daniel, pointing to a building marked "approach" that ran perpendicular to the warehouse.

"Orlando already opened the door on our side. You just have to go through the length of the building and the door on the other side will open from the inside. Then you'll only be about fifty feet from the warehouse entrance. At ten minutes 'til 2:00 you'll enter the warehouse, locate Doyle, and wait for the first shot to be fired. They're only a block away, so you'll hear it."

"What if the key's not there?"

"I thought you had it worked out."

"Not exactly. It's supposed to be hidden close to the door."

Octaviano studied Daniel for a moment, then spoke sternly, "With no key, there's nothing you can do. Come back as fast as you can."

They reached their destination and waited on a small rise with an overview of the warehouse and the adjacent building. After reviewing the plan one last time, the men fell silent. A couple of minutes later Daniel asked, "Octaviano, what happens when you die?"

"I don't think about it."

"That's why I asked."

Octaviano looked to the front seat, "Orlando, where are you going when your time's up?"

Orlando flashed a wide, toothy grin, reached into the top of his shirt and produced a gold chain with a cross.

"You too," sighed Octaviano. "Enough of this, what time is it?" He glanced at the dashboard clock. "It's time to go."

Daniel checked his watch as he pushed his phone and a flashlight deep into his pocket. At 1:20 he left the car and worked his way to the approach building. Upon reaching the door, he stopped to catch his breath and glanced back over the ground he'd covered. The car was now a couple hundred yards away cloaked in dark shadows.

The metal door was ajar, having been pried open by Orlando. He slowly pushed inward, trying to smother each creak with purposeful quiet. The door moved enough for him to slide through into the darkness where the slightest sound seemed to echo throughout the cavernous expanse. He moved quickly through the building and exited the far side.

He crouched down against the outside wall, facing the warehouse. He was not more than fifty feet away. It was thirteen minutes until 2:00. His deep breathing seemed uncomfortably loud in contrast to the eerie stillness of his surroundings and the distant muffled sounds of the city.

The minutes ticked away... 12 'til... 11 'til... He tried not to think, just act. Take the next step, don't think of why – not Philip, or Katherine, or explosives, or Marcos – just act... 10 minutes 'til. He sprinted across the opening and into the warehouse.

Once inside he froze against the concrete block wall. He was searching for an oil drum and a door but the darkness hindered his progress. Pushing

94

forward, he kept one hand on the wall and the other out in front until he discovered a stairwell going to a lower level. Marcos had said, "at the bottom of the stairs."

He descended into total blackness, quickly, sensing he was running out of time. He felt each step with his foot, his back and hands pressing against the wall. His hurried movement caused him to misjudge the last step. He tripped and fell, sprawling across the floor. He lay still, waiting for the echoes to be swallowed by the darkness. His face pressed down against the cool, grimy concrete that smelled of fuel oil.

He had to be able to see. On his knees he bent forward and pulled his jacket up over his head to cloak the light coming from his flashlight. First he checked the time, only three minutes left. Then he allowed some light to leak out. The door was about four feet to his right. A fifty-five gallon oil drum was a few feet straight ahead.

He turned off the light. It had only been five or six seconds. Hopefully, no one was watching the monitor at precisely that moment.

He crawled to the drum and leaned against it with his shoulder. It didn't budge. He stood up and took hold of the drum's top edge, held it against his body and rolled it on its edge just far enough to expose what was underneath. Dropping down to his knees, he ran his fingers along the floor. It was damp and oily to the touch, but there was no key. He was forced to turn on his light.

Again he tried to block the light by holding it under his jacket. The space where the drum had rested was clearly marked by a well-defined circle, and there was nothing to be found.

He couldn't believe this was how it would end, but he didn't have time for despair. Footsteps broke the silence. Someone was running into the warehouse towards the stairwell. Daniel quickly ducked behind the oil barrel as a man started down the stairs. He carried a light, apparently unconcerned about being detected. When the intruder came off the last step, Daniel leaped out, grabbed his shirt and swung him towards the wall. Just before the man's face smashed into the concrete block he heard, "Daniel." It was too late. He tried to hold back, but the momentum sent the man crashing into the wall with a thud and a groan.

Daniel spun him around. The young man appealed, "It's Marcos."

Daniel spoke in a hushed whisper, "I'm sorry. Are you all right?"

Marcos murmured, "I couldn't get here sooner."

"Are there cameras?"

"Not here. Upstairs and in the hallway past this door."

"Where's Philip?"

Marcos pointed to the door, "In a room past…"

The sound of gunfire, coming from a distance, abruptly ended the conversation. Daniel switched on his flashlight, revealing Marcos' face and shirt covered in blood, his head cocked, eyes wide, as though striving to glean some meaning from the ominous sound.

Daniel grabbed his shoulder, "Do you have a key?"

"Yes."

"Get me to Philip fast! We've got to get out of here."

Marcos pushed open the door and raced down the hallway, stopping at Philip's room. He looked back at Daniel. "You know about the explosives?"

"Yeah." Daniel pounded on the door as Marcos inserted the key. "Philip, it's Daniel Stone. We've got to run for it."

The door swung open, and the beam from Daniel's flashlight sliced through the darkness and found Philip sitting on a bed, rushing to put on his shoes, squinting into the light.

"Hurry, Philip! We've got to go, now!"

Philip jumped up and rushed for the door.

They ran out of the room and started down the hallway. The gunfire continued in overlapping bursts.

"Not that way!" shouted Marcos.

Daniel and Philip turned to see Marcos frantically waving a light from the opposite end of the hall.

"That way has explosives!"

They bolted towards Marcos and through a door he held open, down several steps into a narrow tunnel. They hit the dirt floor on the run just as an explosion rocked the tunnel, throwing them against the walls, into each other and onto the ground.

The explosion echoed in Daniel's ears. Thick dust made breathing difficult. Blood was on his face, as he lay stunned from hitting his head. Two strong hands grabbed his jacket and turned him over. He still held the flashlight. Through the illuminated swirling dust he looked into Philip's bearded face with a gash above his left eye.

Philip spoke urgently, looking down at Daniel with his hands still gripping his jacket, "Can you get up?"

Daniel attempted to smile, "I think so."

Philip rocked back and pulled Daniel to his feet.

"Where's Marcos?" said Daniel, looking back towards the door. Spotting a light under the debris, they feverishly worked through the broken concrete and rocks until they were able to lift Marcos out and help him to his feet.

"Can you walk?" asked Daniel.

Marcos nodded, "Why was there shooting?"

Daniel answered, "Someone attacked RAJ."

"The police?"

"No, someone else. I'll tell you later," stated Daniel. "We've got to go."

Marcos took the lead as they stumbled quickly over the rubble and into the tunnel.

Chapter 29: The Missionary

Marcos, Philip and Daniel concentrated on moving through what appeared to be part of a storm drainage system. Within a few minutes they came to a place where an upward shaft cut through the ceiling. About ten feet up the wall was an opening with a metal grate. The night's light increased visibility and provided ventilation within the area directly beneath the opening. They stopped in appreciation of breathing the cool night air.

After a moment, Daniel signaled they needed to keep moving. But Marcos didn't move. He stood motionless, held by a desire to speak, his eyes glossy with tears.

"I'm sorry," Marcos barely whispered.

Daniel paused to study the young man. There was enough light to see the blood and gray dust caked on Marcos' face and shirt. His deep brown eyes were actively seeking, pleading, intently watching Daniel.

"I'm glad you're sorry, Marcos," said Daniel. "You saved our lives."

"Does God hate me for what I've done?"

Philip heard faint voices echoing through the tunnel, coming from behind them. He almost said something, but he knew Daniel and Marcos heard them as well. He moved closer to watch, observing Daniel's calm.

Daniel spoke, his voice relaxed, "Marcos, you're the reason I'm here."

He reached out and touched Marcos' cheeks, cradling the youth's face in his hands. He spoke peace as Marcos silently cried. "God wants to rescue you. He loves you and you're forgiven. He's your Father. You belong to him."

Philip was caught by surprise. Daniel's words and touch, and the young man's response, crashed into the walls guarding his heart, and the walls crumbled before a revelation of love.

Daniel put his arm around Marcos' shoulders, as both an encouraging hug and a prompt to keep moving. Marcos understood and resumed their journey with renewed urgency.

Not more than twenty minutes later, they ascended a flight of stairs to a door boarded shut from the inside. The voices they'd heard earlier had not followed them. They yanked off the boards and forced open the door into an alley. A graveled path with deep ruts and overgrown weeds twisted its way along the rear of concrete block industrial buildings, lined up on either side.

Standing in the alley, Marcos responded with animated hand motions to Daniel's request for general directions toward downtown Mexico City and the U.S. Embassy. When he finished, Daniel put his hand on the young man's shoulder and spoke firmly, "Marcos, don't go anywhere near the RAJ base." Marcos nodded.

Daniel continued, "Go home and get your mother and sisters and take them to the U.S. Embassy. When you get there, ask for Jack Price. He's head of security. Tell him you helped me rescue Philip tonight... remember, Jack Price."

Marcos nodded, repeating "Jack Price," and ran off into the night.

Daniel and Philip began their journey, running through dark alleys and back streets, out of the industrial district towards the embassy in downtown Mexico City.

Daniel explained their situation. "I lost my phone somewhere in the rubble. I don't know how to find my friend. He probably took off when the building blew up. I'm sure he thinks we're dead, and the way we look, I doubt we'd get a cab to stop, even if we could find one."

"Is someone following us?"

"I don't know."

"What were they going to do with me?"

"Execute you, probably tomorrow."

"Tomorrow?"

"Yep."

"You cut it kinda close."

"I was busy."

"Thanks for making the time... I have lots of questions."

"Hold them for later."

Philip remained silent for a minute, "Thanks again for coming."

Daniel smiled, "I'll explain later."

Philip let go of his questions and celebrated the exhilaration of being able to move. He felt good enough to be struck with an idea. With a sly grin, he shared his inspiration. "How far to the embassy?"

"Probably four or five miles."

"Remember how coach never ran us against each other?"

"To protect your fragile ego?" said Daniel.

Philip grinned in response, "How do you feel? Are you in shape?"

"I feel great."

"No excuses?"

Daniel shot Philip a curious glance. "No excuses."

Though amused by the thought, Philip was nevertheless serious. "Then I propose a race, to see who's best. Stone verses Doyle, finally, after ten years."

Daniel again glanced at his friend, and this time smiling in reaction to Philip's confident grin. "You're on."

Running side by side, they settled into a rhythm that carried them forward – step and breath synchronized, pacing each other, with each stride an encouragement to push through.

Daniel's graceful stride expressed his sense of deliverance from the threat of Philip's death and the burden he'd carried for the past month. Fading away was the haunting possibility he would somehow fail Philip and Katherine – that he wouldn't do enough or make the right decision.

In contrast, Philip's motion was strained, driven by the strength of his long stride. He, too, celebrated freedom, but much more, his hope for the future.

An hour later they entered the Bosque de Chapultepec from the south. The expansive park marking their entrance into the center of the city. Philip veered off the trail into a grove of trees and leaned forward with his hands on his knees, trying to catch his breath.

"You okay?" Daniel struggled to ask as he leaned down beside his friend.

Philip responded between deep gasps. "Either we're slow… or your estimate of five miles is way off."

Daniel smiled while still breathing rapidly, "We were lost."

"Lost?"

"Yeah, a couple of times."

"At least no one else could find us," responded Philip through strained breathing. "What about now?"

"We're close."

"How close?"

Daniel pointed ahead. "Through the park and a few blocks up the main boulevard."

They jogged back to the path. "Are you ready for the final lap?" Philip asked, renewing the challenge.

"I thought you gave up?"

"Just a pit stop made necessary by a lousy navigator."

The pace quickened for a quarter of a mile until a sudden sharp pain sliced through Philip's right hamstring. He pulled up limp, struggling not to fall. Grasping his calf, he looked up to see Daniel standing beside him.

"I'm done," said Philip between painful grimaces.

"It's hardly a victory." He offered Philip his shoulder for support. "You're too stubborn to lose unless injured."

"You might not believe this," said Philip holding onto his friend, "but I didn't care who won. I wanted you to keep up," he said as he limped towards the street.

"Well, there's hope for you after all."

Passing slowly through the remaining trees, they entered a wide boulevard lined with office buildings. Daniel pointed up the boulevard. "We'll go towards a column with a statue called the 'Angel of Independence,' and then the U.S. Embassy is only a little bit further."

"I don't think I can make it. You'll have to go and come back for me."

"Not a chance. I'm not leaving you," responded Daniel while trying to flag down a cab. "Let's keep moving."

Philip nodded with more hope than conviction and hobbled forward. When they stepped into the street, they froze as a car's headlights sped towards them. The car swerved across the avenue, almost hitting them as it screeched to a stop. There was no escape. Daniel never let go of his friend.

The front window rolled down, revealing a familiar face. "You guys need a ride?" The driver was Jack Price.

Daniel waited for his heart to leave his throat. "Jack! How did you know?"

Price and another security agent jumped out of the car and helped Philip into the back seat. "I got an anonymous call on *your* phone. Did you lose it?"

"Yeah, earlier tonight."

Price continued, "A guy told me about a gun battle involving RAJ and some other gang. Then he told me about the explosion and you and Philip escaping. He said you'd be coming up from the southwest, and he thought you'd try to make it to the embassy.

"Then we received a call at the embassy from a fellow named Marcos Diego. He said he helped Philip escape and you told him to ask for me. He was panicked when he couldn't find his family. But your sister had already brought them to us."

"Katherine's at the embassy?" asked Daniel as he climbed in beside Philip.

"Yeah," answered Price, "She went to the Diego's and convinced the mother that she and the girls weren't safe, so they came to us. You can call her from the hospital and then see her in the morning after you've both been checked out and answered some questions."

Price turned around and looked directly at Daniel in the back seat. "It was a real mess. Besides the explosion at the warehouse, we've been told there were at least eight dead at the RAJ base. Do you know what happened?"

"We were at the warehouse. I don't know anyone involved in the shooting," answered Daniel.

"How did you find Philip?"

"Marcos showed me the room."

"I already talked to Marcos. How did you know Philip was in the warehouse?"

"Word on the street."

"Is that an answer?" responded Price with a grin.

"It'll have to be. You know how these things get passed along."

"That's okay by me, but the Mexican authorities might want more."

"There was a rumor the group splintered, and they were fighting each other."

"I heard that."

"What can you do to help Marcos?" asked Daniel.

"Probably a lot. We'll do everything we can."

Daniel looked over at Philip as they drove up to the hospital. "That's an impressive cut above your eye."

"It's all right," said Philip smiling. "We have a lot to talk about."

Chapter 30: Siren's Call

With dawn approaching, Berry and Gordon were the only two people dancing in the villa's ballroom. Gordon had made a business proposal to the orchestra and they were happy to play as long as he desired. Since it was much earlier in New York, their night was still young. Berry directed the conversation while they danced.

"Gordon, we need to talk about Chad."

"I'm listening."

"You know I see him often and have gained his confidence."

"It's appreciated."

"I don't think what you're hoping for is going to happen."

"What's that?"

Berry answered, "He recognizes he needs your help to further his political career, especially his desire to someday be a senator. He hates to lose, just like you, but he'll only accept your help on his terms, and he's not very flexible."

"Why's he so guarded? I've never asked him for anything."

"Once Chad shared a comment his mother made about you, that he needed to guard against losing his soul. Of course, implying that you've already lost yours," Berry added with a teasing grin. "Her warning hinders your influence. Even though it hurts his career, I don't think you can overcome it."

"Why not?"

"He fears being close to you and where it might lead, and there's really nothing you can do. Even if you're declared St. Gordon, his arms-length response will remain. He doesn't expect to agree with you, and if he does, he immediately becomes suspicious."

"Is there anything else?"

She smiled as his exasperation showed. Before continuing she sang softly with the orchestra while resting on his shoulder. When the song ended, she explained the most important reason.

"The tools you use to attract ambitious people and bring them into your sphere of influence – power, money, and prestige – don't work with Chad. He's not oblivious to these things, but he's not motivated by them either."

"You're probably right, at least presently."

"And this business with Philip Doyle has only made things worse."

"Does he realize he could lose his re-election bid?"

"Not exactly, but he's aware it'll be close."

"You don't think he'll accept my involvement?"

"Help, yes… but not involvement. He'll accept money and favors from the media, but if you undermine his opponent in a way he recognizes from you, his instincts will drive him further away."

Gordon stepped back and searched her face. Her soft expression reflected the music's romantic mood, but her eyes were cast down, looking away. He waited until she met his gaze. His response was immediate.

"Okay," he said with a wide grin breaking across his face, "What's the plan? The mischievous sparkle in your eyes gives you away."

"I'm not sure you'll like it."

"Try me."

"Let me ask you. What's most important to you concerning Chad?"

"To undo his mother's influence. She filled his head full of nonsense and turned him against me."

"And your grandchildren?"

"I'll most likely lose them too."

"Then you'll have no heirs?"

Gordon's eyes sharpened. "Chad is still his mother's son. You've made your point."

Gordon studied the young woman in his arms, her eyes bewitching under the spell of melody and dancing. But even more, he was fascinated by the mind behind her eyes – fanciful yet compelling. Without limits or norms, she freely projected solutions from the far reaches of imagination. Her solutions readily exposed the thinking of others to be prisons of convention.

"I know Chad's weakness," she explained, "and it's not power, or money, or even his career. He's an incurable romantic, the same as he was in college. He's drawn to mystery and passion. As much as his life is about routine and responsibility, he still longs for romance and the freedom of the wind. And as a mariner, driven by the filling of a sail, he's also drawn to the Siren's call."

Berry closed her eyes, losing herself in the melody. She soon looked up and smiled. "Chad's smart enough to avoid jumping into the sea to his own demise. His instincts are keen. As Odysseus before him, he's tied himself to the mast. Yet he wants to follow his heart, and his heart will lead him to me."

"You?"

"Yes. Chad now suppresses how he feels, but if I go to him, he'll give me his heart."

Gordon's quiet curiosity gave way to disbelief. Her audacity elicited one response. He laughed, and his laughter echoed to fill the empty ballroom. So genuine and infectious was his reaction, she was forced to smile.

"How long have I known you?" he asked.

"Almost four years."

"I've observed you say and do things that have left me amazed. But this, with my son... even from you. What are you thinking?"

Berry answered, unhurried and confident, "I'm thinking of recreating our relationship into one of greater significance, of transcending the pleasure of being your lover, of becoming even closer... to be your daughter and the mother of your heirs."

The fascination in Gordon's eyes encouraged her as she continued, "I'm thinking of Chad, no longer estranged from his father, becoming a future President, which I believe he can accomplish with our help... you, his father, and me, his wife.

"Think of us, Gordon. For three years I've been your secret mistress, and I haven't objected. But even if I were to become your wife, I'd still only be your mistress, your toy, never taken seriously because of my age, cast into a prison of prenuptials.

"You've said many times that we're alike. How much more perfect that I become your daughter, the mother of children who will be true heirs of their grandfather."

A good-natured suspicion overtook Gordon. "What do you want out of this?"

"Well, of course, I'd love Chad, and you, whatever our *new* terms of endearment."

"What else?"

Berry smiled, relying on the connection between them. "First, I'd like thirty million in my name when I marry Chad and another thirty million the day our first child is born. Secondly, at least half of your estate will go into a trust for my children, your grandchildren, with Chad and me as trustees."

Gordon walked towards the exterior ballroom doors. Berry followed close by his side. They passed through an open door onto a brick terrace. The approaching sunrise unveiled the mountains and the valley stretching out before them. His first deep breath of the crisp morning air cleared his head. He trusted the language of the mountains more than the seductive melodies of the dance floor.

"Will it distract us from our objectives?" he asked, more as a preliminary question.

"No, in the long run it will give us even more leverage and influence."

Gordon looked to the Alps rising before him. "You've done it again. It's perfect." He glanced at her and grinned, "What about us?"

She playfully answered with a demure innocence, "I'll be a devoted and loving daughter. As for anything more, you'll have to ask my husband."

Gordon smiled as he slowly shook his head from side to side. "I don't think Chad would approve of more."

Berry stood quietly smiling up at him. The sun's rays found their way through the mountain pass, flooding the terrace with a shining mist. He gazed down into her pale blue eyes, so bright in the morning's first light that they appeared a silver-gray. He was bewitched, wanted to be, enjoying that her eyes mocked his pretense of decision, made fun of every convention, and ridiculed those who cared. He understood her look: knowing, laughing, contemptuous of any abstract construct that dared challenge her imagination.

"Okay, we'll work out the details," he said with a smile that suddenly faded as his eyes hardened. She'd witnessed this intensity before, but never directed at her. His icy stare punctuated his warning.

"Berry, know this to be true. If you fail, if you drive him further away, you're out... with nothing."

Berry pressed for his consent. She didn't intend to fail. "Agreed, then we have a deal?"

Gordon's relaxed affection returned. "Yes, a deal." Then with a suggestive grin he added, "We can begin our new arrangement after we return to America."

"Good," she said, nestling against him. "I'm in no hurry to leave."

Chapter 31: The Impassable Wall

Between showers, medical tests, and stitches above Philip's left eye, Daniel shared details of the search and rescue. Philip could tell some parts were vague, but he felt no need to press for details.

As for what had been happening in the world of PD Tech, Daniel asked Philip to save those questions for the people in Austin. The one shocking detail he did share was the death of Ezra Levi.

After more than an hour of escape talk, Daniel entered a more reflective state of mind. They were finally left alone to enjoy a late night meal.

Philip offered, "You'll never guess what I did to keep my mind occupied all that time."

"I can't imagine."

"I'd have gone quite mad if I hadn't found an old copy of *Ben-Hur*."

"In that room?"

"Yeah, I kept my sanity by escaping into the story. Ever read it?"

"No."

"A terrific story. I was on my third read. I thought *Ben-Hur* might help me understand Ezra Levi and Katherine, and the different ways they think of God. Also, the story helped to clarify my own thinking."

"How's that?"

"I'd always considered science and faith to be incompatible. They were an either-or, but my opinion changed while reading the story." Philip could tell he had Daniel's undivided attention. "Also, for the first time I understood the complex problem Jesus posed for the Jews and Romans. The Jews believed the coming Messiah would be their long-awaited king, like David, to rule the world. But Jesus proclaimed a different kind of kingdom.

"To use a science analogy: the Jewish people expected classical Newtonian physics, and, instead, Jesus gave them a quantum view of reality."

"Newtonian versus quantum physics?" repeated Daniel to make sure he was following.

"That's right," said Philip. "Newton announced his laws of motion and gravity around 1700. His theories were mechanical and determinist, the logical consequence of cause and effect, and his material world with a solid atom at the center offered a reasonable explanation of what was observed. But Newton was unaware of the invisible, quantum nature of matter."

"Go on," said Daniel. "You haven't lost me yet."

Philip continued, "To most people, quantum physics doesn't make sense. It's an invisible world perceived by mathematics, which often exhibits a behavior that's paradoxical to our sensory, everyday experiences. Unlike Newton's idea of a solid atom, in the quantum world matter is not readily reduced to a solid particle, but is often more accurately described as a field or a wave that contains information.

"As a consequence, in a quantum world, scarcity and entropy disappear, and we find billions of computations carried out on chips of sand, streams of light performing delicate surgeries, rivers of information flowing over threads of glass, with millions of people connected to each other because the invisible world of the microcosm is guided by what seems more like intelligence than mindless matter."

Daniel quipped, "And to think we were worried you'd be bored."

Philip smiled, "Armed with a quantum understanding of matter, we're transforming our world. The materialist, industrial age manipulated and changed the physical world from the *outside-in*. In contrast, quantum physics allows us to change the world from inside the atom, from the *inside-out*, and in doing so, to overcome barriers and create wealth and abundance never before imagined."

Daniel asked, "And how did this help you understand Ezra Levi and Katherine?"

"The Jews expected the coming Messiah to impose God's kingdom from the outside-in. Now I admit I don't understand how God's doing it. But quantum physics demonstrates the superiority of change initiated from the inside-out. The kingdom Katherine presents in her letters is one that begins in the human heart, from the inside-out. Her view more accurately represents the true nature of the physical realm as revealed in science."

Daniel was in awe, "What you're saying is fascinating. Was there anything else?"

Philip paused and then spoke from memory, "Katherine wrote in one of her letters, *God's invisible qualities... have been clearly seen, being understood from what has been made, so that men are without excuse.* She said that with an open mind I could discover this."

"Yes, of course it's true," said Daniel. "God's hand is evident in creation, but one point needs to be clarified. A man's entrance into the kingdom can only come through the person of Jesus, on a personal level, from what you referred to as the 'inside-out.'"

Philip responded, "I understand you and Katherine have this personal connection, but who initiated this experience, you or God? Will a person's nature allow it? Can we reason our way to Jesus as God?"

"Reason only goes so far," said Daniel.

Philip spoke reflectively, "In *Ben-Hur*, the Greek wise man said the mind can only reason to a certain point, and then it reaches an *impassable wall*. Is that what you're saying?"

"Yes, it is," agreed Daniel. "What else did the Greek say?"

"He said once you reach the wall, all that remains is to stand and cry aloud for help." Philip looked away and spoke quiet and low. "The Greek believed it was possible to yearn so much for him, with all our soul, that God would take compassion and give us an answer."

Daniel wondered, "And what do you think of that?"

"I can accept Jesus as a great teacher, and even there being a God who's creating some kind of kingdom in the world. But as far as Jesus being God, my mind won't let me go there. I can't bridge that gap."

Daniel felt his exhaustion as he leaned back in the chair to rest for a moment before addressing Philip's comment, but there'd be no immediate response. He fell asleep.

Philip studied his old friend, as though seeing him in a new light. He'd always thought of Daniel as a 'missionary,' which didn't mean anything specific, other than it somehow meant that Daniel had settled for less than he could have been. Now, he knew better.

His thoughts flowed easily to Katherine. He allowed his memory to drift past recollection, past missing her, to dwell in a place where he felt the pain of separation.

He knew they'd not been kept apart by distance or locked doors or even abductors' guns. They were separated by an idea, an understanding, a decision. The cause wasn't visible, yet the chasm was wide, as wide as the east is from the west – as far as belief is from unbelief. For to admit that Jesus was who he claimed to be was to admit that he, Philip, owed everything to someone else.

Chapter 32: A Desperate Fool

The phone rang as Brenda Hanover struggled to wake up. She peered at the clock. It was much too early on a Sunday morning for someone to be calling.

She stretched for the phone as her attitude dissolved into an irritation she intended to share with the obtrusive caller. Only one person ever called her at this hour, and that was… the thought that the caller reminded her of Philip annoyed her all the more.

"Hello, and it better be good."

"That depends. Have you become spoiled working without the boss?"

Brenda gasped, "Philip?"

"Who else dares to call this early?"

Philip held the phone away from his ear in reaction to her scream. After some unprofessional crying and attempts toward composure, she filled him in on the events of the past four weeks. Much of what had happened surprised him, and it was obvious he had a lot of catching up to do. He proceeded to give her instructions to set up for his return. Then he called his father.

****

Berry Fields had finished dressing when she heard the door close. It was 3:00 Sunday afternoon. They'd slept in after their late night dancing. She thought it unusual for Gordon to leave their suite without saying anything, but he'd been on the phone with Darius Cain in Washington. There was an intensity in his voice that wasn't a good sign. She decided to find him and see what happened.

She made her way to the main floor and followed the hallway towards the ballroom and terrace. Before reaching the ballroom, she passed an open door to Marone's private library. The antique Renaissance furnishings, gilt-edged books and hand-carved mahogany woodwork drew her in for a quick look. Upon entering the room, she faintly heard Gordon's voice through a pair of beveled glass doors that were open onto the terrace.

He was talking to Leo, his voice irritated. Her first response was to leave, but curiosity trumped good judgment. Instead, she quietly approached the opening until she could hear without being seen.

Gordon was speaking, "How did you manage to lose that much in the futures market?"

Leo didn't respond, so Gordon continued, "And then you convinced the Arabs to invest a hundred million in a new algae company to cover your losses? Exactly what business were they supposed to be investing in?"

Marone avoided the question, "I just need some time to cover their investment. The Arabs appreciated the potential."

"The potential is what I will control. How it is used will depend on the new Worldwide Food Security program," countered Gordon. "Did you purposely betray me?"

"No, that was not my intention, but I do believe your desire to not alienate your son caused you to underestimate Doyle."

"So you hired RAJ to kill him… against my demand that he *not* be harmed?" stated Gordon in disbelief.

Berry could feel the rising disgust in Gordon's tone. "Well, Leo, I have bad news for you. Philip Doyle escaped and made it to the U.S. Embassy, and most of the RAJ are dead."

There was a long pause and Berry started to leave until she heard Gordon again. His voice was low, "Foolishness begets desperation which begets more foolishness. You've set yourself against the Arabs and powerful interests in Washington. You're in the middle with both flanks exposed. You and I are through."

Berry moved to the window and peered through a space between the glass and the drapery. Marone stood motionless, his neck stiff, eyes narrowed, lips drawn tight, with intense angst jamming his desire to speak.

Gordon calmly stared at him, without emotion, except for the pity one might have for a former ally who has self-destructed. "Berry and I are leaving. I won't be talking to you again." Gordon left the terrace and walked into the ballroom.

Berry turned to leave, but was startled by the presence of Marone's personal assistant, observing her from the door to the hallway. The woman didn't speak, just watched without expression through lifeless dark eyes set on a hollow, colorless face. Berry gathered her composure and walked directly towards the door. The woman said nothing, only leaned enough to one side to allow Berry to pass into the hallway.

Gordon called her as she hurried back to their suite. "I need you to pack our things. We're leaving immediately."

"I'll be ready in ten minutes."

"One of our security people will come upstairs to help with the bags," said Gordon.

When Berry reached the front, a waiting car was being loaded with their luggage. They slipped into the back seat and as they drove away Gordon continued looking at the villa.

He mentioned in a matter-of-fact tone, "There was quite a firefight in Mexico City last night." Then he turned towards Berry and with relaxed self-satisfaction added, "Philip Doyle's alive."

Still standing on the terrace, Marone watched Gordon's car drive down the side of the mountain.

He spoke to his personal assistant, "I have to convince the Arabs they can't trust Gordon before they suspect the loss of their investment."

"Will Connelly contact the Arabs?"

"He still needs me to encourage them to keep the pressure on Israel until the election. I'll continue helping with that strategy, which should buy me the time I need."

"What about the girl?"

"As long as she's with Gordon, she's safe. But if they split, or something happens to Gordon, I want her silenced."

Chapter 33: The Girl Next Door

At Chad's request, Daniel agreed to attend the evening's fundraiser, a black-tie dinner for five hundred people at the Washington Hilton in DuPont Circle. The atmosphere was festive as the orchestra played music from the Big Band era. Also contributing to an interesting evening was the circumstance of his current renown. It had been two months since Philip's abduction and many people knew of his role in the rescue.

Chad pulled Daniel away from another round of questions and led him to their banquet table. He was first introduced to the Corwins, cattle ranchers from the Austin area. He then met Raymond Preston and his wife, Joanne, business owners from Atlanta.

While conversing with the Prestons he heard Chad behind him, "Daniel, I believe you'll recognize this old college friend."

He turned and was surprised to find Berry Fields, who was amused she'd caught him off guard. He returned her grin as they exchanged greetings. Although never a fan, college was the one time in his life when he could appreciate someone who referred to herself as Strawberry Fields Forever.

Chad and Berry moved on just as Daniel was distracted by a figure moving among the party's guests.

The distraction was a graceful young lady of about thirty. Her bright smile, easy movement, and the light bounce of her short blonde hair conveyed a youthful spirit. At the same time, her confident interaction with the wealthy and powerful spoke of experience and competence. He enjoyed her as one would absent-mindedly gaze upon a butterfly, gliding effortlessly from flower to flower with charmed, quiet efficiency, giving and receiving what was needed.

Her continuous motion radiated a certainty of purpose. For Daniel, his attraction was conceptual as well as sensory. She appeared as the essence of an ideal he was unaware he held. Each observable feature and mannerism was as the piece of a puzzle coming together to define a desire previously unknown.

Daniel noticed Chad approach this 'mystery girl' and direct her towards their table. She headed straight to the Prestons, apparently recognizing the couple from Atlanta.

The Texas couple seated at their table asked Daniel a question concerning his work in Mexico. After answering, he glanced up to see his new fascination looking at him. Her eyes were bright and animated, and she looked great in red.

Chad took her arm and led her directly towards him.

"I'd like you to meet…," started Chad.

"You're Daniel Stone," she stated with zestful curiosity, not feeling it necessary to let Chad finish. "I've heard about you from Chad. I'd love to hear the inside story of how you rescued Philip Doyle, if you're not tired of inquisitive strangers."

Daniel felt immediately drawn to her contagious joy and looked to Chad to finish. "Daniel, I'd like to introduce one of my favorite people in all of Washington, the congresswoman from North Carolina, Macy Southerland."

Daniel appeared at ease but felt out of his comfort zone. It was a long way from the Mexico City barrios, so he remained an observer during dinner. Macy was seated beside the Prestons, and Berry sat across the table next to Chad. He enjoyed the conversation and soon found himself contrasting Macy to Berry.

He had been relieved when Chad and Berry broke up in college and she left Austin to finish her degree at Cal Berkeley. She'd been disingenuous in college, but now it was harder to discern, for her insincerely was artfully masked behind a subtle, refined elegance. But what betrayed Berry were her eyes. Only by refusing to be spellbound by their luminous, pale blue glow could one detect her critical gaze.

By contrast, Macy's warm blue eyes were openly honest to a soul with nothing to hide. Her eyes revealed a winsome nature, inviting new friends to share in her joy and sense of wonder.

Daniel was certain Macy grew up as the cute "girl next door," wearing jeans and a T-shirt, playing basketball and riding horses, and most especially, a "daddy's girl." Then one day she put on a dress, and to everyone's amazement, she had transformed into a beautiful young lady.

He appreciated that the pressure of Macy's career hadn't eliminated her youthful enthusiasm as she spoke from across the table. "Daniel, please tell us of your escape with Philip Doyle."

"There's nothing to add to what was in the papers."

"We all want to hear the inside scoop."

Realizing avoidance was impossible, Daniel answered, "I followed a lead that seemed reliable and found Philip at the same time a firefight broke out. We escaped during the confusion."

Macy responded with a light-hearted tease, "That's not an answer. You ought to go into politics."

Daniel laughed, "I'll share one thing I thought was fascinating. Philip, who'd always rejected religious faith, found a copy of *Ben-Hur* where they held him. He read it a couple of times and had many questions about Jesus and the kingdom."

Macy added with the touch of an experienced tour guide, "*Ben-Hur* was written by General Lew Wallace, whose statue is in the Capitol building."

The Texan, Daryl Corwin, joined in, "Too bad he didn't have Allen Wilder's new book if he was interested in the coming of the kingdom."

"I don't think that was the direction Philip was going," answered Daniel.

Raymond Preston offered his opinion of Wilder, revealing an underlying frustration, "Allen Wilder has been claiming those same things for thirty years."

"And the Rapture and Second Coming are closer than ever," said Corwin. His wife added, "Look at what's going on in Jerusalem. Aren't those clear signs?"

The music started and the Corwins and Prestons opted for the dance floor. Daniel was more than happy to find himself alone with Macy. He asked, "When did you know you wanted to follow your father's path?"

Macy shared, "From my earliest childhood, my father would take me to the Capitol building. We'd walk across the marble floors and I remember the sound of my clicking heels rising to fill the vast space above. I was awestruck.

"When I was about twelve, he took me through Statuary Hall. He described the statutes as the silent guardians of history, men of moral courage capable of creating a great nation. He called them "self-governing." He said that because freedom first existed as a reality inside each of them, they could share this freedom as a gift to the whole world. The work wasn't finished, and isn't yet complete, but the building had begun on a firm foundation. That's when I knew."

Daniel smiled, "It looks like our nation wasn't the only thing started on a firm foundation."

Macy returned his smile, "Yes, I was very fortunate."

When a new song began, Daniel stood and offered his arm, "Would you like to dance?"

"I'd love to."

He couldn't decide if it was his long absence from the dance floor or the closeness of his new acquaintance that accounted for his awkwardness. Regardless, he hadn't forgotten the basics. He slipped his arm behind her and gently drew her near.

She asked, "Chad said you're leaving tomorrow for Austin."

"Later, around 4:00."

"Would you like to join me for church tomorrow?"

"Yes, but only if I can take you to lunch afterwards."

"I'd like that," said Macy, "and if there's anything in Washington you haven't seen yet, I'm an excellent tour guide."

"Yes, there is," responded Daniel, smiling.

"And what would that be?"

"I'm not sure, but I'll think of something by tomorrow."

Macy's dream had come true. She was presently serving as a congresswoman in the U.S. House of Representatives. She loved her work, which fulfilled the goal she'd chosen for her life. Her work absorbed all she had to give. The tasks needing her attention presented themselves in a continual stream. Yet this wasn't a problem. It seemed only natural, and she was happy – for the most part.

Her lifestyle did concern her family and friends, especially her mother. Did she ever date? Was she interested in a family? And most recently, did she want to live alone all her life?

'Sure, I'll get married, as soon as I find someone like dad,' she lightly protested. Except for a few college flirtations, dating was never a priority. After a near miss in grad school, there had been no serious relationships. She wondered, as a flickering thought, if maybe her expectations were too high, or she needed to look harder or be more accessible. After all, she'd soon be thirty-two.

Then the duties of Congress called, and the flicker was extinguished by a wave of responsibilities. This state of her life was acceptable. Her days were filled with good work that confirmed the direction she'd chosen.

Yet nothing validated her story more than the reality of Daniel Stone.

On the dance floor, she leaned back and looked into Daniel's face. She offered her eyes, soft and open, without apprehension. She laid her heart bare before her Heavenly Father every night, and so she was confident about what Daniel would find – nothing divided, no contradictions, no fear, no confusion.

Then a thought amused her and brought a smile. She wondered if he also knew.

Chapter 34: Preparing for War

Philip sensed he was different since escaping his captivity in Mexico City. The small daily occurrences, like the inconvenience he was presently experiencing, functioned to remind him of the change.

He and Lydia Shafran, the newly-appointed CEO for ARD, had been waiting at a police roadblock as they approached the vehicle inspection point for entrance into Jerusalem. What had changed for Philip was his newly acquired patience for interruptions that affected his goals. Instead of focusing on the event as though he could somehow will it to be different, he chose to ignore the delay, roll down the window and enjoy the sun's warmth on his skin.

When they finally reached the inspectors, Lydia's credentials appeared to satisfy the officer and they received only a cursory inspection. The officer provided an explanation as a means of sharing his own frustration, "Another raised alert level."

As they moved through the roadblock, Philip asked, "What has caused the riots?"

"Any excuse will do," answered Lydia with a hopeless gesture. "But the latest flash point has been the new Jewish settlements."

Philip said, "Is that what our President was complaining about?"

"Part of it. Many critics of Israel believe we should pull back to pre-1967 borders."

"He doesn't seem committed to Israel's defense," offered Philip. "At least not the same as previous administrations."

"That's our growing fear. We don't believe the Muslims will launch an all-out war against Israel. They know we have nuclear weapons. Their strategy's to isolate Israel by pressuring the U.S. to withdraw aid. Much of what happens in Jerusalem is to validate a pro-Palestinian agenda."

"What do you think will happen?"

Lydia became animated, momentarily revealing a suppressed anger, "The world keeps telling us to solve the 'Jerusalem problem.' What problem? Israel has successfully governed Jerusalem since 1967, to the benefit of all people. If there's a problem, it's caused by those who seek to divide the city. They want to drive us out, and I can guarantee you that's not going to happen."

"What about war?"

"As I said before, I don't think most Muslims or Jews want a war that

117

would destroy the entire Middle East."

"You said *most*."

For the first time Lydia understood where Philip was leading the conversation. "There are some who want war. They are evil, so filled with hatred they either don't care what happens, or they seek a god who wills it."

Philip continued his line of thought, "And those who want war, do you think they have a time line? Is there anything they're waiting for?"

"I don't know. What do you think?"

Philip answered, "We're not waiting to find out. I'd like the entire ARD operation duplicated in Austin as soon as possible. We can maintain the operation here, and no one will be laid off, but everyone should have a current work visa. If things fall apart, we'll get as many people out as possible."

Lydia remained silent while driving along the outskirts of Jerusalem.

Philip asked, "Will you come to Austin?"

"I'll spend significant time in Austin. But if war breaks out… I don't know if I can desert my homeland."

"Then let's hope you never have to decide."

Lydia left the highway and turned towards a security gate marking the entrance to Algae Resource Development. Once past the gate they entered a six-acre compound surrounded by a ten-foot chain link fence. The main offices, connected to research labs, were of gray stone, three stories high with steel bars protecting the windows.

Lydia escorted Philip into the main lobby where he was greeted by a distinguished woman in her mid-forties, with dark hair highlighted by wisps of natural gray. Her warm brown eyes and cheerful smile conveyed confident hospitality.

Lydia introduced him, "Philip, I'd like you to meet Deborah Levi."

Philip was thankful to meet the woman who'd fought so valiantly for her husband's final wish. After Philip expressed his gratitude to her for saving the algae initiative, she took his hand. "Come Philip, I want to show you something."

She led him to the far side of the lobby where they walked up to a large architectural model displayed in a glass case approximately eight by ten feet. Deborah and Lydia watched with interest as Philip stared in awe.

"So this is Ezra's new temple?"

"Yes, it is. A dream that became his obsession." Deborah directed Philip's attention to the display cases along the wall. "Here we have reproductions of the sacred vessels and ceremonial tools painstakingly researched and crafted for temple worship."

"These are amazing. What's this?" asked Philip.

"It's a gold breastplate to be worn by the high priest," said Deborah. "It's covered with twelve gemstones, each engraved with a Hebrew letter to represent the twelve tribes."

Deborah continued the tour, "This is the Table of Shewbread. It's made of wood with a gold overlay. It's said that the Divine Presence in the Temple supernaturally kept the bread fresh all week."

"Shouldn't they go to a museum, or… something?"

Deborah smiled, "We're working on it."

Philip followed Lydia and Deborah into a conference room where ARD's management awaited their visionary leader. He laid out opportunities and expectations in an atmosphere that felt more like a celebration than a commitment to accomplish the impossible. But after weeks of uncertainty, the talented group at ARD welcomed the challenge.

As Philip closed the meeting, he expressed his satisfaction, "Our critics claim we'll fail because the algae production isn't scalable. But they missed our strategy. It's the ARD units that are scalable, especially when placed in the hands of motivated operators. Everything's in place – now to implement. I believe we're ready to set sail on a remarkable adventure."

Chapter 35: Gog and Magog

Daniel walked through PD Tech's main office building to the patio area next to Philip's office. Chad had arrived ahead of him and was seated with Philip.

"Welcome," said Philip, "you're just in time for lunch."

Chad asked Daniel, "Do you talk with Macy very often?"

Daniel responded with a boyish grin, "I'd guess you already know."

Chad offered a defense, "Asking Macy if she likes my friend would be a little high schoolish."

"And?"

Chad smiled, "She told me to mind my own business. That's why I'm asking you. And remember, I introduced you."

Daniel acknowledged Chad's claim. "We usually find a reason to talk every day."

Philip joined in, "Chad, you may have started something." He turned to Daniel, "But don't consider anything serious for at least five years. You have a big job ahead of you."

"I'll make sure you both approve," said Daniel with a grin.

Chad took exception, "Don't delay on our account. You'd be nuts to let her get away. That's if she'll have you."

Chad turned to Philip, "How was Israel?"

"American weakness emboldens the Muslims and makes the Israelis more desperate," answered Philip. "Both of which increase the danger of war."

Daniel noted, "Rob says Allen Wilder believes a war over Jerusalem will be a fulfillment of prophecy?"

Chad offered, "Wilder was recently on the cover of *New Evangelical Thought*. They chronicled his meteoric rise from obscurity to the most recognized prophetic voice in America. In the article, Wilder said that the signs of the times point to a battle for Jerusalem, Ezekiel's War of Gog and Magog. According to Wilder, God is supposed to deliver Israel from an attack by Muslim nations allied with Russia. He teaches that Israel's victory will enable the Jews to build a new temple which paves the way for the Rapture and the Antichrist."

"Does anyone really listen to Wilder?" asked Philip.

"You'd be surprised," said Daniel.

Chad added, "Even though *New Evangelical Thought* has a circulation of less than forty thousand, over two million reprints of the article were sent out to churches and Christian leaders."

"Who paid for it?" asked Philip.

Chad glanced at Daniel. The irony of the answer produced a slight grin. "Maybe my father."

"Gordon?"

"There's a strong rumor…"

Philip asked the obvious, "Why don't you ask him?"

Chad responded, "Not until I know the reason." Recalling something else he continued, "Rob recently told me that Wilder's conferences are now drawing eight to ten thousand."

Philip tried again, "So why would Gordon finance an end-times prophet?" His question was greeted with silence until he added, "It's not rhetorical."

"It had better be," said Chad, "Because we don't have the answer."

Philip was ready to move on. "You'll need to find out. As we all know, Gordon doesn't do anything without a reason."

Chapter 36: A New Paradigm

Chad had been in Washington long enough to recognize when someone was using a committee hearing to carve out a strategic position. The chairman of the House Agriculture Committee had offered a cursory explanation as to why he'd scheduled a summer hearing during an election year. Chad had trouble recalling the reason. He felt like an extra in a political play entitled, *Biotech Agriculture and the Challenge to Feed the World.*

Instead of listening, he wondered about his father's interest in Amber Grains and the meeting at the ranch with Blake Merrill. And then there was the follow-up at the Georgetown restaurant with Darius Cain and Andrea Clark from the White House, Clifton Roberts of Eden Global, and the political activist, Reverend Buzz Nelson.

Something was going on. He suspected his father was guiding the events involving Amber Grains in some elaborate plan to benefit his interests. Chad's natural suspicions were heightened when he received word that Darius Cain was seen leaving the committee chairman's office the previous afternoon.

Chad intently watched the drama unfold. The first three speakers were pro-biotech scientists who enthusiastically sang the praises of genetically modified organisms (GMOs).

The first presenter after lunch was Samuel Bonds, a former senator from Massachusetts who proved to be a tenacious critic of Amber Grain. He advocated for government control of all GMO producers, and concluded with an emotional assault against free markets and privately owned farms, warning the committee that a greed-based business model ruled by profit would inevitably lead to food shortages and global catastrophe.

Next was Andrea Clark, the White House administrator for Worldwide Food Security. Her plans for promoting GMOs in developing countries were eye-opening. The U.S. government had always advanced American agribusiness, but Clark's proposals went far beyond marketing and influence peddling. Apparently, total global penetration had become an administration priority.

Something was beginning to bother him, a lot. The academic scientists had done their part, bathing GMOs in the light of scientific progress, and Clark's goals for Worldwide Food Security were typical bureaucratic meddling. But what was the deal with Samuel Bonds? The committee's hearing had certainly been constructed to achieve a desired effect. But how did Bonds' criticism of markets, capitalism, and Amber Grains fit in? Chad figured he wasn't as yet seeing the real objective of the hearing.

The fact that the final speaker was the Reverend Buzz Nelson was noteworthy in itself. If one looked at the hearing as theater, which Chad did, then the previous presenters were setting the stage for the final act which he could not believe was to be a political activist from the religious left. And now Nelson, a socialist agitator for wealth redistribution, was to be elevated to the status of an expert for world biotech food production.

Buzz Nelson began, "The Declaration of Independence states that men are endowed by their Creator with certain unalienable rights... Life, liberty and the pursuit of happiness. It's our government's stated responsibility to guarantee that all people living within our borders have food to eat."

Nelson spent a couple of minutes offering a context for his preamble, and then he continued...

"In 1980, the U.S. Supreme Court ruled five to four that not only could someone use existing life forms to create a new life form, but they could also claim legal ownership of the new genetically modified organism. Let's now look at the unforeseen consequences of this bizarre decision – in two words, Amber Grains.

"At their present rate of acquiring new patents and opening additional markets, one day soon Amber Grains will not only feed the world, they'll also control world food production. Did Amber create this promising new industry by itself? Have they not depended on public research institutions, government protected patents, the sweat of farmers and the fertile farmland that's the birthright of all Americans? Who gave them the right to operate a monopoly that bleeds our nation and the people of world?"

Nelson droned on, but Chad had heard enough. He finally understood. The reason it had taken so long was because his thinking was trapped by convention, probably like everyone else. The fight surrounding Amber Grains had previously been between those who objected to GMOs and those who believed the scientific progress of the Green Revolution was the only realistic hope for feeding the world.

But now a new paradigm was being created. Genetic engineering was still the hope, and no dissenting voice on that point was allowed into the present discussion. Yet the argument was being radically changed. The new target was the company, Amber Grains, and the economic model of private property and free enterprise.

Two questions raced through Chad's mind. Who was orchestrating the attacks on Amber Grains? And what did they hope to achieve?

Chapter 37: Convention

Election: 75 days

Chad rested against the second floor railing, watching the bustling activity on the convention floor. Excitement filled the air, carried on waves of sound, spoken from diverse perspectives, yet coming together as a common goal. Ben Thomas, the governor of Ohio, was the party's nominee to run in November. A reliable insider had just whispered that Senator Rose Dalton, the energetic conservative from Tennessee, was going to accept the offer to be Thomas' running mate.

Chad was satisfied with the choices. Ben Thomas was not perfect but good enough, and Rose Dalton was an excellent debater and a fiery defender of the Constitution.

Looking out over the convention, he soon discovered Berry standing among the Tennessee delegation talking to Rose Dalton. He grinned while slowly shaking his head. Of course Berry had somehow found out.

He thought of all he should be doing but instead kept watching her. She was wearing a stylish, white silk blouse with ruffled front and sleeves, and black slacks that fit snuggly around her hips. Her strawberry blonde hair with large, loose curls was partially pulled up, allowing the unrestrained remainder to fall upon her shoulders in what seemed to Chad as casual perfection.

She must have sensed someone watching because she glanced up in his general direction. With an inviting smile and a subtle wave of her hand she motioned for him to join her.

Chad took the stairs to the floor level and walked in the general direction of a large Tennessee sign. When he reached the area, Berry stepped out from the circle surrounding Dalton, hurried towards him and grabbed his hand.

"Come on, do you know Senator Dalton?"

"Yes, we're acquainted," he said to no avail as he was dragged along.

When they reached the circle, Chad made eye contact with the senator.

"Hi, Chad," said Rose Dalton, shaking Chad's hand.

"Hello, Senator. Looks like an exciting evening."

"How are things in Texas?"

Chad tried to carry on an intelligent conversation with the woman who could quite possibly be the next Vice President of the United States. But he wasn't able to focus. Berry was standing beside him, holding his hand while resting her other hand on his arm. Her body lightly touched his, and she

124

seemed unaware the physical contact signaled an elevated degree of affection. He both noticed and recognized its meaning, and to complicate matters, he liked it and wanted it to continue.

The noise level in the building increased simultaneously to Berry asking him a question. He looked down when he asked Berry to repeat what she'd said, and she responded by leaning up against him. Her hair brushed his cheek and the fragrance prompted him to breathe deeply. The sensation of her body pressing against him, and her breath caressing his neck and ear, overwhelmed his sense of propriety.

This one act, performed with apparent innocence, crashed through every protective barrier he'd carefully constructed during his time in Austin.

Instead of letting go, his hand gently lingered on the small of her back. She responded by remaining close, which caused any movement to become another point of contact.

Chad received a text message. The chairman of the Texas delegation needed to talk with him.

"I have to go to work," he explained. "How about meeting for a drink after the convention?"

"I'd like to but I'm catching the red eye tonight for San Francisco."

"San Francisco?"

"Yeah, I have to be at the airport by 11:00."

"I'll give you a ride."

"You should stay here."

"I don't think so. Everything will be settled by then and they won't even know I'm gone."

He leaned towards her and with a soft smile settled the issue, "I'll be out front at 10:30."

As he walked towards his meeting in the Texas delegation room, he realized he was excited, confused, and apprehensive... all at the same time.

Chad stood beside his rental, waiting for Berry to make her way from the front of the convention center to the VIP pick-up area. She pulled a roller carry-on and had added a soft, black mid-length jacket to her attire.

"Thanks for the ride," she offered as they headed for the airport.

"I was ready to leave the noise and crowds behind."

"Do you think Thomas and Dalton can win?"

"Of course, but it'll be close. By the way, how did you know Rose Dalton would be Thomas' running mate?"

"What makes you think I knew?"

"I could tell when you were talking to her."

"You know who I work for." She turned towards him and laughed, "Do you really need to ask?"

"Is Gordon sending you to San Francisco?"

"No, I'm going to see family."

"I hope everyone's all right?"

"Everyone's fine. Just the usual drama."

"Is that why you left Austin College after your junior year, because of family?"

"No, I was ready for a change."

"Did you like Cal Berkeley?"

"Yes, I loved it. It was… liberating." With a quick glance and a teasing grin she added, "It made me the girl I am today."

Chad pulled into the drop-off zone. Berry was facing him, smiling. He wasn't sure what to say.

She soon broke the awkward silence. "I'll be back in D.C. in a couple of weeks. I'd love to cook dinner for you at my place. It's one of my hidden talents."

"Sounds great." He meant it, but what he really wanted was for her not to get on the plane and instead have that drink with him.

Berry reached over and squeezed his arm, "I'll let you know when I'm back." She slipped out of the car and disappeared into the terminal.

Chapter 38: Strategic Denial

Daniel was purchasing fresh fruit at a Mexico City farmers market. It was early evening, moments before closing, when a teenage boy approached him. He waited until Daniel noticed him, "My uncle would like to talk to you."

"Do I know your uncle?"

"You're his favorite American."

Daniel smiled. "Where is he?"

The youngster motioned for Daniel to follow and led him to the familiar black SUV parked on a side street. Daniel peered through the open window, "Octaviano, it's good to see you."

"Come in, mi amigo. I have something to show you."

"You do live an unusual life."

Once on the road Octaviano reached down between the seats and pulled out a black binder, about a hundred pages thick, and handed it to Daniel, "I think you'll find this interesting."

Daniel read the title page. It was a U.S. government report, *Controlling World Food Production through Genetic Engineering,"* by Andrea Clark of Worldwide Food Security.

He reviewed the table of contents and then quickly read through the brief introduction, 'Biotech Agriculture as a Means to Global Government.' Daniel asked his friend, "They can't be serious. Have you read this?"

"Two days ago."

"How did you get it?"

"A guy named Buzz Nelson."

"I know who he is." Daniel flipped through the pages. "He gave it to you?"

"Not exactly."

"How do you know him?"

"Buzz and I go way back. He was an advocate for revolution in Central America. We weren't friends, but we ran in the same circles.

"About six months ago, Buzz came down to Managua and called together some of the guys from the old days who are still around... kind of a reunion of revolutionaries. About thirty of us gathered at a hotel. It was fun, and it gave Buzz a chance to gloat about being an insider, a personal friend of the President."

"Sorry I missed it."

Octaviano smiled and continued, "Everyone was drinking. Buzz started bragging about big changes coming, stuff that would surpass anything we'd ever dreamed of. He flashed the report you're holding, but no one was in any shape to look at it. We were too busy sharing old war stories. It was quite an evening.

"When I left the party the report was on a chair, partially hidden under Buzz's coat. No one was looking and I was just drunk enough to be curious, so I put it in my bag. I actually forgot about it until a week ago when Buzz was in Mexico City, delivering a speech before some kind of unity conference."

"What kind of unity?" asked Daniel.

"I have no idea. He was claiming the world was on the verge of a great upheaval that would advance global consciousness. But what intrigued me was his comment, 'biotech agriculture will be the Trojan horse of world revolution.' It reminded me of the report, so I read it."

Daniel asked, "Don't you and Nelson sort of agree on things?"

"Remember, I no longer seek power as a solution. Yet I still expected to find us on the same side. Buzz was always critical of crony capitalism and you know how I feel about the ag business. But after reading the report, I realized he doesn't oppose what Amber does. In fact, he wants to use Amber to advance the cause of world socialism. You'll see when you read it."

Octaviano spoke from deep frustration, as though taping a long suppressed anguish, "That bastard doesn't care about the family farmer, or a dying village, or some poor guy longing for a little dignity. These faceless souls are just fodder for his glorious revolution."

Daniel asked, "What do you expect me to do with this?"

"Read it. Then it's up to you."

Daniel had been reading and re-reading the report all day. When he was finished he placed a call to Chad. "I have something to show you."

"What is it?"

"You'll have to wait until I get there."

"Okay."

"I've asked Macy to come to Austin to meet with us."

"Don't tell me you guys are engaged... already."

Chad's wild guess shocked Daniel because of how far off he was, and yet it was a surprisingly creative guess. Daniel burst into laughter, "I wish it was like that... I mean I don't wish that, well not exactly..." Daniel laughed again. "No, it's not to tell you we're engaged. It has to do with food, but not wedding cake."

"That's too bad. When will you be here?"

"Tomorrow. I'll pick up Macy at the airport and we'll be at your place about 7:00."

"I'll have the kids stay with friends." For the first time Chad's voice conveyed a more serious tone, "Should I look forward to your visit?"

"No."

"I was afraid of that. See you tomorrow."

"Put on the coffee. We'll be there."

****

Daniel and Macy were seated at Chad's kitchen table sharing personal news. After allowing a few minutes to settle in, Daniel directed the conversation to the point of their trip. He handed Chad the black binder given to him by Octaviano. He also gave Macy a copy he'd printed.

Chad opened the cover and read the title. He glanced at Daniel, "How did you get this?"

"I can't say." Daniel offered a suggestion, "Read the introduction and then I'll give you a summary."

When they'd finished reading, Chad stated with exasperation, "Do they really think they can get away with this?"

"They do," responded Daniel. "I read the report for the third time today. I believe it's the final phase of a comprehensive strategy that's been taking shape for several years."

Macy asked, "What are the main points?"

Daniel answered, "First of all, Clark stresses how the Pentagon and State Department have used food, ever since World War II, as a strategic asset to advance U.S. interests. She then discloses how they've accelerated the growth of American agribusiness to not just dominate world food production, but to monopolize it.

"Next, Clark explains how they can maintain world leadership by controlling the distribution of GMO seeds. She calls it the power of 'strategic denial.'

"In the fourth section, the report reveals a step-by-step strategy for placing Amber Grains and the GMO industry under direct government control."

Daniel noticed his friends were a little shocked. "Would you like a few details from this last section?"

Chad answered first, "Sure, but how many can we handle?"

"I'll mention just a few," said Daniel, smiling in sympathy. "Clark praises GMOs while attacking Amber Grains for profiteering from world hunger.

As soon as they have the votes in Congress, genetic seed producers will be absorbed into a new government entity to be called the Agency for Worldwide Food Security.

"Amber Grains is the big prize they're after, but did you notice that they're not proposing to stick Amber under the Department of Agriculture?"

Macy took the bait, "And why not?"

"Because the governing board of Worldwide Food Security is to eventually include foreign directors, making the agency international."

Daniel paused as Macy commented, "We can see where this is going."

Chad added, "And we can see my father's agenda, but he knows Congress would block this."

"It gets worse," said Daniel almost as an apology. "The final section lays out their vision for the future.

"Clark concludes that those who disagree will be labeled "anti-science" obstructionists who support "inefficient farming" that condemns the poor to lives of starvation and poverty.

"To quote from her conclusion: 'A new spirit of unity will sweep across the nations, creating a collective consciousness for the common good. A lever will exist to ensure rogue nations cooperate with social programs created by enlightened global agencies. Population control, wealth equality, environmental initiatives, and freedom from religious and cultural intolerance are within our grasp. No longer will nation-states be able to shield their people from the will of the world community. A new world order is rising. The dream is becoming a reality.'"

Chad stated with emphatic disgust, "And what if we don't embrace their dream of a one world government led by a bunch of global elitists?"

"Then you'll be standing in the way of their paradise on earth," responded Daniel.

Macy added, "If they win public support, then, for the common good, they'll be obligated to purge the nation of whoever opposes them… by whatever means necessary."

Chapter 39: Terminator Technology

Election: 69 days

Late the next morning Chad finished reading the White House report. He was convinced a government-led takeover of Amber Grains was exactly what Gordon had in mind. Gordon and his friends would find a way to make money on the deal, they always did, but the stakes were much higher.

The shadowy one world government, always the boogeyman of conspiracy kooks, was now in play, for real. An actual strategy existed, brilliantly devised and patiently implemented by many willing and powerful participants. Men and women driven by the will to power to accomplish what the Caesars of history had only dreamed, to bring all peoples of the world under one global rule.

Chad found it hard to believe that Blake Merrill, President of Amber Grains, was one of them. Nonetheless, he placed a call to set up an appointment to meet with Merrill.

****

Two days later, Chad and Philip entered the headquarters of Amber Grains in Omaha, Nebraska. Merrill had agreed to the meeting, but asked Chad if he could bring Philip. He wanted to meet the man behind the controversial algae initiative. Chad was glad to have Philip along for support, and Philip looked forward to spending time with the legendary scientist.

Chad and Philip were escorted into Merrill's office. The décor was modest by corporate standards, but appropriately furnished. Family photos occupied the corners of his desk, and a few pictures, magazine covers, and mementos of Amber Grains' history were on display without fanfare.

There was also a collection of black and white photos of a young Blake Merrill working with indigenous peoples from Latin America and Africa. Some evoked a strong, emotional appeal, while others celebrated humanitarian relief efforts.

The photographs covered both sides of a sitting area with windows straight ahead, providing a vista to hundreds of acres of Amber Grains' test plots. An assistant motioned for Chad and Philip to have seats on matching dark green leather chairs that were arranged on a West African tribal rug. But before they could be seated, Blake Merrill entered the office through an interior door.

A handsome man in his late fifties, Merrill was of medium build with slightly graying hair, fit though not athletic, warm brown eyes and a pleasant smile that made him appear to always be relaxed. He was confident, yet unassuming, with a serious nature and polished manner that seemed more practiced than natural.

But it was Blake Merrill's reputation for being brilliant in both business and science that caused Philip to insist that Merrill had to know what the government intended to do regarding Amber's future, whether he was party to it or not.

Merrill greeted Chad, expressing concern for the kids and asking about his father. He then turned to Philip as Chad introduced them. Chad noticed that Merrill seemed to be weighing everything he'd heard about Philip against what he saw.

After sitting down, Merrill directed the conversation exactly as Chad had anticipated by asking about PD Tech's Algae Initiative. Chad expected that Merrill would be content talking about algae genomics for the rest of the day, which is why, fifteen minutes later, he jumped in, "Dr. Merrill, I'll be direct. We've come because of an extremely troubling White House report called, *"Controlling World Food Production through Genetic Engineering."*

Chad saw a hint of surprise in Merrill's expression.

Merrill asked, "You have the report?"

"Yes, we've both read it."

Merrill shifted in his chair. "Who gave it to you?" he asked casually.

"I don't know where it came from originally, but I believe you should be aware of what they plan to do."

"Who?"

"The current government... or at least some elements."

"You believe this information should be important to me?"

Philip broke in, "I believe you already know, and your silence betrays a tacit approval."

Chad was dismayed, unsure of how to soften Philip's approach. He hoped for the best.

A wide smile captured Merrill's expression, as if he couldn't help himself. "Now I meet the real Philip Doyle. What I've heard is true: bold, direct, and intuitively intelligent."

Philip replied, "Although some answers are not black or white, that's no reason to make everything gray."

Chad quickly brought the discussion back on track, "Do you know about this report?"

Merrill was studying Philip. "Yes, I know about it."

"Have you read it?"

After a long pause, "Yes."

"What do you think?"

"About what?"

"They're planning to take over your company."

Merrill again focused on Philip, "Who's going to stop them?"

"Why don't you try?" asked Philip.

"Why would I?" Merrill spoke to Philip as though issuing a challenge.

"Your answers are bullshit and you know it," said Philip. "You profess to love them," Philip paused and looked at the pictures on the wall. "But it's not love... you feel sorry for them. *You* are the center of every picture, cloaked in patronizing superiority. You don't help them stand on their own because you don't believe they can. Instead you create dependencies in these people that destroy their dignity and freedom."

Merrill was stunned. Enough had struck a cord to restrain his response, "You're ignoring what's at stake."

Philip continued, "I couldn't understand why you'd allow a takeover until I saw these pictures. You don't object because the government will accomplish what you lack the resources to do. They'll feed the world. Even though it won't be you directly, you'll know your work made it possible."

Merrill tried not to be defensive, "What's wrong with ending hunger?"

"But you won't. They'll still be hungry for the dignity that comes from feeding yourself. Instead of helping them, you're giving their would-be masters the means to enslave them."

"Enslave them?"

"I'm aware of the new terminator seeds."

Merrill stood up, his face showing deep concern as he slowly studied the photographs on the wall. Then he spoke quietly, almost as a supplication, "But I do love them."

"Then set them free."

Merrill glanced at Philip with a curious expression. "I don't know how."

"You need to figure it out." Philip stood to signal he was finished. "Offer them a hand. And one by one they'll provide for themselves and regain their pride. Then they'll no longer be hungry, and they won't need you to feed them."

Philip turned and walked out of the office. Merrill didn't acknowledge Philip's exit. His attention remained fixed on the photos. Chad followed Philip out the door.

Chad caught up with Philip in the lobby. "Make sure I don't invite you to my next meeting with my father."

"Did you think I was a little rough on Merrill?"

"No, not at all… I mean, you could have shattered his knee caps with a ball bat."

Philip smiled but defended his course of action. "Merrill needed to hear those things. He lives in a bubble of his own creation, and either the people around him don't see it or they're not willing to confront him."

"Probably both. By the way, who'd call something a "terminator" seed?"

"You don't want to know."

"Things can't be any worse, can they?"

They climbed into the rental car and headed back to the airport. Philip explained, "Amber has a patent on what's called "terminator technology." The seed's embryo self-destructs, making it sterile. It prevents farmers from using seeds from previous harvests. And it can also be used to infest and destroy native crops. There's no evidence Amber has done this, but it's always a threat. Especially if it's used for the goals laid out in the Clark report."

"I'm sorry I asked," said Chad. "I've got to find out what's going on."

Chapter 40: *A Wall of Sound*

The morning after his trip to Amber Grains, Chad called Macy.

"Hi, Chad. How did it go with Merrill?"

"Very interesting, I'll give you the details later. Is there any chance of talking to Darius Cain about the Clark Report."

"When?"

"I'll be in D.C. tomorrow."

"I'll give him a call."

"Can you be there?"

"Wouldn't miss it."

****

Election: 63 days

Chad and Macy entered the Longworth House Office Building for their 2:00 p.m. appointment with Darius Cain. They made their way to a small conference room on the second floor. The neutral site was chosen to avoid questions.

Darius was waiting for them when they arrived. He was about forty, short and slightly overweight. His skin tone and posture revealed he spent too much time at a desk, in florescent lighting. But when he started talking, it was easy to see why he'd risen to prominence within White House circles. He was engaging, intensely focused, and possessed a hyperactive temperament that controlled conversations.

He directed a question at Macy the moment they settled around the conference table. "Did you say you've read the proposal written by Andrea Clark?"

"Yes," she looked inclusively at Chad, "We both have read the report." She noticed he called it a 'proposal.'

"What did you think?" Darius asked with a disarming, Cheshire grin.

Macy countered his boyish ploy with a stern rebuke, "You know what we think and why."

Darius seemed to enjoy sparring with the pretty blonde from rural North Carolina. "If you know what we're doing, and I already know your reaction, then why are we here?"

"It's not my desire to inflate your ego," said Macy. "But why does the President have you heading up a project that will be dead-on-arrival in Congress?"

"What about the next Congress?"

"That one either," she quickly responded, "Unless you achieve a supermajority in both the House and the Senate. And you and I know that's not going to happen this November."

"Then you have nothing to worry about."

"Darius, do you really think you can starve the world into submitting to a global government?"

He answered with a disarming grin, "Macy, you sound conspiratorial."

Chad reinforced Macy's position, "We intend to prevent it from happening."

"Prevent what?" he asked with a curious chuckle.

Chad asserted, "We'll make the Clark report public."

"Do the American people really care about Washington squabbles over GMOs?"

"Some will."

Darius dismissed the report's importance, "The paper's an unsolicited proposal by a low level administrator. Andrea Clark will either resign or be fired. Then she'll have to suffer by making more money at a private foundation, probably doing the same work."

Chad offered, "We'll also put the agriculture industry on guard."

"On guard against whom? As long as they keep getting their farm subsidies, few will object."

Darius paused, looking out towards the Washington Mall. Then he spoke to Macy through a self-satisfied grin. "Besides, you're too late. No one will listen because they won't be able to hear. We're about to put into operation a billion dollar wall of sound. From now until the election America will experience one continuous noise, composed of sound bites, wrapped in images, and music, and emotion... coming through every media channel. We'll construct people's sentences for them. Our thoughts will be in their heads, continuously."

Darius stopped, as though finished, but then seemed to remember something. "I almost forgot. Next week Buzz Nelson launches his 'Starving for Profits Tour.' It's brilliant. He has teams of progressive religious leaders and musicians conducting free concerts at all the major universities before the election. They'll teach an entire generation how we're going to end hunger through biotech agriculture guided by a compassionate world government. If you'd like, I'll send you a copy of the *Starving for Profits* documentary that will be available to every high school and college teacher in the country."

****

In Mexico City, Daniel reviewed the evening news for September 7 on a favorite website:

"Today, standing on the steps of the Capitol Building, Chad Connelly, Macy Southerland, and eight other Congressional Representatives made public a White House report entitled, *Controlling World Food Production through Genetic Engineering.* Conservative news sites and talk radio provided coverage, but the mainstream media ignored the report.

"The White House denied any knowledge of the proposal's contents. Andrea Clark, the administrator for a program called, Worldwide Food Security, announced her resignation. Clark took full responsibility for the policy suggestions outlined in her paper. She stated that she was disappointed to leave the President's staff, but was looking forward to her new position in the Washington, D.C. offices of Boston-based, Solutions for Humanity."

Chapter 41: Hero of My Own Life

Daniel knew when he answered the phone that the conversation would be frustrating.

"Hi, Katherine."

"Did you have a chance to talk with Philip?"

"No, but I'll be with him tomorrow."

"Daniel, you have to talk to him. I think about him all the time and I'm driving mom crazy. First the kidnapping, then his discussions with you about Ben-Hur. Now the memories. I've got to see him. There has to be a resolution."

"I'll talk to him."

"Please. I need to know what to do."

"Katherine… I promise."

****

After a tour of the genomics lab, algae test ponds, and the new ARD facility, Philip and Daniel ended their journey with iced tea on the front porch of the Doyle family home. The ranch, located about an hour's drive from Austin, was where Philip grew up and his parents still lived. The rambling stone and timber ranch house sat on a knoll overlooking a meandering creek running through prairie and grazing cattle. Although he'd built his own house on the outskirts of Austin, the ranch was still home.

Philip felt no regrets avoiding the office as they enjoyed the view and the late morning breeze. More importantly, he wished to share with Daniel the issues pressing on his mind.

Philip was momentarily silent, recalling a memory. When he was ready he shared, "My favorite opening line to any novel is from *David Copperfield*. It reads: '*I am born. Whether I shall turn out to be the hero of my own life, or whether that station will be held by anybody else, these pages must show.*' I was in high school when I first read that thought by Charles Dickens. I still recall looking out into the blank space of the distant future and making a vow that I'd be the hero of my own life.

"Daniel, I've made a decision to rescind my vow. Things are different now: the assault on my heart I assumed to be caused by memories of Katherine, the dream on the plane, the strange experience walking the streets of Jerusalem. Then there was *Ben-Hur*. It's as if I was put in that cell just long enough to read it. The book provided a way for me to receive the message. And I have you to thank for helping me to understand.

"The night of my rescue we talked about faith and you asked me what I thought. I couldn't answer. But a miracle did take place that night. Through what happened to Marcos during the turmoil of our escape, I witnessed love as something real, as though love were a tangible presence. Something inside me changed. Love broke through and it pierced my heart.

"I discovered faith, like a gift, enabling me to receive and understand a revelation made directly to my soul. Then I knew what to believe concerning Christ, and why to believe it. I realized I was a rebel and a prodigal son, and he had ransomed me, to bring me home.

"Yet, for a time, my will resisted surrender. But a change had occurred that I'm now prepared to embrace. As an act of my will, by the mystery and grace of God, I've decided to relinquish my role as hero and submit that station to someone else, the new hero of my life, Jesus Christ."

Daniel wanted to jump and shout, but wasn't sure Philip could handle it, so he settled for a smile.

Philip asked, "Will you baptize me in the lake this Sunday afternoon?"

"Yes, I've looked forward to this for a long time."

"I'm going to invite a few friends to the house to witness my commitment."

"What about Katherine?"

"I can't tell her yet."

"Oh no, Philip," Daniel responded in disbelief. "You have to."

"I don't want to disappoint her. I have a lot to learn."

"Do you love her?"

"I don't deserve her after what I've put her through."

"Philip, you never deserved Katherine and you never will. You can only graciously accept what she wants to give you."

"I'll talk to her when I'm ready."

"I don't think you should wait." Daniel's comment was greeted with silence. He didn't want to cast a dark cloud over the baptism so he concluded, "I'll be at your house by 4:00. Some of us have been looking forward to this for a long time."

On his way back to Austin, Daniel called Katherine, "I talked to Philip."
"And?"
"He wants to be baptized Sunday in the lake by his home."
"Oh, Daniel..." Her voice carried a sudden relief.

"He said he didn't want you to know."

"Why not?"

"Katherine, I'm not sure what he's thinking. He said something about not deserving you, and of course I told him he never deserved you." After a brief pause he asked, "What are you going to do?"

"I don't know."

Katherine sat on the bedroom floor, leaning against the wall. She remained still until ten years of sadness lifted and tears of joy floated to the surface.

Chapter 42: Wilder Conference

Chad called Macy to discuss the upcoming election. "I've noticed something that troubles me, and I can't tell whether it's just my campaign or something beyond my district."

"What is it?"

"I'll call it apathy, but it's not the lazy, I-don't-care kind. It's more like it doesn't matter who wins, and I'm not talking about the typically uncommitted."

"Then who's the problem?"

"Our polling shows it's mostly with evangelicals. Past supporters still say they'll vote for me, but there's no sense of urgency. It's not the majority, but certainly enough to raise concerns. As I said before, they act like the election's not important. Is this occurring anywhere else?"

Macy answered, "The committee has no polling data to confirm your experience."

"Well, I have a hunch. When are you coming for Philip's baptism?"

"I'll be in Austin Saturday morning."

"Allen Wilder has a conference here on Saturday night."

Macy shared, "It's interesting you mention him. He was just in Charlotte. A friend who attended told me that Wilder effectively convinced twelve thousand people that America was lost, war was coming to Jerusalem, and we should turn our eyes towards the heavens."

Chad concluded, "I think we need to see for ourselves."

****

<u>Election: 38 days</u>

The Austin Prophecy Conference began with a band playing contemporary worship music. The crowd rose to their feet, clapping and singing in joyful celebration. The worship leaders fed off the energy, creating a continuous feedback loop. Daniel and Macy reached the rear of the stage and joined Chad and Rob Martinson peering out from behind the back curtain wall.

"This is incredible!" shouted Rob above the music. "Over ten thousand people are here!"

Daniel, along with Chad and Macy, took their seats in the VIP section cordoned off along the front. The overpowering noise ceased when Rob came out to introduce Wilder. His brief introduction ended with, "Brothers and sisters – the man of the hour – Dr. Allen Wilder."

The mention of Wilder triggered an explosion of sound as ten thousand admirers rose to their feet. The thunderous applause washed over the stage, enveloping Wilder in a massive swell of affection sent forward as respect and admiration.

Wilder stood patiently until the roar subsided. But the assembly remained standing, for everyone knew what was coming. Wilder stepped towards the front of the stage and declared, "We live in exciting times!"

A second roar exploded from the crowd. With his life's work affirmed, Wilder stepped back, confident and smiling. He soon raised his hand to signal he was ready to begin:

"The evil of this world is coming to an end. There will be dark days, but they will be few. God's glorious kingdom is approaching. I can see its light on the horizon, just as day follows night, the kingdom is coming – first the rapture, then seven long years for those left behind, and finally the glorious appearing of our Lord and King.

"Stand firm and don't be shaken. You know what's coming. Don't fret over your daily struggles. Don't be troubled by elections or the fall of nations. The world is entering the throes of judgment and will have to go through darkness to reach the light. Take heart, for things will get worse before they get better. But know that everything has its purpose.

"The war for Jerusalem, prophesied long ago, is a path we must travel. History's most evil dictator will lead a rebellious world into the throes of great tribulation, unlike anything ever experienced. But by the grace of God, we shall meet the Lord in the air. We shall be spared earth's judgment.

"And out of the ashes of a terrible destruction, a new kingdom on earth will be born when King Jesus appears to claim his throne on the Temple Mount in the Holy City of Jerusalem."

With this introduction, Wilder launched into a full-blown multimedia presentation viewed on large screens located throughout the auditorium. Raw news footage of violence in Jerusalem provided a backdrop to Wilder's mesmerizing story of Ezekiel's imminent war of Gog and Magog. Wilder predicted an alliance of Russia with Iran and the Muslim nations against Israel and God. He lamented America's forsaking of the Abrahamic blessing for abandoning Israel. And then he passionately described God's miraculous deliverance of the isolated Jewish nation.

From war to a short peace, a story was spun of the world coming under the rule of the Antichrist. Computer animation projected a walk through the anticipated new temple on the Temple Mount.

Daniel found Wilder to be an enthusiastic advocate for the faith, and very persuasive. He didn't doubt his sincerity, but he did question Wilder's tendency to draw concrete conclusions from vague scriptural constructs. Daniel also questioned Wilder's use of current events to interpret scripture. But more than anything else, Daniel felt that Wilder disregarded one of the great themes of Scripture – Jesus will come back for a victorious Church.

Daniel noticed that the audience appeared to embrace every word, but this was understandable. The crowd wanted to believe what Wilder was saying because his story made sense of the world. Finally, after two thousand years of silence, God was going to deal directly with evil and set the world right. There'd be no more talk about when and how. To the applauding crowd, the future was now and deliverance was on the way.

At the close of the presentation Chad started for the back stage and motioned for Daniel and Macy to follow him. "Come with me. Wilder has agreed to meet with us. And by the way, Rob found out that Gordon has been funding the ministry for almost two years and is responsible for the media coverage from WBC."

Rob led them into a small room where Wilder was seated with his wife and several staff people. After brief introductions Wilder's people left and Chad laid out their concerns, including the implications of funding by Gordon.

Wilder dismissed any problem with Gordon's involvement. "Your father has never tried to influence my work. In fact, I've never talked to him personally. Maybe you don't know him as well as you think?"

As Chad and Macy explained their concerns about voter attitudes, Wilder appeared unmoved and skeptical of the conclusions they were drawing from circumstantial observations.

Chad came to the point. "Even evangelicals' commitment to vote is now suspect. They say things like, "the time is short" and "politics are divisive and inhibit the sharing of the gospel.""

Wilder offered, "I only interpret prophecy. I'm not concerned with governments."

Chad countered, "Are you sure you're right?"

"Watch the news. Then ask yourself if I'm wrong."

Daniel asked, "But what if it becomes a self-fulfilling prophecy?"

Wilder paused before answering, "No man causes what God ordains."

Daniel concluded his thought, "But what if it's not ordained for this time?"

Daniel, Chad and Macy walked along the Lady Bird Lake Trail on their way back to the hotel. Macy broke the silence, "Our political strategists need to be aware of a new potential category of nonvoter, a possible Wilder factor."

They paused to enjoy the view of the city's lights reflecting off the water, Chad asked, "I wonder how much influence Wilder actually has?"

Daniel answered, "Books, primetime television, news, packed conferences. Many are listening."

"I'm afraid so," agreed Macy.

Daniel and Macy settled near the hotel pool's gentle waterfall. The dim landscape lighting with melodic music flowing through the open patio was more in line with what Daniel had hoped for their evening together.

Although he'd not intended to discuss his past, Daniel soon found himself sharing stories of his life with Maria.

"She died six years ago. At the time of her death, in my greatest need, the Lord healed me with his presence. He calmed the storm and gave me the peace to know that all things are as they should be."

Macy wanted to know. Her warmth encouraged him to continue.

"I know what Chad's going through. It's an ever-present, soul-deadening sorrow. It's like standing in sorrow's shadow, the continuous dull ache of something missing, something incomplete, something that was to always be, suddenly gone forever." Daniel gazed without particular focus towards the sound and motion of water striking the pool's surface. "Often Chad will embrace the memories, and then, at other times, he'll desire relief."

She spoke softly, "I wish I had the right words... I'm sorry."

They remained silent, living a moment in time. Enjoying Macy's presence, he possessed no desire to move. But tomorrow's challenges required a decent night's sleep so he escorted her towards the hotel lobby.

At the entrance Macy hesitated, still holding the moment. He basked in the luminous glow that lit her face and touched his heart. In a motion as natural as the breath he breathed, he stepped forward and lightly kissed her cheek. She smiled, said "good night," and left for her room.

Watching her walk away, he realized that some things in life shine so brightly the world's problems fade to light.

Chapter 43: Love Thy Neighbor

Election: 37 days

Philip had purchased thirty wooded acres on the lake's east side, allowing the sunset to be viewed from his back patio. He chose the roughest terrain available, he explained to his architect, in order to hide a six thousand square foot home, stables and a cedar carriage house within the natural environment. For the exterior, he selected light gray stone with banks of windows and a clay tile roof. The landscaping was a mixture of woods with meandering paths, horse paddocks, and glades filled with wildflowers.

The interior continued the same preference for natural materials. The floors were earth-toned marble and hardwoods. The ceiling heights varied for effect. Three guest cottages were in frequent use. The living area, with its stone fireplace focal point, dining room, and adjoining den, allowed for more than a hundred guests.

Philip moved next to the fireplace beside a large easel with a covered board. "May I have everyone's attention please," he stated loudly enough to be heard above the dozens of conversations. "I have a few words to share."

Philip was ready to explain his purpose for the gathering. "I'm sharing with you this afternoon as a scientist, businessman, and friend. We have a lot in common. We've worked together in the past, and many of you are involved in our latest project. But today I also come to you as a changed person. I am now a follower of Jesus Christ, and as a new Christian, I've asked the question, 'What is the meaning of my work?'

"God has gifted each person with unique abilities. As scientists and business people, I believe we are to use God's gifts of creative imagination and reason, gifts bestowed on a people made in his image, to transform scarcity into abundance, and to meet the material needs of the world. From abundance the hungry will be fed, the weak cared for, and the homeless provided shelter.

"Could this provision happen once again as manna falling from Heaven? It could, but God has allowed us the privilege of participation, that through our productive work we can help fulfill his great command to *love our neighbor as ourselves.* As a result, our work escapes the curse and becomes a "calling" that draws us closer to the kingdom he is preparing for us on earth as it is in heaven."

Philip removed the drape from the easel, unveiling the official new name of their algae project: Stone Mountain Initiative. The logo was a drawing of a large rock jutting out into space. It was a sketch of Daniel and Katherine's

Stone Mountain.

Philip finished his remarks over the rising chatter. "This afternoon I'm going to be baptized. I'm asking you to witness my statement of faith and to hold me accountable to the Lord. I'm aware some of you are surprised by my decision." Philip smiled. "And for those who don't understand, I'm asking you to share my personal joy.

"Would everyone please move down to the lake, and thank you for coming…"

Chapter 44: *Born of a Struggle*

Katherine reminded herself to breathe. The tightening in her stomach signaled she was close. She'd not seen Philip for ten years, and yet he did not seem a stranger. He was ever-present in her thoughts, and she had the articles to read. Philip's success provided an unending stream of news reports, magazine articles and pictures that had been faithfully collected and forwarded to Mexico City by her mother.

Saving them all, she reread many until memorized. A favorite was from a tech publication that had placed Philip on their list of America's most eligible bachelors. The article was fun, sharing information from Philip's private life. She loved a comment by Brenda Hanover, comparing time with Philip to "traveling with your older brother." And Katherine's most prized quote from Brenda, "Philip Doyle is the most married man I know."

Did Philip want to be with her? She had severed their relationship, and she was certain she needed to take the first step.

She pulled through the gated entrance where Daniel had left her name and proceeded to Philip's home. Although she'd never seen the house, she knew every detail that had ever been published.

Two security guards met her in the driveway. When she said her name, they both smiled. The older man commented, "Your brother mentioned you might be coming. We're glad you made it."

She thanked them and started up the stone path to the front entrance. Her stomach churned and her hands began to shake.

What was Philip thinking? Did his future include her? Was her absence from his life the same 'something missing' that haunted her?

Daniel stepped into the lake. Maintaining his footing on the rocks, his thoughts turned to Mexico City, from Marcos bringing the key down the stairs, to the expression on Philip's face after the explosion. These events seemed a lifetime ago, and for his friend standing before him, they were a different life.

Katherine paused at the oversized front door. Colored glass of earth tones, with a dark green vine and leaves woven throughout a geometric pattern, glistened as light passed through.

Taking a deep breath, she firmly grasped the brass handle. The door opened easily, inviting her to enter. She squinted into brilliant sunlight flooding the long, broad hallway leading to a wall of windows overlooking the lake. The marble floor shimmered with dazzling explosions of light playfully skipping across the glassy surface. Turning to close the door, cut glass caught beams of white, refracting them back as prisms of color.

From the foyer's center she looked upwards to exposed beams and skylights and down to a plush circular rug of deep burgundy, beige, and blues that cushioned her feet. She turned to the right, towards the living area, and entered the space slowly. She didn't hesitate. She was oddly comfortable breathing the air. Every detail was of interest: the richness of hardwood floors, custom woven rugs with western motifs, and hand-finished wood furniture, holding cushions of soft leather and natural fabrics. She loved the colors – deep, rich blues and vibrant greens resting on backgrounds of beige and tans, with highlights of English burgundy and sunflower yellow.

Her vision drifted towards the warm, gray stone fireplace, and what she saw caused her to gasp, the room disappeared. The house no longer mattered. Katherine approached a large board, resting on a wooden easel. The words across the top read *Stone Mountain Initiative*.

She focused on the new logo. Reaching out, she touched the figure of a boy standing on the front edge of Stone Mountain, his sword drawn, facing the distant horizon.

Slowly her fingers moved across the drawing until coming to rest where the huge stone jutted out from the surrounding rocks. There, sitting along the side, was a barely visible little girl. The setting was just as she'd described to Philip, the day she and Daniel had visited Stone Mountain after church.

She was ready to find him, for she now knew all she needed to know. But her decision to leave was interrupted by three large oil paintings hung symmetrically on the opposite wall. She recognized the style as Philip's, although his skill had much improved since college.

Each painting featured a mature young man, working, actually, defined by his work. One, a cowboy, relaxed on his horse, watching over a cattle drive. Another portrayed a young farmer walking behind a team of horses, plowing his field. And third was a railroad conductor standing on the back of a red caboose.

The paintings captured a Texas landscape – rugged and barren, yet majestic and beautiful – with each man pausing from his work to gaze towards the sun setting into a breath-taking sky, bathed in color. Katherine studied their faces. Although the three young men were strong and self-assured, gone was the youthful expectation of conquest and adventure. Vigor and confidence had been replaced by a weathered, steel-hard resolve, and a grit born of daily trials and the determination to overcome.

The three young men were searching the horizon – eyes lonely and yearning, mouths closed tightly, faces open to the sky, seeking an answer from beyond – wondering if something were missing, or had been forgotten. Another world? A person? A feeling? A reason to be and to do… what?

For all his success and competence and self-sufficiency, Philip's art laid bare an empty longing and questions of why.

Katherine swallowed hard. She wanted to cry, to hold him and love all the sadness away.

She quickly stepped into the bright marble hallway and then out the back through a wall of sparkling sunlight. She stopped when she saw Philip and Daniel standing in the lake. Daniel was speaking to the guests gathered at the water's edge.

Katherine hesitated, watching. She ached to see Philip, but was it okay? The answer overwhelmed her doubts, sparking a joyous smile. She no longer needed to resist. Her long wait was over.

Standing in waist deep water Daniel asked his friend, "Philip, do you accept Jesus Christ as your Lord and Savior?"

"Yes I do," answered Philip.

"I baptize you in the name of the Father, and the Son, and the Holy Spirit."

As Daniel lifted Philip out of the water, he noticed Katherine quietly standing in the back with the sun highlighting her smile and sparkling tears. He glanced over to see his friend's shocked expression. Philip remained motionless, staring. The door he'd once tried to close had opened wide – a ghost, a deserter, an empty ache in his chest stood at the threshold.

It was as though time stopped and angels paused. Clouds hung motionless as the lake breeze held its breath.

Philip's confusion quickly melted into a grateful, open, tearful smile. He saw his heart, brought back to him by the one who'd treasured it and kept it alive. He saw her face, ever more beautiful, with faint traces of a decade of laughter and kindness and giving.

He now knew what he'd been missing: mystery and joy and love and life. He knew why efforts to purge her memory had failed, and now his future stood before him. Once, during a dream, he'd been unable to move, but whatever had restrained him was gone. He started towards the shore and opened his arms.

Katherine ran to the water's edge and without hesitation took a full stride into the lake. She was later to say she slipped, although from her brother's vantage point it appeared she never intended to stop. Regardless, her momentum carried her into Philip, knocking him backwards off his feet as they both went tumbling into the water.

Daniel glanced at Macy and smiled, her face beaming with delight. Then he turned to the shocked and cheering onlookers and celebrated, "That's another way to be baptized."

When they surfaced to a delighted ovation, Philip was holding Katherine with her arms wrapped around his neck. He whispered something to her. She relaxed her grip and studied his face. She smiled, responded softly and kissed his cheek.

Philip spoke directly to him Daniel, "We want you to marry us."

"I'd love to perform the wedding."

"We'd like you to do it now."

"Now? Don't you want a wedding?"

"We sure do. Right here. We don't want to wait any longer."

Daniel turned to Katherine for help. Her face glowed with expectation.

"But, Katherine…"

"Daniel, we don't want to be separated another day. We want to be bound together, now, for as long as we live."

The answer from Katherine brought a cheer from the shore, accompanied by a chorus of "Do it. Tie the knot. Marry them!"

Daniel laughed as he surveyed the setting. "An eager bride and groom, good friends, and a beautiful afternoon *in* the lake. I'd say it's the perfect day for a wedding."

Again the cheering of friends spurred them on.

"And please hurry, Daniel, the water's cold," begged Katherine with a kid-sister smile.

"Right. Okay. First we need a wedding party," said Daniel. "Chad, Brenda, Charles…" The list grew as friends jumped into the lake to join them.

"Great. Here we go. Dear friends," Daniel began, talking through his boyish grin, "we were first gathered by the water's edge to witness the end of Philip's old life and the birth of a new life. Just as God brought the Israelites through the Red Sea as a sign of new birth and through the Jordan

River into the promised land, baptism is a sign of salvation, a crossing to safety and into abundant life."

His introduction was greeted with a few shivers, "You go, Daniel," "Tell them brother," and a host of "amens" amidst restrained enthusiasm. Daniel proceeded with haste, realizing their ceremony was about to erupt into an impromptu celebration.

Standing next to Katherine and Philip, he spoke to their friends, "We're also about to witness another birth made possible by this work of redemption, two people joining to become one, with the one together greater than the two apart.

"As Katherine's co-worker in Mexico, I can tell you that while serving the poor, she prayed for Philip with unwavering persistence, teaching me the meaning of steadfast love and hope. For this giving spirit, Philip and I are thankful.

"And from what I've heard, Philip has also been faithful to this love." His friends smiled, recalling memories of Philip's stubborn dedication. "He imagines that he's concealed his love for Katherine, but we've heard how he reads her letters at the diner. We know about the track, and why he wished to build a new one." Smiles became laughter.

Friends broke into "Amazing Grace," which gained momentum and they ended with the singing of a variation on "Philip, row the boat ashore, hallelujah" and the next verse began, "Katherine, help to trim the sail…"

Soon after, Daniel concluded with, "I now pronounce you husband and wife. You may kiss the bride." Neither a splash nor laughter could be heard in that gentle and sacred moment. Daniel then turned to their friends, standing along the shoreline. "It's now my great pleasure to present to you, Mr. and Mrs. Philip and Katherine Doyle."

Chapter 45: Celebration

Philip relaxed into an upholstered chair and watched Katherine emerge from the bedroom dressing area, showered, wearing his clothes as hers dried – running shorts that came to the top of her knees and a short sleeve shirt that looked more like a sundress. He smiled at the sight, wondering how so much happiness could originate from the presence of another person.

He found his love to be more than attraction, more than the passion to hold and possess. His thoughts brought forth a picture of their two hearts 'knit together.' To lose their love would have required the two hearts be torn apart. Only he and Katherine, not circumstances or the passage of time, could have performed the tearing. Their love, having endured a ten-year separation, was now given flight.

Katherine settled on the floor. She leaned forward, her forehead lightly resting on his leg. The quiet stillness encouraged her reflection, giving rise to the melancholy of a long separation. She looked up, her eyes searching. A shade of sadness touched her face as the shadow of a lone cloud on a summer's day.

"Philip, what did we lose?"

He shared a gentle smile. She closed her eyes when he lightly touched her hair. Her memory released a vivid intimacy. Her love was once again fully awake. The peace she now sought was his. How could he not harbor resentment against so much being lost?

"That might not be the right question," he spoke softly. "I've come to see that the present is more likely a preparation for our future than a consequence of our past."

Katherine gave him an inquisitive glance, "That's an interesting thought, but hard to grasp."

"Let me show you something."

He disappeared into the closet and quickly returned. "Do you remember this?" He handed her a drawing she instantly recognized. Framed, behind glass, was a ten-year old placemat with a sketch of the front elevation of the house and a floor plan for the living area. Along the bottom was printed 'Glen's Diner,' and in the right-hand corner were two signatures: *Philip Doyle* and *Katherine Stone*.

"I do remember," said Katherine, amazed that Philip had built the home as they'd planned it ten years before.

"I tried to throw it away, but couldn't." He leaned down until his face touched her hair. "Let's talk about the past some other time. Tonight we celebrate the present and the future." He held her hand and whispered, "And thanks for coming to my baptism." Then he kissed her.

The setting sun cast a golden glow across the sprawling back patio. Music enlivened the party. Chad, Daniel and Macy were watching the sunset when Philip joined them.

Philip asked Chad, "Where do you go from here?"

"In D.C. for a few days, then the campaign trail. With only thirty-seven days left, my race is closer than ever. It feels like slogging uphill."

Macy explained, "Chad thinks Allen Wilder's criticism of politics is affecting his race."

"In what way?"

Chad said with frustration, "Wilder separates our spiritual life from earthly concerns, like voting."

Philip looked at Macy, "Is anyone else having this problem?"

"It's hard to measure."

"Why?"

Macy answered with an ironic grin, "People won't admit they're not going to vote because they're expecting to be lifted out of this world any day now."

Philip said, "I'll have Charles Lee talk to the polling people tomorrow to see if he can help them figure it out. Right now I'm going to dance with Mrs. Doyle.

Philip's announcement was greeted with cheers and applause as he left in search of Katherine.

Chad turned to Daniel, "I talked to Charles Lee this afternoon. He's concerned we don't have enough time. But with everyone's full support he thinks we might learn something before the election."

"Then he'll try?"

Chad said, "Yeah. He and Brenda checked out Buzz Nelson's 'Starving for Profits Tour' Friday night over on the Texas campus. Charles said it left him speechless. He expected to hear about wealth re-distribution, government control of food production, and progressive politics. But the event was more like a "religious revival," with Jesus presented as a social activist.

"Brenda made the point that Buzz Nelson has integrated collective salvation, socialism, and emotional moralizing into a kind of socio/political religion that exploits Christian language and scripture to add credibility to his "unity consciousness" movement."

Six-year-old Ruthie interrupted her dad. "Will you dance with me?"

Chad smiled down at her bright face. "Sure, sweetie, I'd love to."

Daniel suddenly felt the rise of profound grief as he watched Chad and his daughter walk hand-in-hand to the center of the patio. He thought he was going to cry.

Macy had been watching. She came up beside him and took his arm. She looked up at him, her eyes also moist with tears. She offered, "Will you dance with me?"

"I'd love to."

Daniel and Macy joined Philip and Katherine, Chad and his little girl, and their many friends celebrating on the patio.

Chapter 46: Solutions for Humanity

Two days after Philip and Katherine's wedding, Daniel received a call from Macy that was unusual only because he normally called her.

He answered smiling, "Hi, did you miss me already?"

"Of course, but that's not the only reason I called. I need you to come to Washington."

"Wonderful. As much as I tried, I couldn't come up with a responsible reason to fly to Washington."

"Do you need a responsible reason?"

"Having been a missionary for ten years, it's hard to justify the extravagance of flying halfway across the country for a dinner date."

"Are you saying I'm not worth it?"

Daniel laughed and attempted to recover, "Did I say extravagant?"

"Yes, you certainly did."

"I meant to say that until I met you, the flight would have seemed extravagant."

"Nice try, but you're in luck. You're needed here."

"What's my excuse?"

"I was contacted by someone whose former brother-in-law works for Buzz Nelson."

"Why you?"

"Mutual friends."

"When?"

"On Thursday afternoon."

"Sure, I'll come to your office."

****

Daniel entered Macy's office in the Cannon House Office Building. Chad was already there, along with a young woman in her late twenties.

Macy greeted him, "Hi, Daniel. This is Stephanie Willis from North Carolina. Her former brother-in-law, named Greg, is a lawyer who works for Buzz Nelson at a Boston policy institute called Solutions for Humanity. Greg and Stephanie's sister recently divorced because of fights over her becoming a Christian. That allowed for Stephanie to share with us today."

After the introduction Macy continued her conversation with Stephanie. "So Greg helped develop a future legislative program called *Tolerance for America*?"

"Yes. He claimed it would protect civil liberties, but it's actually designed to cripple the church."

"How will it do that?"

Stephanie started reading from her notes, "It starts by repealing all tax exemptions. Then many basic Christian moral doctrines will be declared hate speech. Public schools will be instructed to ask children to report their parents if hate speech doctrines are taught in the home.

"Also, it will make it illegal to fire anyone for lifestyle or anti-Christian beliefs – even if the person is a pastor or ministry leader. Parents will be encouraged to sue churches and Christian schools for any emotional distress caused to their children by what will be called, 'threats of hell and judgment.'

"*Tolerance for America* will even go so far as to label the very teaching of the gospel of salvation to minors as 'child abuse.'"

Macy was dismayed. "Don't they realize this will result in the shutting down of thousands of Christian charities that help millions of people every day?"

"That's actually their goal, even though they don't admit it publically. They believe that only the government should provide social services. Greg told my sister, "People don't want to be indebted to some churchman.""

Chad asked, "Do they really believe Christians will let this happen?"

Stephanie took a deep breath and tried to answer, "They have legislators ready to introduce it after the election. Greg called it a 'gold rush' because plaintiffs and their attorneys are practically guaranteed to make a lot of money. Instead of chasing ambulances, lawyers will soon be chasing Christian ministries."

After Stephanie left, Chad said, "This is the second time we've asked why these people would invest time and money on legislation that will never get through Congress."

Macy responded, "Unless they believe that something is going to give them the supermajority they'd need."

"I don't see it," said Chad.

Macy looked at Daniel, "What do you think?"

"I think they're serious about nullifying the Constitution, silencing Christians, and radically changing our way of life."

****

Daniel was in the Capitol Rotunda, standing before the painting of George Washington resigning as Commander-in-Chief of the Continental

Army. He reached back for a distant memory of the only other time he'd been in the Rotunda. He was just a boy, and it was his last vivid memory of his father before his death.

He recalled that as a twelve-year-old he had been standing in the very same spot. His father had come up behind him and said, "Daniel, this is the most important scene in the Rotunda. Do you know why?"

After a moment's hesitation, he responded, "I don't think it's the most important. I'd say it's third."

His father was pleasantly surprised, "Third? Okay, what are one and two?"

He glanced over her shoulder. "Number one, the baptism of Pocahontas."

"Why?"

"First you must have faith."

"And what's second?"

This time he pointed to the Pilgrims, praying before departing for the New World. "The Pilgrims, because next you must act on your faith."

He remembered looking up at his father, seeking approval. His father smiled and then he directed him back to Washington's resignation. "Now this painting of General Washington. What makes it so important?"

Daniel thought for a second and then answered, "He could have been the king or an emperor, like Caesar, but he refused."

"That's right. Millions have been blessed, and future generations will live in freedom, because two hundred years ago George Washington followed his conscience and turned away from such power. We must never forget the story we live in. Why do you think he did it?"

"Because after you have faith, and you put your faith into action…" Daniel said thoughtfully while turning full circle to take in the entire room. Coming to a stop, he looked up once again at General Washington and concluded, "Then you must do what is right."

Chad and Macy joined Daniel in front of the Washington painting. Suspended somewhere between a memory and a future hope, Daniel shared, "General Washington was issuing the world a challenge. Political messiahs are not the answer. He showed us that we must turn away from power as the means to achieve the good."

Daniel looked from Macy to Chad, and then back to the painting. "Now it's up to us. Will we rise to accept his challenge?"

Chapter 47: The C.U. Movement

Election: 32 days

Sitting at a window in D.C. Books and Café, Chad absent-mindedly observed people walking by as he waited for a phone call from California. His anxiety could have been attributed to any number of things. Not only were there his campaign, Amber Grains, and the reports coming out of Israel, but now *Tolerance for America* was thrown into the mix.

And if that weren't enough, he was having dinner at Berry Field's apartment on Saturday night. Although he had much to brood over, his thoughts often drifted to her. He was terribly unsettled, wondering if he should fight the attraction or surrender. But the debate raging in his head was pointless because he knew he was going. Whenever good judgment tried to intervene, his desire to see her rose up to snuff out any objection.

His phone rang. Max, the "Light in a Dark Corner," was calling from California.

"Hello, Max. What did you find out?"

"Your father's a busy man."

"My father needs a hobby. What are the details?"

"Let's start with Buzz Nelson's Solutions for Humanity. It receives money from the usual liberal foundations, but the largest donor, by far, is an obscure educational institute called the Consciousness Unity Movement. Their purported mission is to 'support the growth of collective consciousness through science, faith and public policy to advance social justice, economic equality and global community.'"

Chad asked, "What do they propose?"

"Well, not much of anything. Their home page says that unity is found through diversity, and there are the typical attacks against the Church as intolerant. Also, it seems they conceived of some program they call, *Tolerance for America*. But there aren't any details on their website. So it doesn't say much at all. My guess is it's now inactive and it's used as a front for laundering money to Solutions for Humanity."

Chad wondered, "Can you tell who's behind it?"

"C.U. has been connected to people from Cal Berkeley, but there's no history. In fact, everything about the past has been scrubbed clean. The oldest third party reference we could dig up was from about eight years ago. And you're going to love this, the article we found mentioning C.U. was written by Buzz Nelson."

"Where was it published?" asked Chad.

"In a now defunct leftist policy journal. Buzz referred to C.U. in an article he wrote about the evolution of liberation theology into a more mainline political philosophy. In the article Buzz mentions meeting the founder of C.U. who'd written a paper profoundly impacting his thinking.

"The C.U. writer convinced him that trying to achieve collective consciousness by stressing the superiority of one's logic or arguments was destined to fail. The most likely path to success would come through the creative use of language, by *redefining* what people already believed to be true or desirable in a way that fit one's agenda.

"According to Nelson, the C.U. writer made the point that humans willingly embrace abstract concepts of right or wrong, such as love, justice, honesty and tolerance, versus hate, injustice, theft and intolerance. But most people don't think in abstracts. They depend on society to define the terms, to give a concrete meaning to ideas. Therein lies the opportunity to subtly change behavior."

"Do you know who wrote the paper?" asked Chad.

"No, the article was called, *Unity through Diversity,* but Nelson never mentions who wrote it. And there's no record of it anywhere."

Chad pressed on, "What about the funding?"

Max continued, "Not only does C.U. provide funding to Solutions for Humanity, but it also funds several other groups that pass the money through to Solutions."

"And who funds C.U.?"

"Last year they received donations from five different entities that had a common thread... Gordon Connelly."

Chad greeted the revelation with silence. His fear had been confirmed. He couldn't tell if he was angry or disgusted, but he felt sick. After a moment he suggested, "I'm guessing Gordon also gives money to Buzz Nelson."

"That's right. As far as we can tell, Gordon first gave him a grant from his Global Outreach Foundation in order for Nelson to start the Language of Faith Seminars. They teach liberal, nonreligious politicians how to use Bible words to appeal to evangelicals."

"I've heard of it, but had no idea Gordon was involved."

"Gordon has funded numerous projects for Buzz Nelson since then."

"How does Nelson finance the Starving for Profits Tour?"

"It's sponsored by Solutions for Humanity, which means, once again, your father's footing the bill."

"Max, what do you think Gordon's after?"

"I've studied these global elitists for years, and there are any number of motives: power, greed, utopian visions. But the one thing they all have in common is arrogance. They believe they're smarter than everyone else, and it's their privileged duty, even destiny, to rule over the rest of us."

"Thanks, Max."

"Any time."

Chad considered his father's activities before leaving the café. Gordon had devised an ingenious strategy directed at two sides of the same demographic. He was using Wilder to convince conservative Christians to stay home and Buzz Nelson to energize discouraged, younger voters with an exciting new, "Christian" vision of an earthly paradise achieved through political unity.

His father never ceased to amaze him. Gordon wasn't trying to convince Christians their faith was wrong. Instead, he was subtly redefining what Christianity meant.

Chapter 48: Answering a Siren's Call

Chad knocked on the door and waited. A final desperate appeal to reason penetrated his thoughts. The appeal proved fleeting, for reason vanished the moment the door opened to a Berry Fields who'd never appeared more beautiful. She smiled and he chose to enter. Watching her move, his eyes followed the soft curls playfully teasing her bare neck and shoulders. A delicate, black silk dress rested peacefully against her skin, worn as casually as an afterthought. After taking his coat, she led him inside.

He heard himself compliment her stylish décor, though he noticed little while feeling everything. Candles and firelight illuminated warm colors, blending the deep tones of oriental rugs with elegant fabrics and cut flowers showcased in crystal. The only colors to strike his consciousness were shades of red, stirring his soul with unspoken promise.

"Would you like a drink?" she offered softly, her words floating upon the rhythmic jazz that filled the room.

He nodded yes, choosing not to allow his voice to disturb the mood.

"Scotch?"

He nodded again.

He continued his journey into another world, absorbing the ambiance as one would absorb another's spirit. The walls displayed original paintings, sensual abstractions that provided windows to his imagination.

Falling into the couch as an act of surrender, he raised the drink to his lips, inviting its warmth to ease the gnawing ache. These 'spirits' offered their blessing, to disarm any resistance, to overcome any objection. His immersion into her world promised to grant his soul its peace.

Taking another sip, he leaned back, closed his eyes and released himself to the music – soft and melodic – soothing the turmoil it covered. He was aware of what was happening, but the care had escaped him. He was lost. He knew that as fact, for he had untied himself from the mast and jumped into the sea in answer to a Siren's call. He only wished he'd never be found.

He felt Berry sit next to him, her hand resting on his shoulder. His eyes remained closed.

He felt compelled to say something, although he didn't want to hear the irritating distraction of his own voice. The silence was charged with desire. He opened his eyes to her amused smile. Her eyes, laughing, made him want her all the more, to feel her touch, to kiss her mouth and hold her against him.

Berry didn't wait for him to decide. She leaned close to his face, her lips slightly parted. He could feel her breath against his skin right before she kissed him, igniting a vivid desire.

When she leaned back, he noticed she was studying him. The amusement, ever present in her eyes, was absent.

He realized his dilemma. He wanted to forget dinner and hold her next to him for as long as it took for her to fill the hole in his soul. But she'd be thinking of the smoke alarm going off in the kitchen. Or if he asked her to turn off the oven, not only would the spell be broken, but he'd be rude for not appreciating the dinner she'd prepared.

He saw no recourse except to speak, "How was San Francisco?"

The amused grin returned to Berry's face. She seemed to understand the choice he'd made. He wondered if she has already decided to let the meal burn or had turned down the heat just in case. But the course was set.

Berry answered, "The Bay area was beautiful, and I enjoyed getting away for awhile."

"And the family?"

"Everyone's fine… I'm broiling salmon. Are you hungry?"

"Yes. Thanks."

"It'll take a couple of minutes to finish."

He watched her walk towards the kitchen. As she disappeared through the door he said, "I like the music."

Berry spoke from the kitchen, "I heard them at the jazz festival in Lausanne this summer. Could you check the fire?"

Chad stood, carrying his drink. He slowly made his way to the fire where he tossed in another log. Beside the fireplace was an open nook that provided enough room for a study with a desk and bookshelves. Chad stepped into the space. He felt that in a general way, he could tell what people considered to be important by the books on their shelves.

As he scanned the titles, he found what he'd expect from Berry, contemporary biographies, new age spirituality, and a collection of fiction and political books undoubtedly signed by the authors she'd met through Gordon.

Thinking of Gordon, he wondered… yes, there it was, Buzz Nelson's, *Starving for Profits*. Of course, it would be autographed. He smiled, pulling it off the shelf and opening the cover. Nelson had signed it to, *Berry Fields, Thanks for the inspiration that led to Tolerance for America, Love, Buzz.*

Inspiration for *Tolerance for America*… what the hell was that about? Chad reeled in his confusion until he saw another book by Nelson entitled, *Unity Consciousness*. He picked it up and opened the cover. This one also had a note.

To Strawberry Fields Forever, A guiding star in the unity movement. Your paper, 'Unity through Diversity,' and our subsequent conversations, provided the creative brilliance to make this book a reality. Forever grateful, Buzz.

Chad slowly sat on the arm of the chair, stunned. He heard Berry's voice from the kitchen, "Dinner's about ready. Could you open the wine?"

What was he doing? Who was she? He was falling for someone he didn't even know, and from what he'd just found out, she wasn't simply someone who disagreed. She was the guiding star, the creative brilliance and inspiration for what opposed him and his core beliefs.

Conflicting responses confused his ability to think clearly. If Lauren saw him now, it would break her heart... and what about Adam and Ruthie? The still, small voice was neither still nor quiet. Yet his feelings fought back, his desire to hold Berry demanded expression. He wasn't capable of a decision, except to know that he had to get away, to decide some other day, when his head cleared and he could think. But for now the voice in his head kept repeating... run.

He walked to the dining area re-reading Buzz Nelson's expression of gratitude. He left the book on the table, open to the note, grabbed his coat, and quietly slipped out the door.

Chapter 49: The War Against God

<u>Election: 24 days</u>

Although Chad was impatient to talk with his father, Saturday was the soonest he could visit East of Eden. He asked Daniel to accompany him for support.

Chad said, "He knows I won't cave to his way of doing things, but my campaign's faltering and I'm still holding on to a glimmer of hope that he can help."

"I doubt he wants me here," suggested Daniel.

"I insisted."

They walked through the great room, past the towering fireplace to the glass doors. Chad spotted his father seated on the patio gazing at the mountains. The Aspen trees still held their golden leaves. Winter was coming, but the warm afternoon sun restrained an approaching cold front. As they walked out onto the patio, Gordon turned to acknowledge their arrival.

"Hello, Chad, it's good to see you."

"How are you today?"

"Relaxed. My work is finished."

"Do you remember Daniel Stone?"

"Yes, I do. It's nice to see you again," said Gordon shaking Daniel's hand. He asked Chad, "How's the campaign?"

"Not good, as you already know."

"There's still time. I can help."

"How?"

"Some media friends have something on your opponent. They're waiting to hear from me."

"No thanks."

"Why?"

"I care about how I win."

"What do you mean – win?" pressed Gordon. "Without my help you're going to lose. It's just that simple."

"I disagree with his politics, but that's no reason to ruin him."

"Suit yourself. He'd bury you if he had the chance."

"But he won't need to, will he?"

Gordon's peaceful countenance stiffened, but his voice remained undisturbed, "What do you mean?"

Chad answered, "I mean, for one thing, Allen Wilder's message is defeating me."

"Wilder's been around for years."

"You bankrolled him. You and your friends at World Broadcast turned him into a national celebrity."

Gordon seemed amused. "You still haven't given me a reason why I'd promote Wilder."

Chad answered, "To elect a President and Congress sympathetic to *Tolerance for America*."

"I'm impressed. You've been busy."

"Apparently not as busy as you and Berry."

"Did she tell you this?"

Chad stated, "I'm through talking to Berry. I know she's involved."

Gordon's severe stare revealed both surprise and disappointment. "Ms. Fields will no longer be speaking for me."

Chad pressed the point, "What is your ultimate goal?"

Gordon responded, "If we don't save the world, who will?"

"And when you succeed, what will we be left with? A world of joyless slaves?"

"But what if people believe they're happy and free?"

Chad had to satisfy his curiosity, "How did Berry fit into all this?"

Gordon explained, "Berry envisioned the road to unity passing through diversity. After pointing out that attempts to enforce conformity to a particular belief system ultimately fail, she proposed that no one has to change. They only have to acknowledge that what they believe isn't really "true," but only a preference. A person is affirmed by participating in the common good of the group. We no longer strive to unite the world under one ideology. *Tolerance for America* is the cornerstone of our new Tower of Babel. Everyone can speak their own language."

Gordon spoke directly to Daniel for the first time, "In America, who's the major opposition to collective unity?"

Daniel answered, "Probably evangelicals."

"Why?"

"Christians believe God knows and loves each person individually, like a parent loves a child. Liberty and truth come from God. That's why Christians resist surrendering their personhood to a collective will."

Gordon appeared to enjoy explaining his thinking. "We knew global government couldn't happen without America, which we considered to be a political problem. But Berry convinced me it was much more. She understood that because individual liberty is fundamental to Christian political thought, we wouldn't achieve our goals unless evangelical Christianity was negated. Berry's crowning achievement was her advice not to fight Christianity, but instead redefine it as a 'means to a good end.'"

Chad asked, "And that's where Buzz Nelson comes in?"

"I've underestimated you," offered Gordon, smiling at his son. "Yes, Buzz has done a marvelous job. We'll subvert Christianity's influence, not by eliminating it, but by creating a *new* religion that embraces unity through collective consciousness. Then we'll call our new religion, *Christianity*."

Gordon looked from Chad to Daniel, then back to his son. When neither responded he added, "After we destroy the theological basis of the 'I', we'll suppress any aberrations that show up."

"Like Philip?" said Daniel.

"Yeah, a good example."

Daniel asked, "Did you save his life?"

Gordon smiled, "I thought you did?"

Chad's frustration was growing, "What about Amber Grains?"

"I don't think we should discuss it since you're on the Agriculture Committee. Is there anything else?"

Chad ran through the list. "You never explained why you're financing Wilder?"

Gordon explained, "His escapist vision of the future and political views suit our purposes."

"How?"

"You've figured it out."

Chad countered, "Is it working?"

Gordon studied his son and then smiled, "So you don't know either. I wondered. But your presence here today indicates you're feeling it."

Daniel noticed Chad's dazed bewilderment so he decided to ask, "Gordon, what do you think of Jesus?"

Gordon willingly replied, "In the Sermon on the Mount, Jesus was describing a new form of human government, a community of individuals who are to be self-governed by conscience. These are people beyond our control. For how can we control people who give us their shirts after we take their coats... or turn the other cheek? They may stand naked and battered, but they know true freedom. I realized this stood in direct opposition to our vision of a united world order.

"But let me ask you: Why did Jesus refuse to rule the world? He possessed the power to really change things. It appears, by eyewitness accounts, that he had an incredible mastery of the natural world. I imagine he could have turned those stones into bread. But for some mysterious reason, the only person to ever have the power to solve our problems chose not to do it."

Daniel couldn't remain silent, "Because it's not about that kind of power. And besides, Jesus *is* feeding the hungry and healing the sick…"

"Did he heal *your* wife?" interrupted Gordon with unusual intensity. "He abandoned you, just as he's abandoned everyone else. Yet you think we should worship him? Why? What's he doing for the thousands of children who die every day of disease and starvation? Why shouldn't we reject him for allowing two thousand years of human misery?"

Daniel responded, "Human misery is the consequence of rejecting him."

Gordon scoffed, "Wilder claims he'll return to rule the world, someday. But we're not waiting for him. We'll build our own paradise on earth."

He stood to leave. "Snow's in the forecast. This afternoon may be my last opportunity to ride before the weather sets in. If you decide you want my help, call me at the stable."

"I do have one last question," asked Chad. "What's the meaning of East of Eden?"

Looking to the mountains rising in the west, Gordon considered the request. "It's symbolic, obviously, and rather simple. God started a war against humanity in the Garden of Eden. I've planned for many years to fight a decisive battle against the Christian Church. When our victory is secure, I'll enter the Garden of Eden as a representative of mankind." Gordon glared at the mountain. "I'll enter through the east gate, past the flaming sword and the winged cherubim, not on the bent knee of repentance, but standing erect, carrying the banner of victory."

Daniel asked, "What will the banner say?"

Gordon stared at Daniel. The malice in his eyes demanded to be heard. Gordon slowly raised his gaze to the snow capped mountain peak and to whom it represented. "The banner will read," he began slowly and then finished with a strong clarity of intent, "We have no king but Caesar."

Watching Gordon walk away, Daniel was struck with the answer to the question Katherine had once asked him: "Where is Joshua?" He also understood what he was to do with the rest of his life.

Chapter 50: On the Run

Berry stood at the front entrance to the Bay Area Girls Academy. She'd said goodbye many times in the past, but this time seemed different. Both she and Annie sensed it, and the practiced ritual became awkward.

"I have to go now," Berry said, just as she always did. But the response from the distressed face of the ten-year-old standing in front of her was unlike before.

"Will you come back?"

Berry stepped back inside the door, "Annie, don't I always come back?"

"This time isn't the same."

"Of course it is. I won't be long, you'll see." Berry bent over and kissed the girl's soft cheeks. When she saw the swollen eyes, glistening under the foyer lights, Berry lifted her up with a loving hug.

"I love you, Annie," said Berry with tears streaming down her cheeks.

"I love you, Mom. Please come back."

Forty minutes later, Berry was heading south from San Francisco in a dark blue BMW convertible with a black canvas top. She was now on the run, hiding from Gordon. Would he want her dead? She didn't really think so, but she wasn't sure. She definitely knew too much, and it wasn't in Gordon's nature to leave loose ends. Even if he thought he could trust her, there was always the possibility she'd sell him out if the bid was high enough, or if someone forced information out of her.

Her decision was to disappear until after the election. If Gordon achieved his objectives, and her recommendations worked out, he might allow her back into his circle in some capacity.

Berry received a phone call from the only person she'd answer, "Hi, honey."

An unknown man responded, his voice threatening. He spoke with broken English and a heavy Hispanic accent. The man on the phone had taken Annie. Berry strained to understand him and the voice of another man in the background. "Go to woods… creek… by soccer field." She kept asking him to repeat himself. Her voice increasingly hysterical as the man's frustration heightened. "Alone or the girl will die… you come and the girl can go… only one hour."

Berry screamed into the phone, "Who are you? Let her go now!" There was no response as the line went dead. She pulled off the road at the next exit and tried to regain control. She feared she might pass out from her rapid breathing and violent heart beat. She gripped the steering wheel to stop her hands from shaking.

She glanced at the clock. It had taken forty-five minutes to get to this point. On the return trip she'd only have fifteen minutes to spare. That was cutting it too close. She turned back onto the road and headed north towards the city.

She struggled to focus. Calling the police was out of the question. What could they do other than rush in. Gordon had cut off her access to his private number, so there wasn't enough time to reach him. Chad was her only chance to stop his father. She called, "Please answer... please answer... please..." The call was transferred to voicemail.

"Chad, this is Berry. Please call me immediately." Her voice trembled. "It's life and death. I need your help... Please..." Her voice trailed off as she broke down in tears.

Two minutes passed and she tried again, "Please answer..." The second call also slipped into voicemail. All the way back to San Francisco she called, waited, and called again.

Driving into the city, she decided on a course of action. There was a road leading to a secluded ridge overlooking the athletic fields. From that vantage point she'd call Annie's phone and demand they let her go before she'd come to the woods. Then she'd think of something. It was a terrible plan, but it was all she could come up with. Her main hope was that although Gordon was a heartless bastard, she was certain he'd never approve of killing a child. But did he even know their strategy?

She tried to reach Chad again, and this time she was going to leave enough details that he'd be able to have his father indicted. The phone rang until it was transferred to voicemail. But she received a different message, "The mail box belonging to Chad Connelly is full."

"Damn it! Damn, Damn, Damn!" she screamed at the phone.

Berry entered the road leading up the hill to the ridge. When she was close to the top, she turned off her headlights and called Annie's phone. The call was answered just as she turned into an isolated parking area on the edge of the ridge. A quick motion coming from the dark immediately in front of her car caused her to swerve out of the way. She heard yelling coming from the other end of the phone before it went dead with a loud clunk. At the same time she realized she'd almost hit someone. The car drifted as she watched through the rearview mirror. It was the man who'd answered her call, picking up Annie's phone, yelling to someone.

Berry looked ahead. In the deep shadows of tall fir trees she could make out another man holding a young girl's arm. It was Annie and she was being led towards a parked car. Berry rolled down the windows and yelled, causing both of them to look up at her. Annie recognized the BMW and yelled back, waving.

Berry flipped on her brights and sped in their direction. The man shielded his vision from the lights and held Annie tightly, causing Berry to stop. The man shouted for Berry to turn off her car as he hurried to the driver-side door. Berry started to get out, demanding he release Annie. He grabbed Berry with his free hand. During the struggle she fell back into the car, breaking free of his grip. He quickly reached for the door to prevent it from closing. Trying to help, Annie threw all her weight against the door, slamming it on the attacker's hand. He jumped back, screaming in pain as he released his hold of Annie and took a wild backhanded swing at her head. She ducked and pulled free.

Annie ran towards the far end of the parking area with her pursuer close behind, cursing, holding his damaged right hand. Berry drove directly towards them. She was determined to stop him with her car. When she'd almost caught up with him, he broke towards the ridge and avoided her front bumper by sliding over the edge. Berry spun away from the side of the ridge and continued towards Annie who was approaching the tree line.

The car left the blacktop and Berry slammed on the brakes. She pulled the steering wheel hard to the left until the car started sliding sideways across gravel and grass towards the trees. When the front end came around, pointing back towards the road, Berry shouted for Annie to jump in. She leapt through the window, landing head first in the seat. Her legs followed as she twisted herself upright.

Berry stomped on the accelerator and the wheels screamed, spraying gravel into the woods. In a moment the tires found traction, launching the car forward towards the blacktop.

"Get down," Berry yelled, forcing Annie's head below the windshield.

The engine's whine drowned out every sound as the BMW raced across the lot. Berry noticed the kidnapper's car pulling out from her left side, driven by the man who'd chased Annie. She looked forward again and saw the first man who'd dropped the cell phone, standing between her and the lot exit. He was fifty feet straight ahead, squinting into her brights, aiming a pistol directly at her car.

She veered sharply. His first shot glanced off her side view mirror. His second shot ripped through the canvas top. Once again her instincts took over as she automatically swerved to the right to avoid hitting him. The tires screeched in protest as the car's weight leaned hard on the left side. Berry panicked, sure they were going to roll. The gunman dived to his right.

Berry straightened the wheels and the car lurched forward, heading for the road.

She glanced at the rearview mirror. The other car was approaching when, suddenly, the gunman jumped up to fire his pistol at her again. It all happened in a second. The other driver saw his partner too late and slammed on the brakes. His car spun out of control as he tried to miss him. The back end swung around, hitting the gunman, sending him sprawling through the air. The car careened off the lot. Berry heard it smash into the trees just as she reached the road and headed down the hill.

Berry was once again traveling south on Highway 5, but no longer just to lie low. She and Annie were going into hiding. She briefly considered seeking protection from some branch of law enforcement, but she had no evidence it was Gordon. If she accused him and it wasn't his doing, then she would definitely close the door and create a powerful enemy. Besides, how could she seek protection from Gordon? He was the real government, or at least a power within it.

At 11:40 p.m. Chad finally called. Berry had found a small hotel off the highway and Annie was already in bed. She took the call outside.

"Hi, Chad. Thanks for calling."

"What happened? Are you alright?"

"Yes and no. Someone tried to kill me tonight. I escaped and I'm trying to hide."

"Do you know who?"

"Two Hispanics, I think professionals. They might have been hired by Gordon."

"Berry, why would my father..."

"Gordon and I had a falling out. I no longer work for him, but I know much more about his operations than he cares to be made known."

"But enough to have you killed?"

"Who else would have hired these men?"

"Do you think they're after you now?"

"No, I believe one of them is dead. Run over by his partner when I got away. The other has a badly damaged hand."

"How are you?"

"I'm fine."

"What are you going to do?"

"Chad, can you help me. I have no one I can trust."

"Why do you trust me?"

Berry paused in thought before answering, "Because you're trustworthy."

Chad responded, "I'll talk to Gordon, but I have to be careful. I don't want to offend him if he's not involved. But if he is, I don't want him to know I'm in contact with you because then he'll try to find you through me. It won't be easy, but I'll see what I can do. What about you? Do you know where you're going?"

"No, and even if I did, I wouldn't say it over the phone."

"I understand."

"I'll be in contact later, when I decide what to do."

"Okay, I'll let you know if I learn anything."

"Thanks, I'll be in touch."

Chapter 51: New World Order

Election: 18 days

Daniel was working late on Friday night, alone in his Mexico City Life Bridge office. He leaned back in the chair, imagining how much he'd rather be having dinner with Macy.

A loud knock at the front door of the building startled him. He glanced at the clock, 9:32 p.m. He hopped to his feet and headed down a short hallway. Through the glass door, aided by the lobby lights, he recognized Octaviano standing outside.

He quickly opened the door. "Come in. Is everything okay?"

Octaviano's mood was friendly but serious, "I'm afraid I once again have something troubling to share. But this time I think you'll be able to do some damage."

Daniel led him back to his office and motioned towards a chair at a small conference table. "What is it?"

"Remember I told you about meeting with old friends in Nicaragua about six months ago?"

"Yeah, that's where you got the Clark report."

"Buzz Nelson called the group together again. About forty of us met in Managua two days ago. I didn't know the purpose, but I went prepared to secretly video whatever he said. After dinner, some drinks and storytelling, Buzz shared his excitement about the coming of a new world order. He said he wanted those who'd worked so hard with little success to know that our future was at hand. Everything we'd dreamed of was about to happen. I really think he was there to boast. He stood before the group as their leader delivering the kingdom."

"Were you able to tape it?"

Octaviano's amused eyes and wide grin informed Daniel of the contents on the DVD he set on the table. Daniel picked it up, pulled his chair towards the desk, and turned the computer around to face them.

"Are we ready to watch?"

Octaviano first wanted to share some thoughts. "For me, it was a sad night. Many of these people had been friends, comrades-in-arms. We'd fought together many years ago, but as I watched Buzz talk, and witnessed their excitement, I realized they wanted their socialist revolution so badly they've forgotten why.

"You'll hear Buzz discuss a plan to withhold food in order to create political instability and regime change. They applauded his strategy of allowing people to starve as a means of achieving their goals."

Octaviano's expression revealed a deep despair. "Most of these people began their quest years ago with youthful idealism. But over the years they've grown to hate those who stand in their way more than they remember who they'd wanted to help."

Octaviano nodded and Daniel slipped the DVD into his computer. Soon Buzz Nelson was speaking before the group:

"Government is the organized will of the people and thus the only fair and equitable arbiter of human life. It represents the pinnacle of human community. In contrast, individual choices create inequalities and injustice. To restrain government action is to limit the potential for the common good. Therefore, to limit government is to allow evil to flourish.

"We stand at the threshold of great change. For when collective consciousness forms the heart of government, the good future God promises us will come to pass, *"then nothing they plan to do will be impossible for them."*

Daniel paused the DVD and shared his amazement, "Do you believe how he turned God's words upside down?" Octaviano's blank look conveyed he had no idea what Daniel was talking about. Daniel offered, "It has to do with the Tower of Babel." Then he restarted the video.

The Nelson tape continued, "I've come to Managua to tell my old comrades that our time has come. A new world order is rising. The U.S. elections will bring to power a government prepared to end reactionary conservative opposition to global progress once and for all.

"Since government embodies the collective will, individual actions outside the collective are immoral. In the future these independent men and women will be constrained and re-oriented. They will renounce their antisocial behavior and freely submerge their lives, their property, and their hopes and dreams into the common good."

Daniel momentarily stopped listening to jot down some notes. Octaviano was watching him. Daniel appealed to his friend, "Tell me it's just a bad dream."

Octaviano explained, "Buzz conveyed a confidence that bordered on celebration. That's probably why he came to Managua. He was so excited about the coming victory that he couldn't contain himself."

Daniel turned back towards the screen, but from that point on his swirling thoughts competed with Nelson's voice. He only retained bits and pieces.

"The private life, including property, must be abolished in order for people to reach their full potential as human beings. Everything private negates man's socialization. Substitutes like family, church and career will be diminished....

"We're on the verge of creating the "new man," but the burden of this task falls to qualified elites. Their hard work and sacrifices will usher in a new era of human progress....

"Freedom is an affliction the masses will happily lay at our feet in exchange for their daily bread....

"Israel is a thorn in the side of global unity that will be removed. After we win the election, Israel will be isolated and forced to surrender Jerusalem." Nelson laughed at the thought of his next comment, "Even the evangelicals won't put up a fight because many of them see the abandonment of Israel as the fulfillment of prophecy."

Daniel was considering how to get the video to Macy and Chad. What would they do with it? The news media couldn't ignore it. Buzz Nelson was a frequent White House guest and a personal friend of the President. The success of his "Starving for Profits Tour" had resulted in him showing up on every news show and magazine cover in America. In the past month, Buzz Nelson had become a household name.

Daniel's attention was re-directed back to Nelson, "Our C.U. Movement has stepped into the void on college campuses with a new kind of Christian experience. Ours is a dynamic faith of inclusion and acceptance. Hell is reserved for those who believe in it.

"About two weeks ago, we had an amazing occurrence at one of our conferences. At the end of the event, the speaker gave a spontaneous call to faith, asking those present to lay down their individual personhood and take up a spirit of unity for the good of all humanity. Hundreds left their seats and walked forward to the stage. We now give this call to faith at all our events with the same amazing results."

Daniel stood up and walked out the front door. He was standing by the road, looking out towards the night sky when Octaviano walked up beside him and asked, "What do you think?"

"It's all a gift. Buzz Nelson's need to prematurely celebrate, your decision to go to Managua, and then you having the presence of mind to tape his talk and bring it to us." Daniel looked at his friend with a perplexed expression, "But how did we ever get to this point?"

"Maybe you should ask those who speak for your God."

"I just hope we're not too late."

Chapter 52: The Visitor

Late Saturday morning, one of the Mexican Life Bridge interns interrupted Daniel. "There's a lady in the lobby who'd like to speak with you."

"Thank you, I'll be right there."

Daniel left his office wondering who it might be. When he entered the lobby, he was speechless. Berry Fields was standing by the front window, looking across the lot towards the ARD production facility. She appeared unusually plain, no makeup, eyes puffy from lack of sleep, hair pulled back, exhausted.

When she saw him, she smiled in response to his expression. "You seem surprised to see me."

Daniel didn't immediately answer, and Berry noticed him looking at the young girl standing beside her. "Daniel, I'd like you to meet Annie... Annie, this is Mr. Stone."

He responded to her outstretched hand. "It's nice to meet you, Annie."

The little girl smiled as Berry continued, "Annie's my daughter."

Daniel's reaction caused Berry to smile. "Daniel, I need to talk with you, privately." She turned to Annie. "Honey, please wait for me here."

Daniel interceded, "Let me get one of the interns." He soon returned with a friendly young lady. "Izel, please offer Annie something to drink and take her on a tour."

He invited Berry into his office. Once seated, he asked, "Berry, why are you and Annie here in Mexico?"

"I no longer work for Gordon, and I believe he tried to have me killed in San Francisco." She related the story, including her effort to reach Chad and their subsequent conversation.

"So Chad doesn't know you're here?"

"No one does."

One question pushed to the front of Daniel's mind. "How old is Annie?"

"You're right," said Berry, "Chad's her father."

"That's why you left Austin before our senior year?"

"Yes."

"Does Chad know?"

"No, you're the first person I've ever told."

"Why did you come to Mexico?"

"I know Gordon has no influence over you. We need a place to hide."

She then added, "I thought of telling Chad about Annie over the phone, but I kept putting it off, and now I'm here. Do you think I should tell him?"

"Yes."

"I'm probably paranoid, but I don't trust the phones as a result of living in Gordon's world for so long. Will you be seeing Chad soon?"

"I'm leaving for Austin in a couple of hours. We're getting together later tonight."

"Will you explain the situation to Chad and ask him to convince his father to leave us alone?"

"Berry, I'm sorry I can't return the trust."

"That's another reason I didn't tell Chad. I didn't want him to think I'd use his own daughter to influence him. But I'm hoping you and Chad decide to believe me."

Daniel explained his lack of trust, "Did Chad mention our conversation with Gordon last Saturday?"

"No, we didn't talk very long."

"According to Gordon, and Chad, you're responsible for *Tolerance for America*, Buzz Nelson's unity consciousness, and the strategy of using Allen Wilder. Is this true?"

Berry grimaced, "I discovered years ago that people were often fascinated by my observations, even though I was just saying what was obvious."

"Observations?" asked Daniel.

"About how the world works."

"Based on what you believed?"

"Believed?" repeated Berry thoughtfully. "I believed in Strawberry Fields Forever, but even "Berry" was a construct."

Daniel waited for her to continue.

Berry grinned at his perplexed stare. "During my senior year at Berkeley, I wrote an essay about how changing perception could redefine one's reality. My professor and some of his friends were intrigued and eventually invited me into their inner circle. A year later I wrote *Unity through Diversity*, which Buzz Nelson read. He recommended I talk to Gordon, not knowing that I knew Chad. Gordon grasped the implications of what I was saying and incorporated my ideas into his overall strategy."

Daniel shook his head in disbelief.

Berry shrugged, suggesting it wasn't hard to understand. "To me it was more like a game, and my imagination opened doors. Now, it appears I've created a world that's no longer safe for Annie and me."

Daniel asked, "Is it ever about anyone other than you and Annie? How about the truth? What you've done isn't a game, millions of lives are affected."

Berry silently looked away. After a moment's pause Daniel proceeded, "Are there any weaknesses in Gordon's plan?"

"Not really. He's a thorough strategist."

"Nothing?"

Berry remained quiet for a short while. "If Gordon has any weakness, it's that he tends to overestimate people he likes and to underestimate those who disagree with him."

"For example?"

"He's always underestimated Philip, and Chad too."

"Who does he overestimate?"

"Buzz Nelson... Buzz has a huge ego and is a bit of a loose cannon. I think Gordon's been lucky Buzz hasn't done anything stupid so far."

Daniel wasn't about to tell Berry that it already happened. "Anyone else?"

"I've always thought he underestimated Allen Wilder."

"In what way?"

"Gordon doesn't understand people who are guided by principle instead of utility. I tried to explain to him that Wilder teaches what he believes is true, and not just something that helps him get what he wants. I warned Gordon that if Wilder ever discovers what he's saying is not true, he'll turn on a dime even if it hurts his career. To Gordon, a principle is only important if it serves one's interests."

Daniel concluded, "Berry, I have to leave for the airport, and I'm not sure how long I'll be in Austin. You and Annie can stay at my house until we decide what to do. I'll talk to Chad. He needs to know, and I do believe you about Annie."

Daniel stood up and walked to the door. "I'll have someone take you to the house. They'll pick up whatever you need at the store. Is that your BMW?"

"Yes it is."

"It would be best to leave it here. We'll park it in the garage."

"Thank you for helping us," said Berry as she nodded her agreement. "Please tell Chad I'm sorry, for everything."

****

The Buzz Nelson video ended and a dozen conversations sprang up among the circle of friends seated in the living room of Chad's Austin home. Excitement filled the air, for everyone knew they'd just seen the first significant breakthrough since the onslaught had started.

They'd previously hoped the Clark report, outlining the government takeover of Amber Grains and food production would awaken the American

178

people. But the slow public response had been discouraging.

The polling people, supported by Charles Lee and his research team, had been working tirelessly for three weeks to determine what impact Allen Wilder and Buzz Nelson were having on the election. They still didn't have dependable numbers.

Chad stood before the group of friends, including media and political strategists. "This is additional proof that what we've feared is true. Our American experiment in liberty and limited government is seriously threatened. We'll share ideas tonight and then reconvene tomorrow at 1:00 for a strategy session at Philip's home."

At 2:00 a.m. Daniel was alone with Chad. "Before I crash, I have something to share that's extremely important."

With a boyish grin, Chad guessed, "Now you're going to tell me you and Macy are engaged?"

"I wish it were that simple. Berry showed up at my office this morning."

"I talked to her Tuesday night. I wondered where she'd go."

"She has a little girl with her, whose name is Annie."

Chad looked slightly perplexed. "Berry never said anything about…"

"Annie's her daughter."

Chad started to express his surprise but Daniel preempted him, "She's ten-years-old."

Chad sunk back in the chair, staring, suddenly fearing Daniel's next comment.

"Berry says you're the father."

Chad stood up and slowly paced the room. "Is that why she left school?"

"That's what she said."

"Why didn't she tell me?"

"She's never told anyone."

"Where are they staying?"

"At my house," said Daniel. "She thinks Gordon tried to kill her."

"She also said that to me."

"Do you believe her?"

"I don't think he'd do it… but she does."

Daniel asked, "Can you talk to him?"

"Do you know how hard that'll be? I'm scheduled to see him in D.C. late tomorrow night. I told him it had to do with Berry, but that's before I even knew about the girl."

Chad paused for a moment, and then continued, "If Gordon had nothing to do with the attempt on Berry's life, my conversation with him will be a disaster. But if he's involved, then he has to be stopped. There's no good way out of it. I have to talk to him."

Daniel explained, "Since I'm in Austin for a few days, I asked Katherine to go to Mexico City to help Berry and Annie. She leaves in the morning."

"Thanks."

Daniel rose to his feet and headed for the guestroom. "I'm exhausted. We can talk in the morning. It's far too complicated to make sense of tonight."

"Thanks again for helping them. I'll see you in the morning."

"Berry said she's sorry for everything." Daniel left and then reappeared in the doorway. "One more thing, Annie's a precious little girl."

Chapter 53: Preventing the Possibility

Before beginning their meeting with media and public relations strategists, Philip asked Charles Lee for an update on the polling project.

Charles explained to the gathering, "We believe we'll have solid numbers by next weekend, so we've scheduled a presentation for Sunday at 5:00.

"Right now we're detecting major shifts in voter sentiments. Wilder is definitely affecting the way evangelicals view the importance of the election. Buzz Nelson's impact is also dramatic. His Starving Tours are not only persuading students, but these students are influencing their families. If these patterns continue gaining momentum, we could be facing significant losses."

Chad restated their intent to bring the contents of the video to the public. Macy would coordinate activities with the party's leadership and political strategists in Washington. A group of Texas businesspeople led by Art Doyle committed to provide the funding. After they all agreed to go public with the information within forty-eight hours, Chad turned the meeting over to the media people.

Daniel and Macy left the group at 3:00 to drive an hour and a half to San Antonio to meet with Rob Martinson before Wilder's San Antonio Prophecy Conference.

Rob had agreed to discuss the upcoming election and view the Buzz Nelson video. Daniel believed that if they could convince Rob, they'd at least have an ally on the inside. And to Daniel, spending time alone with Macy more than made the trip worthwhile.

They arrived in San Antonio and met with Rob. He tried to explain Wilder's attitude, "Allen simply doesn't believe he's having an impact on the election. He's heard speculations, but there's no polling data to confirm what you think is happening."

Daniel asked, "Can we show you the Buzz Nelson video?"

Rob said, "Sure, I'd like to see it."

After watching the video, Rob agreed that Buzz Nelson's view of America was a disaster, and he was especially concerned about Nelson's comments about Israel. The prospect that Christians would stand idly by and allow America to abandon Israel because they believed it fulfilled prophecy was troubling.

Rob revealed his concern. "Allen would be devastated to find out his message was in any way helping Israel's enemies force the surrender of Jerusalem."

Daniel pleaded the case, "The polling people are working day and night with a research team from PD Tech to measure Wilder's effect. They're going to present their results next Sunday afternoon at Philip's. Can you come?"

"Okay, I'll be there. But I don't think I can do any good. Wilder's leaving next Saturday for Israel, and he'll be gone for about a week."

"When's he coming back?"

"He's due back the following Friday, which is only four days before the election. And he has conferences scheduled three nights in a row."

"But we can count on you for Sunday."

"I'll be there."

The dark road through the Texas night reminded Daniel of his previous drive into Austin for Lauren's memorial service, which seemed like a very long time ago. He appreciated that Macy's presence in the car was a vast improvement.

In a reflective mood, he asked, "Do you ever wonder how things might change if Gordon has his way. What if the election's a landslide, *Tolerance for America* becomes law, and the government takes over genetic food production?"

"I've given it some thought, but I don't dwell on it."

"What would you do?"

Macy answered with a teasing grin, "I'd accept Darius Cain's invitation to dinner."

"If you can't beat 'em, join 'em."

"Yep, instead of being "eliminated," I'd let Darius bore me to death."

Macy followed with a serious answer, "It seems that throughout history, the power brokers keep distorting our God-given desire for community into a counterfeit "unity." It's my nature to push back. I don't like bullies."

"What if we lose in a landslide, will you stay in Congress?"

"What makes you think I'll stay if we win?"

"Is there something you'd rather do?"

She turned towards him with a mischievous smile, "I'd rather home school seven children."

"Why seven?" he asked laughing.

"Because eight would be overwhelming."

Daniel smiled, "That seems like quite a change."

"No, not actually, just a different phase of the same battle."

"Then you probably should get married."

She teased, "I've thought of that. I'm partial to Washington lobbyists, with law degrees and last names for first names."

"Anyone in particular?"

"Not yet, I'm still waiting for God to bring the right guy into my life."

"Do you think he might be someone you already know?"

"Possibly, but the one I'm thinking about is a little slow. Maybe he's shy."

"Or maybe he's waiting for the right moment."

Macy smiled, "Then I guess I need to be patient."

****

Chad flew into Reagan National Airport on Sunday evening and took a cab to Gordon's condo. Gordon was friendly but suspicious since Chad had mentioned Berry as the purpose of his visit.

After fixing Chad a drink, Gordon asked, "How can I help you?"

"I understand Berry no longer works for you."

"I thought you weren't speaking to Berry anymore?"

"Someone tried to kill her."

Gordon paused to consider the statement, "And you believe her?"

"Why wouldn't I?"

"Maybe she's trying to create sympathy."

"That's possible."

"Where and when did this attempt supposedly happen?"

Chad shared what details he had until Gordon asked another question, "She mentioned two Hispanics?"

"Yeah."

Gordon paused long enough for Chad to think something had struck a chord. "Why have you come to me?"

Chad tried to suppress the angst swelling up in his chest. "I wondered if you had any idea who might have done it?"

Gordon's focus was acute. "Berry believes I hired these men?"

"I didn't say that."

"Don't play games, Chad. Did she tell you she thought I did it?"

"She doesn't know what to think."

After a strained silence, Gordon demanded, "Do you think I did it?"

"No... but..."

"But it's *possible*..."

Chad didn't believe his father would have Berry killed, but he had to follow through. "Berry has a ten-year-old child." With his father staring at him in disbelief, Chad asked, "Did you know?"

Gordon responded slowly, trying to remember if there had been any clues. "No, I didn't. I never thought to look." Then Gordon shot a quick glance at his son. "There's more to this. You didn't come here just to tell me she has a child."

Chad responded, "I found out last night I'm the father."

"The father!" Gordon spoke with astonishment, "You've got to be kidding."

Gordon's attitude quickly turned to indignation, "So that's it. You came to warn me that I'd be killing my granddaughter's mother." Gordon's anger grew, and Chad prepared to receive the worst. "For years I've tried to work with you, even though your damn religion's like trying to win a race dragging a ball and chain. But I will not look aside as you smugly accuse me of this absurd malice."

Gordon stood up and continued, "I think I know who's responsible for attacking Berry, and I'll try to stop it."

Gordon walked towards the door. Disgust hardened his voice, "Right now you're wondering if you can trust me, or if what I'm saying is a ploy to find her." Anger flared in his eyes as he held the door open. "We have no reason to see each other again. The person Berry should fear is not me, but the Italian, Leo Marone."

"Why Marone?"

"He convinced the Arabs he could deliver PD Tech. The Arabs paid him a hundred million upfront. He became desperate and tried to force the deal. Berry knows his secret."

Chad wondered, "Could he have had Lauren's plane shot down?"

"It's possible."

"Can I give his name to the investigators?"

Gordon stated emphatically, "I'll take care of Marone in my own way... Give me a couple of weeks."

"Okay," said Chad, understanding that his father wasn't making a request, but was issuing a command. When he reached the sidewalk, he stopped and looked back towards his father, who was still standing in the doorway. "Thanks," he said. Then he turned and continued walking into the chilly drizzle of the D.C. night. He'd accomplished his objective, but the cost was high.

Gordon placed a call, "Darius, inform the Arabs that the money they invested in the new algae venture was used by Leo Marone to cover his losses in the futures' market. He had no algae business to sell them."

"You don't want to wait until after the election?"

"No, do it right away. They need to know they were cheated."

Chapter 54: The Offer

Thursday noon, two days after the public exposure of the Buzz Nelson video, Philip sat in his office watching the wall monitor. The host of WBC's *Midday Show* was discussing the most shocking business story of the year. Amber Grains' stock was down over eight percent for the day due to the surprise resignation of Dr. Blake Merrill, who was stepping down as president of the company he'd founded twenty-eight years before.

The show's commentator, Maggi Tannon, was interviewing a woman from the Department of Agriculture, who said, "Merrill didn't give a definitive reason why he resigned, except to say he would be pursuing other interests."

Tannon politely disagreed, "Blake Merrill was quite clear. He resigned because of former White House Director Andrea Clark's report that detailed the administration's plans to nationalize Amber Grains if they win the election."

The woman objected, "Those were Clark' proposals, not the administration's."

Tannon wasn't buying it. "Ms. Frederick, we're not debating the Clark report. Blake Merrill believes it's true enough to resign from Amber Grains and announce he's staying on as Chairman of the Board in order to fight a government takeover."

Philip smiled at the young woman's handling of the USDA publicist. He was also glad that Merrill was finally taking a stand. He looked up as Brenda burst into his office. She had an excited grin plastered on her face and was bursting with news.

"Philip," she said as though sharing a secret, "You'll never guess who's here." She glanced at the wall monitor and was distracted by a tape from the previous evening that showed Merrill announcing his resignation. She looked back at Philip as though she'd just answered her own question.

He still had no idea, "Who?"

"Blake Merrill. He's sitting in the lobby."

Surprised, Philip admonished her, "Well, don't leave him there. Bring him to the patio and make sure we're not disturbed."

Within moments Brenda led their visitor to Philip's office patio. Merrill appeared relaxed, wearing blue jeans, a dress shirt and casual blazer. Philip offered him a seat at the circular patio table.

Merrill seemed to approve of the fountain and water garden with its

186

impressive collection of flowering plants.

"Very nice," he mentioned.

"Thanks, I enjoy the informality."

Merrill's countenance was unhurried and peaceful, not what one would expect from someone in the midst of a firestorm. He didn't hesitate to bring Philip up to date, "I've resigned as president of Amber Grains."

Philip recognized it was part of Merrill's social manner not to presume Philip would know. Philip responded, "I saw the news. I also heard you're planning to fight a government takeover."

Merrill passed over Philip's comment. "I want to thank you for what you said in my office."

Philip remained quiet, seeing no good way to respond.

Merrill continued, "You were correct. I knew it right away. In fact, I may have known for years, but it took someone actually saying it for the truth to break through."

Merrill paused as he looked about the patio. "When I realized what I'd done all those years, the way I saw the poor in relation to myself, there was no option other than to leave Amber. I'd lost sight of the purpose of my work. In an effort to be a disciple of Christ, I'd become a materialist. Instead of seeing eternal beings made in the image of God, they had become helpless mouths to feed."

Merrill smiled, "Remember you told me to set them free, and I said I didn't know how?"

Philip nodded, "I remember."

"You challenged me to figure it out." Merrill smiled again, "I think I have. It started with resigning. Next was my commitment to lead the fight against anyone using Amber as a tool to enable political control. But I realized even that wasn't enough."

Merrill removed from his jacket pocket a single piece of paper, printed on one side, and laid it on the table. Philip picked it up and started to read, but soon stopped and looked up at Merrill with a curious surprise.

Merrill explained, "It's my resume. I'd like to work for you."

Philip expressed his astonishment, "Amber Grains does more business in a week than we do all year. What can we offer you?"

"Years ago I lost my way, but I'm not too old to learn. You're taking on a huge task, which is quite honorable, yet I believe you're going to need every ally you can round up. I'd like to help."

The two men sat quietly. The sound of running water through the rock garden reminded Philip of the night before going to Mexico City, listening, wondering if he'd ever see Katherine again. Then he thought of Daniel, and Merrill's offer became even more real. Yes, he'd always need "every ally" he could get.

Philip pulled out his phone. "Dad, is Uncle Bret going to be at the ranch for dinner tonight?

"Great. I have someone with me who's joining the company. I'd like to bring him to the ranch to experience a Doyle dinner table initiation.

"His job?" Philip glanced at Merrill and grinned, "I'd say he's a pretty good scientist.

"Thanks, we'll be there by 6:00."

Philip turned off his phone and looked back at Merrill with a broad smile, "Can I show you around?"

"I'd like that very much."

Chapter 55: The Coming Landslide

Election: 9 days

Charles Lee stood in the Doyle living room at 5:00 p.m. on Sunday afternoon, prepared to present the results of a furious, twenty-eight day analysis. Political strategists and the polling people were scattered among candidates, media consultants, and friends. An ominous foreboding had crept into the party's anticipation of the coming election, and everyone was seeking answers. Vice presidential candidate, Rose Dalton, happened to be campaigning in Texas and Chad convinced her to join them.

After some opening comments, Chad asked Charles Lee to make the presentation. Charles began, "For the past four weeks the polling experts, along with PD Tech's research team, have studied both Wilder's message and the Starving Tours in an attempt to measure the influence these phenomena are having on potential voters. We've concluded that they are both influencing expected voter patterns to such a degree that they will dramatically impact election results.

"One aspect of Wilder's influence is to recognize that thousands of Christian leaders agree with him. With that support, his non-voting political message, seemingly validated by the events in the Middle East, has steadily eroded evangelical enthusiasm for the election. The difficulty was to determine at what point the erosion actually resulted in people staying home. Our research marked the tipping point at about three weeks ago when the violence in Israel dramatically escalated. Since then, the number of voters intending to abstain on Election Day due to Wilder's influence has grown considerably.

"Our second task was to determine if the Starving for Profits Tours were having an impact. College students, and young people in general, require a great deal of motivation to get them to the polls. From what we've been able to discern, that's exactly what's happening. The Starving Tours have resonated with the students. The way we established the depth of their commitment was to research their efforts to influence others. The results were profound.

"We'll first provide a brief overview. Then after a short break, we'll come back to explain the details and answer questions.

"Turning to the Presidential election," Charles pointed to a national map appearing on a large display screen. "This map shows the consensus of national polling companies as of three days ago. They show a close race with twelve swing states undecided.

189

"It's our belief that these polls fail to account for the two factors I've just described. The first is the significant number of evangelicals we have identified who aren't likely to vote. Over eighty percent of these people would have supported Mr. Thomas.

Secondly, we expect the voting numbers for young people influenced by the Starving Tour to be huge. When factoring in what we've seen of their ability to motivate their families and friends, the President's party could add another three to four percent across the board."

Charles Lee ignored the murmurs and continued, "The next map shows the electoral changes we anticipate."

The new map was greeted by a strange stillness followed by a spontaneous gasp. Ten of the twelve swing states had all moved to the President's column giving him a landslide total. Four Thomas states were now undecided.

Charles moved on quickly to the Senate and Congressional races. The results were the same. The President's party would be close to achieving super majorities in both the House and the Senate.

Charles closed the initial briefing, "To end our overview on an encouraging note, the public response to the Buzz Nelson video is phenomenal. The message has penetrated the wall of sound that tried to drown it out. Blake Merrill's resignation has brought public awareness to the administration's plans to use food as a weapon to advance their global political agenda. We're just beginning to see the effects of these events during the past week, but the true impact won't be known until the exit polls on Election Day."

When Charles Lee finished, an explosion of chatter filled the room, confirming the importance of their work.

Philip, along with Macy and Chad, led V.P. candidate Rose Dalton and her top political advisor, Frank Kellor, into the library.

"Chad, do you believe this?" asked Kellor.

"Yes, I've followed the polling work from the beginning. I'm experiencing the same results in the field."

Kellor asked, "Has anyone talked to Wilder? Are these the results he wants?"

Rose Dalton touched Kellor's arm. "Frank, have you ever read one of Wilder's books?"

"No."

"I have," offered Rose, "so let me explain the problem. We have a lot of good people looking to the heavens because they're disheartened by the affairs of men. I share their hope, but those of us in this room are wired differently. We feel a responsibility to occupy until he comes, whenever that might be. Until he does return, I believe he expects us to do all we can to prevent legislation like *Tolerance for America* from ever becoming law."

They silently agreed. Rose asked, "It looks like Buzz Nelson has discredited the Starving Tours for us. So what are we going to do about Wilder?"

Chad answered, "A friend of ours who works for Wilder is here today. We're meeting with him afterwards to determine how we can get Wilder to understand the consequences of his position."

Rose responded, "Would it help if I spoke to Wilder? Or maybe Ben Thomas could?"

Chad answered, "We can try to set something up. Wilder's in Jerusalem this week, so we'll have to do something quickly."

"Is there any way to counter his impact?" asked Frank Kellor.

"No, I don't think so," said Macy. "Christians who have decided not to vote won't be swayed, unless…"

"Unless what?" questioned Kellor.

"Unless the message comes from Allen Wilder."

Rose Dalton stood to leave. "Thank you for all you've done with the Nelson video. As for Wilder, please contact us immediately if we can help. I'll thank Mr. Lee and the polling consultants on my way out. They've uncovered a problem we can't ignore."

Philip and Chad met with Rob Martinson at the kitchen table to debrief. Daniel and Macy soon joined them.

Philip shared an idea, "I know two Jewish women in Jerusalem who could talk to Wilder about U.S. support for Israel from a Jewish perspective. To Lydia Shafran and Deborah Levi, it's a much more serious matter than U.S. politics or interpretations of prophecy."

"Why would Wilder meet with them?" asked Rob.

"Because he'll want to see ARD's amazing collection of artifacts that have been created for temple worship. It's like visiting a museum. There's even a huge model of the proposed new temple. Wilder will love it. He'll be stepping into the world of the people he believes will someday build the new temple he's always talking about."

Daniel asked, "Will the women do it?"

"I explained it to them earlier today. They're excited for the chance." Philip spoke directly to Rob, "Can you talk to Wilder in the morning. He needs to know that his message will inadvertently aid those who want to withdraw U.S. support for Israel. Then you have to make sure he visits ARD to see the world's greatest collection of temple artifacts. The rest will be up to the ladies."

"Can you do it?" asked Chad.

Rob agreed, "I'll call Allen in Jerusalem." He assured them, "I think he'll go for it."

Chapter 56: A Burden Too Great to Bear

Election: 7 days

Allen Wilder stared out the window of the van taking his small group to the ARD research center. He was lost in thought as the streets of Jerusalem passed by. These were desperate times. Frustration and pent-up hatreds were boiling over. He was convinced the entire Middle East would soon be consumed in war.

This line of thinking wasn't new. He'd been predicting these developments for several years. He believed that the violence bearing down on Israel was a prelude to Ezekiel's war of Gog and Magog.

He'd always been confident in his interpretation of Scripture, so why was he feeling so unsettled? His uneasiness had started Monday morning with a call from Rob Martinson. Rob had described polling results that showed his message was going to dramatically affect the outcome of the election.

He initially insisted that the polling was wrong, but that didn't explain the video Rob had insisted he watch. Buzz Nelson had said, "After the November election, Israel will be forced to surrender Jerusalem. The evangelicals won't put up a fight because many of them believe the abandonment of Israel is the fulfillment of prophecy."

When he heard Nelson's boast, it nearly crushed him. The enemies of Israel were celebrating their coming victory because of the unintended consequences of his message.

He tried to suppress his distress when they arrived at ARD. With his entourage of eight, he passed through security into a large, open space with a high ceiling and terrazzo floor. The reception desk was stationed in front of several displays of ARD equipment, set up for tours. On the far side of the room, he could see the temple artifacts displayed in glass cases. He was excited to personally experience the Jewish preparations for the new temple.

Two distinguished women in their forties introduced themselves to the group. They were Lydia Shafran, the CEO of ARD, and Deborah Levi, the Chairman of the Board.

When meeting Deborah Levi, Wilder spoke first, "Mrs. Levi, I'm sorry about your husband's death."

"Thank you. These are dangerous times," she said while reaching out to shake his hand. "And please call me Deborah."

"I'm Allen."

"We're so glad you came. Your love for Jerusalem and the Jewish people is well known. We are fortunate to have you as an advocate for Israel with the American people."

"We have the same roots in Abraham and the Old Testament."

Deborah smiled and directed his attention to the temple displays. "I'd like to show you my husband's passion." She led him, along with Lydia, across the room to an eight by ten foot model of the proposed temple.

Wilder studied it carefully, asking many questions. He moved slowly through the displays of painstakingly crafted reproductions of sacred vessels and ceremonial tools. He asked brief questions and listened intently to the answers. Who researched the gold breastplate to be worn by the high priest? Where did the twelve gems come from? Who determined their quality?

He stared at the pure gold menorah as though trying to imagine the light of seven candles reflecting its brilliance inside the temple. Lydia pointed out the altar of incense and the utensils of copper and silver used to carry the incense in the temple.

The tour of nearly a hundred items continued with the table of shewbread, the laver of cleansing, and several silver trumpets inlaid with gold. At the end was a display of garments and robes made for the priests from a special linen thread.

Deborah and Lydia invited Wilder for tea at a small table off to the side. The women directed the conversation to the crucial issues facing Israel including U.S. foreign policy and the lack of commitment by the President to Israel's security. Deborah and Lydia believed the administration's policy was intentional and emboldened Israel's enemies, making peace harder to maintain. But neither of them believed that an all-out war was inevitable. Instead, they saw a subtler goal of leaving Israel with no allies or support, then wearing the Jewish people down through a strategy of constant violence, economic hardship, and the promise of peace to be reached after just one more compromise – the surrender of Jerusalem.

Deborah was convinced that Israel's defense depended on its longtime ally. The ongoing alliance had always been complex, but the surfacing of this strange, new threat was hard to fathom. In order to ensure the active participation of the U.S. in Israel's security, she was about to engage an American preacher in a discussion of end-times prophecy. As baffling as it seemed, she realized the necessity and was willing to do it. She asked for God's blessing as she began.

"Allen, I know you remember that Israel has fought three major wars since becoming a nation – 1948, 1967 and 1973. Do you suppose that there were people convinced at the beginning of each of those conflicts that it might be the war prophesied by Ezekiel?"

Wilder answered, "Yes, but there were differences."

"But isn't prophecy much easier to understand after it's fulfilled? Wouldn't you agree that until it occurs, it's hard to be sure?"

"At times it is," he offered. He felt as though Deborah had targeted his own rising concerns.

She asked, "What about this time? Can you be certain? I'm not asking you to question your interpretation, just the timing. You speak with such certainty, but can you really know?"

Wilder responded, "No one knows the time. I only point to the signs."

"But what if the many people you speak to no longer believe it's necessary to defend Israel because God will do it?"

Lydia interjected, "Because your interpretation of Ezekiel turns war into a blessing."

Deborah said, "Allen, the next war could happen *because* the United States no longer stands with Israel. If your timing is off and it's not the war to fulfill Ezekiel's prophecy, then many people will die in a war that could have been prevented."

Wilder was becoming uncomfortable, "I see your point."

Deborah continued, "I understand how your studies, from the safety of America, can be interesting theological theories. But from the reality of Jerusalem, your speculations are a matter of life and death. The enemies of Israel are transforming your message into a political weapon they're using against us.

Deborah leaned forward, "Allen, God has blessed you to be a great communicator. But you are proclaiming a future you *cannot* know. Despite your good intentions, for those of us living in Israel, your speculations may determine *our* life or death. Is that a responsibility you wish to bear?"

Deborah's peaceful delivery disarmed him as he considered the full weight of her question. His mind was flooded with the realization she was right. Since he claimed to know the unfolding of future events, he was responsible for the actions of those who believed him and his prophetic assertions. He could already feel the pressure. The future of Israel, and Jerusalem, and the peoples of the Middle East, were a burden too great to bear.

Wilder consciously took a deep breath and sat quietly for a moment. Deborah and Lydia remained still until he was ready to speak, "When I sit at my desk in Dallas and read the scriptures, the questions of prophecy are academic theology. But being in Jerusalem, I have sensed the fear of war, experienced the violence, and witnessed people living every day by hope.

As you were speaking, I began to realize that the future is God's. It's my responsibility to live faithfully in this present day."

He paused and then confessed, "You're right. I don't know what's going to happen, or when. But I've spoken as though I do, encouraging others to live in the future and ignore the duties of the day. Now we're about to face the consequences of my error. I have made a grave mistake."

****

Election: 5 days

Wilder was scheduled to speak on Thursday evening before a small audience at a site overlooking Jerusalem. His talk was to be taped at dusk, with the city bathed in evening shadows, and then edited to include some of the current events he'd witnessed during the week. WBC would pick up the satellite feed and broadcast his program across the U.S.

On Thursday, during the day of the speech, Wilder switched production companies, dropping the WBC contractor and selecting a local Jerusalem producer. WBC was unconcerned, as long as the feed was available for the first scheduled showing at 7:00 p.m., EST.

Wilder was introduced and began his presentation...

"For many years, I've shared with you how events in the world, and especially Israel, have pointed to the fulfillment of prophecy. My experience in Jerusalem this past week has shown me that my impatience for the Lord's return has caused me to run way out in front of God. In all humility, I must step back and admit that I don't know if his return is imminent or not.

"During my discussions with residents of Jerusalem, I realized that I was treating God's word as an academic exercise. I'm guilty of a grave error. To the Jewish people who actually live in Israel, what people believe about prophecy is a serious matter because those beliefs affect the very survival of their families and nation..."

Chapter 57: Face of His Adversary

Election: 5 days

Gordon was at East of Eden when he received a call from the president of WBC. He advised Gordon that Allen Wilder was addressing an audience in Jerusalem, and Gordon wasn't going to like what Wilder was saying. Gordon immediately turned it on.

Wilder was speaking, "…When we see signs of war and tribulation, we're required by duty and honor to stand side by side with our friends and allies. We must insist by *every* means possible that America keeps its commitment to the nation of Israel. This includes voting in next week's election. I was wrong to recommend against our involvement in earthly affairs. I must apologize for this misguided advice…"

"What in the hell is he doing?" muttered Gordon into the phone. "Martin, did your people suspect this change in direction? Didn't you tape it?"

The president of WBC responded, "He dropped our production team this morning and said he was going to use a local producer he'd worked with in the past. We had no idea what he was planning."

"You've got to cut the feed. Claim technical difficulties."

"No one will believe us. It'll only create questions and more publicity for Wilder."

Gordon started listening again. Wilder continued, "We must faithfully perform our duties to be salt and light in the world that God loves. Our desire for his return must not detract us from the difficult task of leading our communities and nation. We have every right to declare God's Word in the public square, and insist on a moral environment where we can raise and educate our children. Less than half of evangelical Christians are expected to vote this election, and it grieves me that my actions have contributed to this travesty. I urge you to join me this Tuesday as we exercise our civic duty by voting our conscience."

Gordon's anger spilled over, "Damn that son of a bitch! Get him off the air!" The screen blinked and a sign claiming technical difficulties appeared.

Gordon was already formulating a plan to counter Wilder's about-face. He advised the president of WBC, "I'll call you in the morning. We need to discredit him… like a rumor he was paid off by Thomas' people. We'll show tapes of his previous conferences as though they were current. And we'll run ads of his nonvoting message."

The president of WBC warned, "Gordon, his turn-about will be big news. Our efforts to counter it will only add fuel to the fire."

"It has to be done," demanded Gordon. "I'll have a plan by morning."

When Gordon hung up, he threw his phone across the room, shattering it against the stone fireplace. He was lost to a silent rage. With only four days left, the unthinkable had occurred. He had misjudged the man who had just forfeited his life's work and reputation by admitting he was wrong.

His rage was fed by Leo Marone's betrayal, the self-inflicted damage of Buzz Nelson's boasting, and the emergence of Blake Merrill as an adversary. And there was the lost opportunity to win over Chad, and Berry's disappearance. Victory had been his expectation, but now he was facing a glaring defeat. He paced. No thought brought relief. Betrayal and failure and loss wound tightly into a binding hate.

God was mocking him. Honor could be found in defeat, if by a worthy adversary. But he despised the foolish weakness that opposed him. His actions were being used to advance the very kingdom he'd sworn to prevent. His hatred boiled over and demanded release.

Gordon grabbed his rifle and climbed into the Land Rover. With a snowmobile in tow, he drove towards the entrance of Teton National Park. He consciously knew the park wasn't the Garden of Eden. It didn't need to be, for in his mind and in his war, desire was reality. Symbolism conveyed the true meaning of his actions.

Gordon pulled up to the park's east entrance. The low, gray ceiling began to break apart as the sun descended upon the mountain peaks. The sky blushed, and soft pinks and lavenders melted into a crimson fire. Streams of brilliant light poured over the mountains creating a luminous, yellow haze.

Gordon knew he wasn't alone. For if he were facing Eden's east gate, then winged cherubim were standing as an imposing discouragement to those who did not belong. He stood outside his vehicle and raised his rifle to his shoulder, aiming just to the right of the gate. He fired once. What he shot could only be seen through spiritual eyes, but his desire created the reality of his actions. He shifted his aim to the gate's left side and fired a second time.

He then headed up Teton Park Road for Grand Teton Mountain, cursing Chad and his friends. Although they'd thwarted his grand strategy, they'd never understand. They'd think him mad, but those who understood the war, they knew. The object of his wrath did. God knew his actions were more than the vain rantings of a mad man. Rather, his actions were the deliberate frontal assault of a man tired of fighting from the shadows, frustrated with a war of deception. Gordon Connelly was a warrior, and as he believed was his right, he demanded a direct confrontation. He was demanding to see the face of his Adversary.

Snow covered the mountains, and his progress slowed as he climbed higher. Between worsening road conditions and lengthening shadows, the drive became treacherous. He abandoned the Land Rover at Taggert Lake Trailhead, mounted his snowmobile, and headed up Garnet Canyon. As his path wound back towards the mountain, Grand Teton came into clear view. The sun's rays crowned the summit.

Gordon slowly raised his eyes, cold and determined. Barely above a breath, he pronounced in a spiteful whisper, "You'll *not* defeat us. The meek have rejected you."

Through a contemptuous sneer, Gordon's voice boomed, resounded across the snow-laden ridges. "The world will be our glory, not yours! We will be the conscience of the world!"

Gordon continued, speaking as though face-to-face, "They don't want your freedom. In exchange for bread they'll wear chains forged with their own hands. We will build a new paradise."

Gordon's words were not enough, as his malice demanded more. He lifted his rifle to his shoulder, a weapon built by human hands, personified as an agent of his bidding. Arrogant pride motivated his resolve. His rage was hardened into a consuming spirit of hate, and it was this spirit that carefully aimed at the luminous crown. He smiled and squeezed the trigger, firing once, and then again, and then a third time. He slowly lowered the rifle, his eyes still focused on Grand Teton's summit, listening to the echoes ringing throughout the ridges and valleys.

Within moments his attention was drawn to a new, unfamiliar sound – a low, rumbling thunder, growing ever louder. The ground trembled. Small clumps of snow broke loose from the ridge directly above him. The gentle thunder built to a roar as the earth shook violently. Sensing movement from above, he glanced up to see an avalanche of white powder, pouring out over the ridge as a rushing river, sweeping him off the trail to bury him under a mountain of snow.

No one was to ever know if he was granted his direct confrontation with his sworn enemy. No one would ask if his smile when he pulled the trigger was the result of seeing his Adversary's face. No one would know because Gordon Connelly's war against God was over, and he was lost.

Chapter 58: Called to Account

Election: 4 days

Chad received the news from the county sheriff's office on early Friday evening. They were sorry to inform him that his father had been killed the day before in an avalanche near Grand Teton Mountain.

Suddenly, every issue consuming his life went blank. The struggles, frustrations, and fears caused by Gordon's attitudes and actions faded into the background. All that remained were memories of a father he cared deeply about, prayed for, and hoped could someday see that life was deeper and richer than the world Gordon so tightly held in his grasp.

Often he'd wanted to laugh with his father and encourage him to let go. The world wasn't going to spin out of control. He'd tried to convince Gordon to relax and enjoy a reasonable certainty that life and the world were held in supremely competent hands.

But Gordon refused to see it, and eventually Chad gave up trying.

A new shadow of grief passed over his soul. He yearned for what might have been and for the great joy Gordon could have given to all who knew him, and considering Gordon's talents and resolve, maybe to the rest of the world as well.

But it wasn't to be. Gordon had chosen his path years before, and he'd closed the door to any possibility beyond his own reach.

The park rangers had found his vehicle Thursday night along the roadside. His body was discovered Friday under twenty feet of snow. They wondered why Gordon was that high up on the mountain with darkness closing in. Chad told them he didn't know, and he didn't. He believed it had something to do with the Garden of Eden, but as to the actual reason, he could only guess.

As he considered his father's life and the circumstances of its end, he recalled something the Psalmist had said, "*Why does the wicked man revile God? Why does he say to himself, 'He won't call me to account.'*"

Chad sat alone in the backyard of his Austin home and wept as he embraced his memories.

****

Election: 3 days

The men's prayer breakfast ended and Chad was on his way to the next event. He was to talk for eight minutes about his enjoyment of coin collecting at the annual Austin Antique Convention. A call came in from the

200

campaign office.

"Hi, Maggie, how's the schedule? I'm only ten minutes behind after my first event, so at this pace, I'll only be an hour and a half late for my dinner speech."

Maggie smiled, "I have confidence you can make it up. Just keep answering your phone when I call."

"You've got it."

"I'm going to give you a phone number. It's a New York attorney named Jeremy Lakes. He'd like to talk with you about your father."

"Thanks. I'll try to reach him."

Chad placed the call. Jeremy Lakes answered and introduced himself, "Our firm has represented your father's personal affairs for the past twelve years. We were sorry to hear of his tragic death."

Chad allowed the attorney to direct the conversation, from briefly discussing their firm to making a few complimentary comments about his father. After what Lakes must have felt to be an appropriate time, he brought up the purpose of his call.

"Chad, I know you're busy with the election coming up next week, but we should schedule a time to meet. As the heir to your father's estate, you'll need to make several important decisions as soon as possible."

The will? He hadn't even considered it. In fact, he hadn't thought about it for years. Now, in just one sentence, an attorney he'd never met had placed a life-changing responsibility squarely on his shoulders.

His silence encouraged Lakes to make a personal comment, "Your father talked to me several times about his relationship with you. He told me that you and he often didn't see eye to eye, so you might be surprised that he left you practically the entire estate. But knowing your father's confidence, as I'm sure you did, he always believed he'd win you to his side."

"I know he did," said Chad. "He believed that given enough time, he'd win the whole world to his side. When do we need to meet?"

"Next week, after the election."

"Can you come to the lodge?"

"That'll be fine. Let me know when you'll be there."

****

When his phone rang, Daniel glanced at the clock. He was ready to leave for the 'get-out-the-vote' rally that had been hastily organized by Austin area churches. The rally reflected a national grassroots response to the powerful inspiration coming from Wilder's Jerusalem speech. Daniel had been asked to say a few words about the effects of foreign aid on indigenous cultures, the Buzz Nelson video, and, as always, something about Philip's escape.

As he headed for his car, he answered Philip's call, "Hello, I'm on my way to a rally to tell everyone in Austin how awful you looked when I found you in Mexico City."

Philip laughed, "Make sure they know I was in the lead when I pulled my hamstring."

"I'll also tell them you're a bad loser. What's up?"

"Have you seen the news from Dubai in the United Arab Emirates?"

"No, I haven't had time to watch any news."

Philip shared, "Leo Marone was assassinated by gunmen on his way out of a restaurant at the Dubai Grand Hyatt."

"Do you think this was what Gordon meant when he told Chad he'd stop Marone in his own way?"

"I'm sure it is," said Philip. "He probably let the Arabs know that Marone had cheated them."

"I'll call Katherine. Berry needs to know she doesn't have to hide anymore."

Daniel immediately called Katherine and updated her on the news about Marone's death. "How are Berry and her daughter doing?"

"They're good. Annie's a sweetheart, and Berry's been very helpful at the clinic. They've developed a special bond with an eight-year-old girl named Ariela. She's undergoing surgery for cancer on Monday. Her prognosis isn't good, and there's only a small chance of her pulling through."

"I'm sorry to hear that."

"It's sad, Daniel. I wish there were more we could do. Berry and Annie visit with her several times a day, which gives Ariela's mother time to rest."

"I'm glad to hear Berry's helpful. Hopefully, it'll be good for her. Now that we know Berry's safe, why don't you come to Austin on Tuesday to join us at Glen's Diner for the victory party?"

"I'd love to. I miss my husband."

Daniel teased, "I thought you'd be happy to get away. I can only take him for about a week at a time. He's way too intense."

Katherine laughed, "It's not the same."

"Well, it's your choice," said Daniel smiling. "I've got to go. Wilder's Jerusalem speech has the whole evangelical community stirred up. Tuesday's going to be an interesting day."

Chapter 59: The Clinic

Katherine entered Ariela's room. Annie was sharing exciting plans for after Ariela's surgery. The little girl appeared frail and often afraid. Katherine had seen it before in others. Her thin face, hollow eyes, and weak responses warned of approaching death. Each smile Ariela managed was taken by Berry and Annie as a victory, every attempted laugh filling them with hope.

Katherine asked Berry, "Are you and Annie ready to go? It's late and our wonderful patient needs her rest for a big day tomorrow."

Berry answered while smiling at Ariela, "I'd like to stay a while longer. Why don't you and Annie get some dinner, and then pick me up when you're done. I don't want to leave our brave little friend alone. Her mother's coming in later to spend the night."

"Sure we can." Katherine looked at Annie, "Are you hungry?"

Annie stood to leave, "Good night, Ariela. I'll see you tomorrow after your operation. Then we can decide what we're going to do to celebrate."

Ariela wanted to smile, "Bye, Annie."

After they left, Berry sat on the side of the bed, holding her hand and lightly touching wisps of gently curled hair. Ariela would doze briefly, then wake with restless breathing.

"I'm too tired to sleep," she said with strained effort. After a quiet moment, she struggled to speak, "I like Annie. She's funny. We're best friends."

Berry smiled, "Annie likes you a lot. Now try to sleep." She got up and turned down the lights.

"I can't," she said. "Can you sing to me?" her request barely audible.

"I don't think I know any lullabies," said Berry as she thought for a minute. "I remember a song that's like a lullaby."

"Please sing it."

Berry hummed the melody of her college theme song, and then softly sang the words she remembered, *"Living is easy with eyes closed, misunderstanding what you see. It's getting hard to be someone but it all works out. It doesn't matter much to me."* She continued humming until she closed with, *"Strawberry Fields Forever."*

"Please sing again."

Berry sang the verse once more, as quietly as a whisper. Ariela closed her eyes and fell asleep. Berry, still holding Ariela's hand, moved to a chair beside the bed. She sat still, listening to the child's labored breathing.

Watching, worried, Berry knew she was staring into the face of death. Everything inside her opposed that possibility. Her soul silently screamed "No!" It wasn't right. Death was wrong. It shouldn't happen. She now saw what she'd never seen before. The circle of life be damned. Death was evil.

Immediately something swelled up inside her that cried out in protest. To hell with death, she reached out for life.

"God, if you'll hear me? Not for me, but for little Ariela. Please don't let her die."

Berry let go and leaned back in the chair. She pressed her hands to her face, covering her eyes.

"Sarah."

Berry thought she heard a voice and lowered her hands. She glanced from side to side. The room seemed darker, the shadows deeper. She listened. The machines hummed and beeped. Muffled sounds flowed through an open window.

She relaxed back into the chair, her eyes closed.

"Sarah."

Berry was startled, sure that she'd heard a voice. A quick survey revealed nothing. The room was remarkably still, the background unnaturally quiet. A shadow filled the air like a mist.

"Sarah."

This time she not only heard, but realized someone was using her birth name. She turned in the direction of the voice, towards the far dark corner. She sensed the presence of someone in the room, but felt no apprehension.

"Yes?" she spoke, with growing awareness that something was about to happen.

"I have heard your prayer."

The voice was clear. She somehow knew the meaning and who it was. A stirring moved at the shadow's edge, coming towards her until she saw… His face.

Her response was instant. From deep within, from depths unknown, sprang up a well of life so forceful it overwhelmed her every capacity. A rush of tears exploded into her throat, choking her, pouring through her eyes, flooding her mind with only one consuming thought.

She slid off the chair onto her knees, sobbing, fighting to speak. She had to say something or she would surely die. She finally gasped enough air to cry out, "I'm sorry."

When Katherine arrived at the door, she found Berry sitting on the floor, and she felt the Lord's presence.

She quietly entered and sat beside Berry. The Holy Spirit was so strong Katherine felt choked with emotion. She waited quietly.

Berry looked up, her eyes swollen and red. Her expression and voice carried a peaceful awe. "He knows me. He called me Sarah."

"Did you see him?"

"Yes. His face… for an instant. Then I started to cry." Berry looked into Katherine's eyes, smiling. "I asked God to save Ariela, and he appeared and said to me, 'Sarah, I have heard your prayer.'"

Berry stood up and looked upon Ariela, who was now sleeping peacefully. She turned to Katherine, "Is it possible?"

"Berry, he wants you to know that no matter what happens, he's here."

Berry placed her hands on Katherine's arm and with an open smile and eyes shimmering with tears, she asked, "Katherine, please call me Sarah."

Chapter 60: A Walk

Ariela came through her operation with growing strength. The doctors were cautiously optimistic. Considering the dire expectations, the news was received by everyone as a miracle.

Sarah Fields, the former Strawberry Fields Forever, felt joyfully light and decided she and Annie needed to get out. Despite the overcast sky and occasional light drizzle, they grabbed umbrellas and pulled the BMW out of the garage.

On the way to the Farmer's Market, Sarah thought for a moment that they were being followed. She kept glancing at the rearview mirror, but couldn't confirm her uneasiness.

"Is something wrong?" asked Annie.

"No, of course not." Sarah took a last glimpse into the mirror and, seeing nothing, wrote it off to frayed nerves.

Strolling through the market, arm in arm, Sarah must have seemed preoccupied. Annie asked, "Mom, what are you thinking about?"

Sarah smiled, "I'm sorry if I've ignored you, but a lot has happened, and my mind's a busy place. I'm happy for Ariela's progress, and I was thinking of a good friend of mine who helped us before he died in an avalanche."

"When was that?"

"Just four days ago, in the Grand Teton Mountains."

"Did you like this man?"

"He was Berry's best friend."

"Why did you change your name?"

"It happened last night in Ariela's room."

"What happened?"

"Katherine said that Berry had to die so Sarah could live."

"I don't get it."

"You're not supposed to. It's a mystery," said Sarah with a little laugh.

"Anything else?"

"Your father. Maybe we'll see him, someday."

"Will I like him?"

"Yes, very much. He's a good man."

"Is he married?"

"His wife died in a plane crash several months ago."

"That's sad."

"Yes, it was tragic. She was amazing and her work lives on."

They walked a while longer in silence before Annie asked, "Are you thinking about me?"

"Yes," she answered smiling. "I'm thinking about how I'll never leave you again."

Katherine received a call from Daniel. His voice was troubled, "Octaviano just contacted me. He's been keeping an eye on things, just in case. He said someone's following Berry. I mean Sarah and Annie. Do you know where they went?"

"They were going to the Farmer's Market."

"I'll tell Octaviano," said Daniel. "Can you call the police?"

"Yeah."

"Call me as soon as you hear anything."

"I will. You do the same," said Katherine as she gathered her things and raced to the car.

The cloud cover grew darker and brought a light rain. Holding an umbrella in one hand, Sarah sifted through stacks of vegetables to find the right combination for dinner. She sensed someone watching and looked up to see a man, leaning against a table of produce, under the cover of an awning.

She tried to ignore him but felt drawn to look again. He was about fifty feet away and his posture had not changed. He was Hispanic, with a short stocky build and a ball cap drawn down, his eyes barely visible under its brim. A chill came over her, made colder as the rain picked up and daylight faded.

She hurriedly collected her selections and handed them, along with her payment, to the woman minding the booth. As Sarah turned to leave, she couldn't help but glance once more out of the corner of her eye. He was occupying the same spot, pulling the collar of his jacket up around his neck. That's when she saw his bandaged right hand.

She panicked and quickly looked for Annie. Where was she? She spun around, searching in every direction.

"Annie," she called, trying to maintain control. When her vision crossed where the man had been standing, he was no longer there. She couldn't find either of them.

Terrified, frantically searching, she ran back and forth calling her name.

Which way? She kept moving, expanding her circle.

Katherine pulled up to the front gate and ran through the rain into the market. She moved quickly, searching for Sarah and Annie. The first person she recognized was Octaviano, who disappeared down a parallel row of booths before she could call to him.

She jogged in the opposite direction through mud and standing pools of water, hoping one of them would succeed. A few moments later she spotted Annie running through the booths. Soon a man appeared, following her, coming out from behind a large fruit stand.

Katherine sprinted ahead of Annie's general direction, through produce displays, trying to keep her balance, running along the slippery paths. She came upon a narrow passageway between a permanent, concrete block building and the back of a row of booths. Annie's pursuer had boxed her into a corner against the building. His right hand was wrapped. In his left hand was a steel blade.

Katherine ran down the path towards them. Seventy feet... fifty... thirty... The man looked up and saw her approaching. He grabbed Annie. Katherine yelled, "Stop!" just as her feet slid out from under her and she fell on her back. She was momentarily stunned as the air rushed out of her lungs. She gasped a deep breath and scrambled to get up, her feet continuing to slide in the mud.

The man charged towards her, yanking Annie by the back of her jacket. Annie struggled to get away, screaming, "Help! Let me go!"

He spun around and struck the side of her head with his bandaged hand. He grimaced in pain as Annie slipped to the ground. He resumed his march towards Katherine, dragging Annie behind him.

The momentary diversion allowed Katherine to find her footing and pull a small revolver out of her jacket pocket. She pointed it at the man's chest, holding it with two hands, not more than eight feet away.

"Don't move!" she yelled.

He glanced at her while pulling Annie off the ground to use as a screen.

"Drop the knife!"

He ignored Katherine's command, holding the blade in his left hand with his right arm wrapped around Annie to constrain her in front of him. Annie grabbed his bandaged hand and twisted it with all her might. He shrieked and cursed Annie, lifting his blade, threatening to strike her. In the struggle, his knife sliced across Annie's arm, and she cried out as blood flowed from the wound.

"Stop!" screamed Katherine in horror, seeing the blood. She aimed at his left shoulder and squeezed the trigger, flinching as she anticipated the shot. The pistol clicked instead of firing. Hearing the sound, the man stopped and glared at her.

She hesitated, surprised by the gun in her hand, and then glanced up at the assailant. Squinting through the pouring rain washing over her face, she glimpsed at what seemed like pure evil in his cruel eyes, a mocking grin, and the face of a tattooed snake glaring at her from his neck.

The man shoved Annie to the ground and lunged at Katherine, letting out a grotesque yell. She stepped back, gasped and as a reflex, pointed the gun at the middle of his body and pulled the trigger. The gun jerked when it fired and kicked back in her hands. Shock distorted his expression as the bullet struck his chest. His momentum carried him forward into her, and they both fell to the ground with the man landing on her.

She struggled to get out from under him. She'd lost the gun and couldn't see with the rain and mud in her face. The man pushed himself up and raised the knife, but before he could strike, a shot rang out. He twisted and fell back on top of her. Echoes resounded through the rain, followed by a long stillness.

With all her strength, she pushed the lifeless body up and slid out from under him. She scrambled over to Annie who was sitting in the mud, quivering between sobbing gasps.

"You're okay now, Annie. Let me see your arm."

Katherine glanced at the dead man lying in the mud. She looked around to see who might have fired the shot. She thought it was Octaviano, but he was nowhere to be seen.

Annie spoke in a trembling voice, loud enough to be heard above the rain and commotion, "You shot him."

Katherine ripped the lining out her jacket and tied Annie's wound. "It's not deep. You'll be all right."

Sarah ran up and slid down to her knees. She pulled Annie into her lap and hugged her. Tears mixed with the rain on her face.

Annie pointed. "Mom, Katherine shot the man with the broken hand."

Sarah looked at the body lying on the ground, then back at Katherine, "Are you okay?"

Through her rain soaked face Katherine nodded, "The nightmare's over."

Epilogue: The Fellowship

"Will you marry me?"

"Yes, I'd love to."

Daniel opened his hand, revealing an engagement ring. He took Macy's left hand and slipped the ring on her finger, then leaned forward and lightly kissed her cheek. "I love you."

"And I love you, Daniel. I'm so happy. It's beautiful." She surveyed the interior cabin of the Gulfstream, "I never imagined becoming engaged to a missionary aboard a private jet."

"Nothing is a surprise after the events of the past six months," said Daniel smiling. He opened a bottle of champagne and poured two glasses. "It seems strangely appropriate to be celebrating aboard Gordon's jet, compliments of Chad, traveling from North Carolina to Austin after your victory speech. Now we can announce our engagement and celebrate with friends at Glen's Diner."

Daniel raised his glass, "Here's to you, Macy, the love of my life."

"And to you," offered Macy, "the man I've been waiting for."

Macy slipped out of her seat into Daniel's lap. She wrapped her arms around his neck and kissed him.

Daniel smiled, "I must have done something right."

"That's just a starter. I have lots more." She beamed while playfully teasing, "If you had proposed on the dance floor, I wouldn't have run for Congress."

"When we met?"

"Yeah, that's when I knew."

"I'm a little slower."

"I'm learning that," she offered with a delightful laugh that was followed with a mischievous grin, "So you decided to live in D.C.?"

Daniel answered carefully, "That's not exactly what I had in mind." Then he laughed, "But I love you enough to suffer the Washington traffic."

"Daniel, I love you so much I'd follow you to a Mexico City barrio."

"How about a compromise. I'm moving the Life Bridge office to Austin."

After a brief pause, Macy asked, "So, the next two years I'll be living in D.C., North Carolina, and Austin?"

Daniel smiled, "And vacationing south of the border. Think of all the adventures."

The aroma from the grill and the excited chatter of friends welcomed Daniel and Macy when they arrived at Glen's Diner. Shelly and Glen had closed the diner to host a private post-election party.

The party was in full swing, for good reason. Chad, surrounded by friends, was watching a rebroadcast of his victory speech given two hours before.

The good news began when Charles Lee concluded from exit polls that all across the country, evangelical voters turned out in numbers higher than expected. As of midnight, Charles estimated that they might pick up a few seats in the House with the Senate remaining the same.

Although the presidential race was still too close to call, everyone at Glen's knew they had escaped a potential disaster. There would not be enough votes to pass the radical agenda of Gordon Connelly and Solutions for Humanity. As for now, they'd escaped *Tolerance for America* and a government takeover of food production.

Another cause for celebration was the announcement of Daniel and Macy's engagement. The delighted crowd made the newly engaged couple promise to take their marriage vows a second time in the lake by Philip and Katherine's home. And of course it would be followed by a reception on the lakeside patio at sunset.

Daniel and Macy were sitting with Philip, Katherine, and Chad. It was after 1:00 and many guests had left the diner. They were in a relaxed mood, allowing the conversation to drift, when Katherine recalled something she wanted to ask Daniel.

Katherine mentioned, "Do you recall the question I asked when you were leaving Mexico for Lauren's service?"

"Yeah, I remember. You were frustrated with the lack of direction and leadership in the world, and you asked, 'Where is Joshua?'"

"Well, are you ready?" Katherine prompted her brother.

"I'll give it a try." Daniel began, "As you know, Joshua led God's people into the Promised Land. He was a man who walked by faith and not by sight. But this was only a shadow of what was to come, for the name, Joshua, is Hebrew for Jesus."

"I didn't know that," said Philip.

Daniel nodded, "Yeah, it is amazing, especially when we consider that as the "new Joshua," Jesus leads us into a different kind of kingdom. Not one that's geographical or based on political power, but one that changes the world by changing us from the inside. We've been set free to live by conscience, for the word of God is written on our hearts."

Daniel spoke to his sister, "The obvious answer to your question is that Jesus, the new Joshua, is seated at the Father's right hand. But there's more."

Macy jumped in, "Meaning there's a not so obvious answer?"

Daniel returned Macy's smile, "Since we're joint heirs with Christ, each one of us has also been commissioned a new Joshua."

Philip asked, "What does that mean?"

"Three weeks ago, Chad and I talked with his father at East of Eden. As I listened to Gordon, I felt engulfed in spiritual darkness. I knew I was facing a spirit of antichrist. I asked God how to respond, and in the midst of the world's open hostility and overwhelming power, I was immediately filled with joy as a clear, simple answer swept away all my fears: 'Take up your cross and proclaim the good news that the door to the kingdom is open wide, the strongman has been bound, and the redemption of the world has begun.'"

Finding Hope & Inspiration By Engaging the Battle

The website/blog for
Winning the World
&
Breaking Babel

www.davidkullberg.com

Order *Winning the World* & *Breaking Babel* at:
www.davidkullberg.com

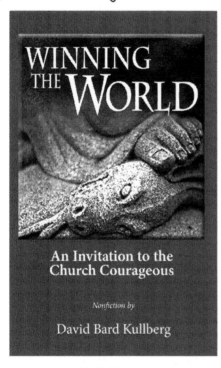

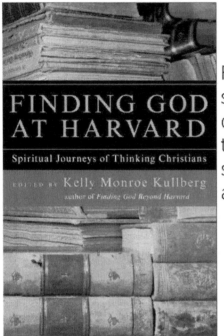

Kelly is a gifted writer with rich insight into what it means to be human... Kelly describes a story that only God, who is Veritas, could weave together.
Ravi Zacharias – FROM THE FOREWORD

An extraordinary, personal story that probes both the beauty and the pain of living... as one very brave soul yearns to please God and live life to the fullest. It made me laugh and brought me to tears.
– **J. Stanley Mattison**, Founder and President, C.S. Lewis Foundation

Kelly's kaleidoscopic quest for veritas is a colorful, poetic narrative filled with heartache and joy - riveting and unexpectedly poignant.
– **Owen Gingerich**, Professor Emeritus, Harvard-Smithsonian Center for Astrophysics, and author of *God's Universe*

Kelly's focus on Jesus Christ as the Truth has also been the focus of her own peripatetic, energetic and thought-provoking life.
– **Mark Noll**, University of Notre Dame, and author of *America's God*

Kelly heralds a gospel which we want to believe, because it is truthful, yet charitable, full of love. Her style is engaging, an apologetic with the warmest possible human face.
– **William Edgar**, Professor of Apologetics, Westminster Theological Seminary

Order *Finding God Beyond Harvard*, visit:
www.davidkullberg.com/store

Spark your sense of wonder

Faith & Culture brings together 70 inspired Christian thinkers who guide us on a journey of intriguing ideas, people and events from science, history, art, literature, philosophy, theology, and contemporary culture.

It's like a college course that covers dynamic facets of a Christian worldview. For 15 weeks, each day offers another unique story that inspires and intrigues. The most common reader response, "I didn't know that about..."

Faith & Culture
The Guide to a Culture
Shaped by Faith

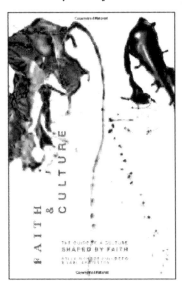

Screwtape on The Da Vinci Code
– Eric Metaxas
The Sleep of Death – Os Guinness
Hearing God – Dallas Willard
The Secret Gospels – Darrell Bock
God's Middle Knowledge
– Wm. Lane Craig
Sodom: What Archaeology Tells Us
– Walter C. Kaiser
The Modern University
– J.P. Moreland
Modern Science, a Child of Christianity
– Charles Thaxton
Darkness – Hugh Ross
DNA – Ray Bohlin
The Strange Small World of Quantum
Mechanics – Michael G. Strauss
A Scientist's Sense of Wonder
– Walter Bradley
Hamlet: Shakespeare's Ingenious
Design – Jonathan Witt
Also entries on Bob Dylan, Picasso,
Rembrandt, van Gogh, Islam,
Michelangelo, Handel, and many more.

Kelly Monroe Kullberg, founder and president of The America Conservancy, editor of *Finding God at Harvard*, and founder of the Veritas Forum.

Lail Arrington, author of three books including *Godsight*.

For more information visit: www.faithandculture.com
Order *Faith & Culture*, visit: www.davidkullberg.com/store

The America Conservancy

Because of love, we cannot be silent or passive.
God inspires believers to build in the ruins of culture,
restoring all things.

Mission: to advance a strategic plan for America's renewal in the 21st century. Strategy: to unite Christian and patriot leaders in 10 pillars of culture, creating projects for America's renewal.

The basis for each project is life-giving biblical and Constitutional wisdom which is the DNA of the American Experiment. The yield of biblical and Constitutional truths include the dignity of the human person, freedom, the rule of law, the nuclear family, creativity and entrepreneurship, generosity to the poor, and a reasoned understanding of the created world.

For more information visit:
www.americaconservancy.org

61391602R00128

Made in the USA
Middletown, DE
10 January 2018